With Love

— Annabeth

SKILANDS

SEAN WEBSTER

authorHOUSE®

AuthorHouse™ UK
1663 Liberty Drive
Bloomington, IN 47403 USA
www.authorhouse.co.uk
Phone: UK TFN: 0800 0148641 (Toll Free inside the UK)
      UK Local: (02) 0369 56322 (+44 20 3695 6322 from outside the UK)

Published by AuthorHouse 04/18/2023

ISBN: 979-8-8230-8230-3 (sc)
ISBN: 979-8-8230-8229-7 (e)

PART 1

The window covers always jammed whenever I tried to open them. Throughout my life, I never had the strength or skill to open them slightly. Eighteen years later, I still struggle to get them halfway.

My parents had built the window themselves. They cut through the wooden walls and created the window because my sister and I always loved looking at the view. The scene of the floating islands and the sun's rays worming their way through the centre still gives me a sense of peace. Jagged rocks and dirt were hanging from below each island, varying in size and shape. Shadows of the isle were projected off each other, and the bridges linked between them. Some islands even had roots from trees and plants protruding out the side.

The top of the islands was almost always flat. This was due to humans building houses and other various structures on top of them.

Although, some were left alone and had mini mountains or groups of trees on them. Some islands were so small it was only big enough to fit a single shed. A few islands were hundreds of feet above and below us. Yet most of them were within twenty feet of the other islands.

I finally bashed open the covers and took in my favourite view of our farming island. I sat on the step that was put there so the younger me could reach it. I felt a cool breeze flow through the room, then finally closed my eyes and let my mind wander for a few seconds.

Today was the day that could change my life. I was taking my flying license test today. When you turn eighteen, you're allowed to take it. Most people do. It helps them navigate between the islands easier. You don't have to rely on family and friends to see people. The biggest problem was having your skier or skipper.

A skier is a thing people fly with. They're little jetpacks with skis at the bottom to stand on during the flight, straps to keep you in and some, depending on where you were, have weapons. The weapons were only meant to manage pests like birds, but some people used them to kill others. I have yet to hear too many stories involving those, as that is more of a middle and inner island thing. Out here, we don't have enough money to afford weapons.

Our family has a couple of skiers because we use them to navigate between our farmlands. As it was a private air space, my sister and I got plenty of practice with them. The real test would be the skipper test, but I would only take that test for a while.

Skippers are a cross between what people called aeroplanes and cars six hundred years ago. At least that is what it says in my old books from my mum's library. Oh yeah, she collects many books and runs a small community library to keep outer islanders educated.

Skippers are much more robust and hold multiple people with a wheel at the front. We had an ancient one somewhere, but it could barely move, so we never used it. It was too expensive to fix. Back in the day, it was used to help move essential farming things, but years of wear and tear got the better of it.

The outer islands needed more skiers and skippers that were expensive. Our ones were more like floating bits of metal held together by scraps. The inner islands were a different story. They have skiers so fancy that they're worth more than a whole cluster of islands.

Only the royal family, upper-class rich people and owners of clusters lived in the inner islands. Middle islanders sometimes venture in and get special treatment, but we outer islanders never got close. We were too far out for anyone to care about us, so we were often left to handle things independently.

We also had a lot of crime happen. No one tried to support us. I bet the Inner Islands don't even know about the Island Pusher. Nobody knows who it is, but someone in the Outer Islands has built a reputation for raiding islands and pushing people off the edge. That is one brutal way to go.

Below the islands was a blue void. I don't know what is down there, but rumour has it the air is so toxic it melts your skin. A few people have built suits to try going there but have yet to return.

Now and then, a few flashes down there cause whole islands to fall and disappear. Another rumour is that the Inner Islands know what it is and has things to prevent it. Again, Outer Islands and some Middle Islands aren't so lucky.

We also have clusters of islands. They consist of hundreds of islands within a particular area, given a name. Ours is The Marhalm Cluster. We weren't the poorest places but weren't the richest ones in the outer islands either.

I checked the time and saw I had a few minutes to prepare before my ride was here. It would take me to the test centre. If I missed it, I would have to wait two more months to do it again. I knew I had to wear something smart, but I didn't want to overdo it. I haven't got anything too good in my wardrobe; however, I was able to dig up a black, long-sleeved shirt. It was a little screwed up, but I didn't care. It was better than the usual plain grey shirt I wore near enough every day.

When dressed, I grabbed my leather pouch, shut my window, and opened my front door to wait outside for my ride.

My island was a little small, but my parents are both farmers. They own a few islands that were different. We were lucky because we had a decent house and a small garden. Most people didn't have a garden in our area.

I didn't have to wait very long. A long yellow skipper skipped through the air and slowed down as it approached our land. The engine spluttered, and thick black smoke puffed out the back. Whispers of smoke rose and flew down to the void, carried by the wind.

Four metal feet emerged from the bottom of the skipper. They touched the ground, then ended up winding down into silence. I knew I would ace the test, but it didn't stop me from getting nervous.

I studied the yellow skipper carefully. It was rusty and had a black glass dome over the seats. As I was admiring the glass, it started to move. The dome peeled back, sunk somewhere into the back of the skipper and revealed four seats. One seat was already taken up by a man who wore travelling goggles. The moment I saw him, I recognised him. Ray Wilhelm.

Ray often brought bread from my mum, and I have known him for as long as I can remember. His job was some taxi thing. He lived on the outskirts of the Middle Islands, though he spent most of the time in Outer Islands. He probably feels sorry for us. Even so, he is very well appreciated and loved by our cluster.

"Hey, I'm here for mister Amphorn Aozora," Ray said seriously. His voice was very squeaky and sounded like an older man on helium. He took off his goggles and looked at me with his grey eyes. The first thing I noticed about Ray was his white moustache and beard. Somehow, he always kept it so white and fluffy.

"Hey Ray, I didn't know you were taking me," I said, and he smiled and waved me into his skipper. I hopped in and buckled up. Once I had my goggles on, Ray powered up the engine. It whined into motion, and before we knew it, we were off.

"I saw your name on the list of people doing your flying license test today. I wanted you to feel less nervous," Ray explained to me, still very smiley.

"Thanks. I feel like I will easily pass. I have been riding skiers for years now to help out Dad. Though I am not as good as Skye," I said, leaning slightly over the edge of the skipper door. Ray had left the windows open as he knew I always loved the feeling of the breeze.

I studied the void that loomed below us and watched a few streaks of white float across. My younger sister, Skye, and I had agreed that one day, we would find out what was down there. She wanted to do it, but I've always had to tell her no. She tried taking a skier to below the islands several times and got caught in a gust of wind. She almost flipped over once, and if it weren't for her skill with a skier, she would have fallen. You'd have thought that being that close to death; you would stop and think again. But she is even more determined to get down there for some reason.

To keep a conversation flowing, Ray asked, "How is Skye? Is she still causing trouble at school?" He then chuckled in a high-pitched squeak.

"Yeah. My parents were there not long ago, actually. She stole books from the public library. Something about the old world."

"Typical stuff, then?" She will end up being one of the first adventures to discover what is in the void," Ray announced. Then he said, "So, where is the first place you'll fly to when you get your license?"

I thought for a second. I had never given it a thought. I have always wanted to travel to the inner islands. The journey can take months, if not a year, which would only get you to the outskirts of them. Well, if we were using the skiers, we have available in the outer islands, at least anyway. They would fall apart in the crosswinds of the Gully.

The Gully is a vast gap between the middle and inner islands. It has powerful winds, so any cheap, fragile skiers or skippers would get swept away. Several people have lost their lives there. So, the Inner Islanders chose to set up pathways that carefully navigate around the Gully. It still isn't safe, but it's the best they'll ever get. The safest way would be to travel around the whole circle of islands. Going around would come up on the Northern side of the Inner Islands. That'll take even longer. We're talking about a year and a half to get there. One day I'll try it but certainly not soon.

I ended up telling Ray that I wasn't too sure and that I'd probably stick with helping my parents out with the farm. Perhaps do runs to the market for them.

Ray slowed down the corroded skipper a little later as we approached the busy areas. Lines of traffic were formed between tightly packed together islands. We were in the main centre of our cluster, located on the Southeast side of the Ring of Islands.

Buildings made from rusted abandoned metal and wood were tightly crammed onto smaller islands. Some facilities even had bridges. Most looked like they would fall apart if even the slightest weight landed on them. The bridges were built between islands, so people didn't need to rely on squeezing a skier onto each island. There were also some bigger islands with more shops side by side. Their condition wasn't much better, but they still held together.

In the centre of all clusters, the islands are always much closer, as if they used to be a single island that fractured and split. Some places would have huge metal support poles attached from below the island. The other end would connect to another island, keeping them close together. Once in a lifetime, they would break and tear out chunks of the ground and cause significant problems to a few islands. Somewhere under the islands had something that kept them up; I am sure of it because sometimes they would fall randomly.

As our skipper weaved between islands, we eventually slowed to a near stop. Ray fiddled with knobs and sticks, and we lowered into a large island. From where we were, I could see a bunch of skiers all lined up in a row, one of which I am guessing I would be flying shortly. We touched down, and I hopped out. I thanked Ray for the ride, and he said that he would return in an hour to pick me up. Then we wished me good luck before trundling away into Marhalm Centre.

PART 2

I waited for a little bit and stared at the building. This was a very solid-looking building. It was well made, the wood being sanded planks with insulated windows. It stood out a lot compared to all the other facilities nearby. I think the middle islanders funded it, but then the inner islands probably took all the money from it.

I took my first couple of steps, and I will admit, now that I was here, the idea that I was going for my official license was starting to loom over me. I felt my stomach flip as I pushed open the door. I could smell some cleaning product that hurt my nose. So, I avoided breathing in through my nose as much as possible, despite making myself look like a dog panting. A huge, sparkling white desk with a woman standing behind it. She wore a light grey dress with black sleeves. She also had a writing I couldn't understand on her chest.

"Hello, sir, are you here for your test," the woman asked with a beaming smile. Her accent was unique; I could tell she wasn't from the Southeast. I said yes and gave all my details. She tapped a monitor a few times, and then there was a clunk. Behind her, a small locker popped open and revealed a key ring with two keys. She handed it to me and told me I could put my things in a locker. I looked down at myself and realised all I had was my ID card, which was all I needed. People would bring snacks to help settle nerves, but to me, that is pointless. I'd throw up everything I ate if I were that nervous.

The wait took a while. I sat on a metal chair, one of the only things that looked like it belonged in the Marhalm cluster. It was rusty scrap metal but still, despite its look, was surprisingly comfy. Too comfy. I was beginning to slouch when my name was called by a man whose beard was tickling his chest.

He was dressed in a brown cloth tunic with a brown leather jacket on top. He also had a brown helmet with round goggles around it.

I stood up, the feeling of nerves hitting me even more. I was fine until now. I wasn't even sure why I was getting worse because I knew I could easily handle a skier. If I could manage the ones we had at home, these would be much easier. At least, that is what I thought.

I was led by the man outside who looked down at me. I waited.

"So, you are Amphorn Aozora. I don't suppose you're related to the farmers?"

I nodded. Our family was well known because we were one of the only farmers here. At least our name and parents. Skye and I were usually called 'the farmer's kids.'

"I have seen you kids flying between your islands before on those dodgy-looking skiers. You sure look like you're more than competent. Don't worry, kid. You'll do fine. Do you have your key?" Again, I nodded and felt the keys in my pocket. One was for the locker I didn't use, and the other was for the skier I will be flying. I took it out and showed it to him.

"That is great. So, my name is Winston. I will be your tester today. Do you know how these tests work, or would you like me to explain them?" The truth was, I knew exactly how these tests go, but I was still nervous. I had a habit of procrastinating, and now was a chance to push back the inevitable an extra minute or two. I asked Winston if he could go over what we planned to do, which he did without care.

"No worries. It will work if I ask you to perform an essential check on the skier. Then I will ask you to get on and do a basic take-off. Once you are up, I will hop onto my skier and fly side-by-side with you. Our helmets will have a voice connection so you can hear my instructions. Throughout the flight, I will ask you to perform some basic tasks. Overall, we will take about half an hour. At the end of the test, I will give you a rundown of how you did. Do you have any questions?" I shook my head. I regretted asking him to explain the test because I wanted it to end. After doing a little bit of writing, we were finally ready.

The first thing he asked me to do was to check the skier. It was simple enough.

Lights worked, the thrusters weren't blocked, landing gear wasn't broken. All the straps were secure, and the helmets and goggles fit well.

It was then time to take off. My skier was shiny and white, with red lines down the back. These were commonly known as learner skiers.

These skiers were much more potent than what I was used to, and when I pushed the button to take off, I took off a little too fast. Luckily, I could quickly stabilise myself and hovered on the spot. I could tell these were well-built because I wasn't getting the feeling that the standing platforms were about to give way and the thrusters were going to stop. Instead, they felt solid. Eventually, we got moving.

The turning was a lot more sensitive than I was used to, but I adapted quickly. I could feel the vibrations from the thrusters through my feet and the air on my face. The hardest part was going over the edge of the island and flying above the void on a skier that was all new to me. A pit formed in my chest on the initial exit of the island. However, it didn't take long for me to relax and remember to breathe. I could do this.

I heard a voice in my helmet that instructed me to perform a one-eighty turn in the air. I was confused about whose voice it was but remembered it was Winston's. I followed the instructions given with ease. I turned my handlebars to the right and lifted my legs forward slightly. The skier stopped in the air and turned to the right, quicker than I thought but still manageable. I was then asked to proceed through the Cluster Centre. I was taken through a couple of streets, slower than most people. It was the first time I had flown anywhere this busy, and that is when things went wrong.

I was getting ready to pass under a bridge between islands when Winston commanded me to turn around as it was a one-way flight zone. I did just that but too much. I accidentally leant too far back and temporarily lost control. In my attempt to correct myself, I accidentally accelerated and flew straight down towards the void. I got faster and faster, and my mind went blank. I was panicking as air whipped my face, and the blue got closer and closer. Then, there was a jolt up my whole body as the thruster disobeyed my commands and automatically turned itself the right way up and hovered on the spot. I didn't know what was going on. I was dizzy and heavily breathing and still shaking.

I took hold of my handles and took a deep breath. Above me, a skier was approaching slowly and then hovered in front of me.

"Are you okay," Winston asked, getting close to me. I didn't know what I was feeling. Shock, confused, cold. I wondered how the skier corrected itself and Winston explained that the learner skiers had emergency connection buttons that the examiners had.

"I guess that means I failed the test, huh," I stammered, trying to joke about my failure. Winston grunted, "We will talk about that when we return to the centre. Okay, kid, head back up to the islands when you feel ready, and we will head back to the test centre.

I composed me, did the appropriate checks, and then climbed again.

Every movement I did was slow, as I was paranoid I would overdo it again.

It felt like everybody was watching me, knowing what I had done, when in reality, no one probably noticed, let alone cared too much. People just got on with their days, but it didn't stop me from hating the flight home.

I have never been so relieved to get back. I carefully landed and stepped off of the skier. The ground couldn't have been any better. Solid floor, no vibrations. Winston also landed and said he would return in a moment before darting off into the test centre.

When he came back, he was holding some paper.

"So, how do you think you did," Winston asked, inviting me to sit down on one of the benches I didn't notice outside.

"Um…failed I guess." I felt sick and wanted to go home.

"Hmm, you did well. Until the one incident. You are a very competent flier, and I could see that. That mistake was regrettable. However, despite that, you still passed." I didn't hear what he said at first. I hung my head down in shame, then lifted it quickly.

"Wait…what," I questioned, not sure if I heard him correctly.

"You passed. It was unfortunate that your skier wasn't up to standards," Winston explained, winking at me. I was so confused. Winston turned his paper around for me to sign something. When I read reviews on the test, I saw what he had put.

There was an incident where the emergency correction system malfunctioned and forced the pupil towards the void. The pupil was still able to correct himself and return with no faults

I read over the text again and again. That wasn't what happened. It was my fault.

I lost control. The emergency system saved me. I went to protest, but Winston winked again. Oh…it clicked. He lied on purpose. I wasn't too keen on lying about how my test went, but I wasn't about to complain. I signed the paper, confirming that was the truth. I was then handed a telepad.

Telepads were small cubes, about 2 inches in each direction. They had a lens on the top and a button on the side to turn them on. They were used for almost everything.

TV, games, light shows, you name it, they could do it. They also had ones that only had one purpose. I turned the telepad on, and light emitted from the lens.

In between Winston and I was now a holographic image showing a certificate.

"This is yours to keep. Well done," Winston explained, wearing a devilish smile. I stood perplexed, holding the telepad, happy but also feeling guilty. Before I could say anything else, Winston shook my hand, and I was waiting out the front again. How was I meant to explain my test to my family? All I need to say is that I passed. They wouldn't ask for details, indeed. On second thoughts, Skye probably would. She is always nosey and wanted to prove she was better at flying than me. She is right.

I found a small wall that I could sit on out the front of the test centre. It was closer to the edge than I would have liked, but I wanted to sit briefly. I stared down into the blue abyss below. Did anything live down there?

I could see a few white fluffy things floating about far below. Nothing unusual. However, only people who go to school in the inner islands or some middle islands learn about it. It is called a cloud, and they hold water that pours over the people who live in the void. That sounds like it would be awful. Floods would ruin everything.

My trips to the library are often more educational than school. Before my mum met my dad, she travelled between islands, collecting as many books as possible and learning as much as possible. Even now, sometimes she would take trips and be gone for days to learn new things. She is originally from the middle islands, but my mum settled down when she met my dad in the outer islands. The wealth from my mum's side went towards my dad's family farm and helped expand it into what it is today. They then had two kids. Skye and me.

Both my sister and I probably got our adventurous side from my mum. It was she who let us first step foot on a skier and convinced my dad to let us give it a try.

Skye looks a lot like my mum too. Long, light brown hair and hazel eyes. Also, not very tall. Skye had slight curls in her hair, whereas my mum didn't.

Me, I am more like my dad. I have dark hair and dark brown eyes and am a little over average on the height front. All of us were very fit. That is probably because of our work on that farm, especially since my grandparents died.

I sat on the wall for ten minutes before I saw Ray's rusty yellow skipper spluttering towards the test centre. He hovered for a brief moment and then touched it down carefully.

"Hey kid, how did you do?"

"Hey, I uh…I passed," I answered back, fake smiling. I wasn't about to tell Ray about the details.

"Ha, ha! I knew you would. I bet you aced it. Hop in, and I'll get you home. Tell your family the good news!" I chuckled silently. Aced it. Funny. I did the opposite.

I almost died, but sure, I aced it.

I got into the skipper, and off we went. We went past where I had my incident, which made me feel queasy. I hoped Ray didn't notice. When I looked at him, he was smiling and looking forwards. Good. He didn't see the colour from my face drain away.

PART 3

I thanked Ray for dropping me off and gave him some money. He then congratulated me again and headed away.

I saw my parents' skiers were back, which meant they were home. Skye was probably home too. She would have gotten a lift from a friend, as our skiers could only hold one person. I opened the front door, and Skye immediately appeared, wearing her red and white wrap dress. Her belt with gold-coloured buckles was tied around her waist.

"So? Did you embarrass the Aozora name," Skye asked in her usual innocent but sarcastic tone. She placed her hands behind her back and waited for my answer.

"I passed obviously. I'm not that bad, you know," I told her. Straight-up lying, easy. I pushed her aside and stepped into the house.

"I expected no different," Skye answered. She then did something weird. She started to hum and skip around the house.

"What about school? Did *you* embarrass our name? Also, where are Mum and Dad?"

Skye kept skipping around and humming. She opened the cupboard, took out some bread, and ate a slice.

"Mum and Dad went off with Frankie to help with building a fence. Also, no, I didn't.

I was told I was behaving myself and that I should be proud. Mum and Dad almost passed out when they heard that."

"You're telling me you actually followed…rules. Wow, we must be close to the end of the world."

"Oi, I know how to be good. I find it boring. You weren't much better than me!"

"Yeah, well, I...have nothing. Dang, it!" I'll admit I wasn't the most well-behaved kid.

It's just around Skye that makes me look better.

As annoying as Skye is, she is amusing. Watching her push people's buttons is always fun because she somehow knows how to walk the fine line without crossing over. It is her secret superpower, and she knows it. Luckily, I know how to push her buttons. That is my power.

Skye giggled at her small victory and started eating away at her bread. She skipped into another room and returned with a book called 'The Settlements of the Void People.' She was always reading, but I couldn't help but focus on her being overly happy. As I got myself juice, I asked Skye, "What have you so happy?"

"Huh," Skye replied, a mouthful of bread. I forgot how quickly she got engrossed in books.

"You have been humming and skipping. Why are you so happy?" I expected her to moan that I interrupted her reading, but instead, she placed the book down, spun around on her chair and sat on it backwards, facing me. She had an evil smile that meant she was either planning something or had already done something.

"What have you done," I demanded, now extra cautious.

"Nothingggg! Not yet, at least," she grinned, now her eyes matching her evil smile. Now I was feeling scared.

"Let I ask you, how often have we been left alone," Skye asked me as I sat down on a chair opposite her. I took a sip from my drink and placed it down. Skye spun back around and went back to sitting as usual.

"Not too often...why?"

"Well, Mum and Dad will be out for a while, and you now have your license. We could try fixing up the double-seat skier, and you can take me to Marhalm Centre. Is that all she wanted? I was expecting way worse. The only problem is that our double seat was ancient and had not been used since I was six. It was left out in a shed on the island behind us. There is a small bridge linking our home island and that island together, so Skye could easily hop across. I was just not ready for me to put Skye and myself in a situation that could go wrong.

"Do you think that we can get it working before they get back? We don't have many parts to fix it, and they'll be home in six or seven hours."

"Really! Come on, Amp! Do you think I would suggest such an idea without any previous preparation? I have been working on it for a while, and the only bits left to do will only take an hour if we both work together. Please! Be the best brother ever." I forgot to mention that although my name is Amphorn, most people call me Amp as it is a lot easier. It's also how I introduce myself.

"I guess it wouldn't hurt fixing it up. Plus, it would be great to go somewhere without Mum and Dad with us all the time. We could properly explore places we are always told are not good places to go!" Skye's eyes lit up, and her smile grew even more extensive. This was genuinely the most excited I have ever seen her. I genuinely thought she would cry. She squealed and bounced up.

"Ah, are you serious! Okay, I am so excited. I have been waiting for this moment for ages!" She then told me everything she had been working on and everything that needed to be fixed. The duel thrusters were blocked with muck, and handles needed new handlebars, then oiled up. Just a couple of things out of many that Skye told me.

I followed her as she skipped outside through the backdoor. She didn't even bother putting on a jacket. She was eager.

"Hurry up," Skye shouted as she danced over the small bridge. I followed behind quickly but a lot slower than her. I was not too fond of this bridge. It felt way too weak, but somehow it survived all these years. Skye opened the shed door when I got to the other end. The shed was remarkably robust, considering it was made out of old wood and metal. The high winds had never really bothered it.

I joined my sister and entered the shed. I had been in here a few times. We store farming tools and equipment here. Also, we used it for spare storage space for anything in the house. To the left, Skye was already uncovering the blue plastic sheet covering the double skier.

The double skiers looked like single skiers but longer. Like all single skiers, they varied in shape and design, but for the most part, they had the driver at the front, a bar that connected the vertical bars for the driver and passenger, and four dual thrusters instead of two single thrusters. The passenger would usually stand at the back.

"So, all we need to do is secure the landing stilts properly, but I can only get underneath properly with someone holding it up. Also, the connection bar is secured on but just needs someone slightly stronger, aka you, to tighten it up a little more. I need help with getting the grips on the back handlebars too. I chose to have the back skier facing the front and secured it that way as the rotation gear was loose. I couldn't fix it as it was too broken. So yeah, the back is only facing forward."

"Skye, I get it! Let's get to work and stop wasting time." Skye seemed to be surprised but didn't complain. Instead, I let her be what she wanted me to do. I picked up the appropriate tools and started following her instructions.

Skye and I had learnt a lot about fixing up skiers because of my dad. He taught us how to fix broken farming equipment, eventually skiers and skippers. It is all machinery and similar stuff, anyway. My knowledge is good enough to fix things, but Skye showed a massive interest in it and read loads more. She also studied mechanics in her own time and was way more advanced than me. When it comes to stuff like this, I just let her tell me what to do. I wouldn't doubt her and don't tell her this, but I would trust her with my life if it came to building or fixing something.

About forty minutes later, we had done everything Skye had mentioned. She also added a few additions and then asked me to give it a test run. I hopped in and strapped myself in. Skye handed over the plastic key to get the skier started.

I pushed it into the slot on the side of the headrest. I then covered it up.

There was a loud noise as the thrusts just about managed to kick in. We still needed to fuel it up, but it was running. I then pushed the accelerator button on the handlebars and felt the thrusts vibrate. The more power I gave it, the more I felt the thruster's vibrator. It didn't take too long before I thought the thruster lifted off the ground. It felt cumbersome compared to single skiers.

It also felt less likely to spin over. I was surprised by how much control I had too. One of the additions Skye had given the skier was that the back passenger could also help control the skier. It was a common thing to help the driver stabilise it. Again, it would be Skye if I had to trust anyone in the back.

Skye's excitement was through the roof. When I turned the engine off, she yelped with delight.

"I will grab some fuel and fill it up. You can get our helmets," Skye said, darting to the other side of the shed.

"Are you sure you want to go now? Do you not want to eat something first or, like, get dressed?"

"Oh, shut up. I want to go now! We can always buy something when we're out! Hey, even I will pay for it." I was nervous as my parents wouldn't know where we were, but at the same time, the idea of going out ourselves has always been on my bucket list. I couldn't wait.

"Fine," I told Skye, "I'll be back in a moment." I then carefully went back over the bridge and entered our house. The first thing I did was search my room.

Somewhere I had my helmet and goggles. I found mine in the top cupboard above my bed. Then I grabbed another money pouch from my drawer and entered Skye's room. It was similar to mine, except she had flowers by her window. They also gave her room a pleasant fresh smell. The room was also elegant and tidy, which often was a talking point. How can a rebellious girl have such a clean room is beyond me!

I found her gear pretty quickly. It was on a shelf neatly next to a couple of books. We got our stuff for our birthday a few years ago, and Skye and I treated them like babies. She had a dusky pink helmet and goggles, whereas mine was light brown. I didn't mind, though. I searched through her drawers, being careful I didn't find anything I didn't want to see, and when I discovered her money, I left her room. I ensured I locked the house too, but it wouldn't matter. If someone tried to travel here to rob us, they could kick the walls down.

I then made the last trip over the bridge I needed to make. When I got back, Skye was bouncing on the spot. She snatched her things from me and got herself ready. I did the same, tucking my money deep inside my pockets. I wouldn't want that falling into the void. I saw that Skye did the same.

"We will carry it through the doors outside and then go. Are you ready?" I'll admit, I was nervous.

"Skye, when we go, promise me something," I said, wrapping my hand around the skier.

"Um...okay."

"Don't go off too far. I am responsible for you. …stay near me… please."

"I will look after you, don't worry, Amp," Skye laughed, then lifted her end. I did too. Together, we lugged the skier of the shed and placed it gentled on dying grass in front of the bridge. Skye had given the skier so many support parts and reinforced almost everything. I wasn't going to ask how she found time to work on it, but somehow, she had.

"Let's do this," she said, closing the shed before us. She then stepped onto the back and strapped herself. Fuelled with excitement but nervousness, I buckled up and powered up the skier.

PART 4

I checked Skye was ready; I don't think she could be more prepared. I pushed the accelerator we rose off the ground slowly. I then moved the bars forward, and we floated over the top of the void. This was it; Skye and I were on our own.

I carefully guided the skier forward and away from our Islands. I felt sick, but at the same time, I was ready for our trip. I went slower than Skye was happy with, but I didn't care. I wanted to make sure that I wasn't about to flip over.

I joined a flying lane and followed the traffic. I tried not to look at the void and focused on where I was going and other skiers. It didn't help settle the sick feeling I was getting. What am I doing? I should have at least waited for my parents to come home. What if we fell into the void? They would never know what happened to us. Despite my doubt, I powered on.

"Land over there," I heard Skye shouting behind me. I glanced as far behind me as I could. Skye pointed to a massive island with tons of market stalls. From above, there looked like hundreds of individual tents and booths. To the side was a parking zone for Skiers. With the help of my sister, I guided our skier down. I pushed the landing gear button just before we touched down. At first, nothing happened, but there was a creak then they flung out. When we were down, I switched off the engine, took a huge breath, and released the handlebars. First trip alone, done.

Skye quickly got off, and she leapt off the skier. I joined her shortly after, ensuring I had taken the key out.

"You did very well for a newbie! Come on, let's check out the stalls. I have always wanted to go here," Skye squealed. It must have felt like her birthday or something.

Mum and Dad rarely came here. They always tell us how it looks charming, but it is a rough place. The people are not very nice at all. It is why they hardly sold their farming stuff here. I've been to the market several times since I was a kid, but Skye has yet to. She has begged a lot but never got the chance…well, until now. Luckily, we did choose a good time for the market. It was The Skiland Festival.

The Skiland Festival happens once a year and lasts about a month. It is to celebrate the day the Skilands were created. Everybody celebrates it, but no one ever questions what was before the Islands. I have a theory that all the Islands were once joined together. Anyway, during this time of the year, places like the market were decorated with lights. Some people host parties and share gifts. Shops also have discounts on all their products, a bonus for us at the market.

"Hurry up, Amp," Skye said as she began running towards the crowds of people.

"Wait up, Skye. Don't go too far!" She acknowledged me, which was better than I was expecting. However, she still carried on running without slowing. I doubled checked the skier was off before I chased after her.

I pushed through the crowd, that only got thicker the further I got. I kept getting made aside by random people, but I kept my eyes on my sister. My parents were right about one thing; the people were so disrespectful. I could see people fighting, pushing each other around, and not even apologising for accidentally hitting anyone else. Straight away, I felt anxious about leaving Skye alone, so I sped up as quickly as possible.

There was a little moment where I lost sight of Skye, but it was only a short time till I caught up with her. She was standing still, staring at something. I placed my hand on her shoulder, out of breath. Honestly, I have no idea how she wasn't exhausted. Then I saw what she was looking at so carefully.

A large bridge connected to another large island with only one pathway. Either side of the path had the usual scrap metal buildings. However, they were more than one floor but three. About eight buildings on either side in a row dotted the side of the path. In between the buildings had lights strung up, and the pathway had lamps that lit up the trail.

"Whoa! This is so pretty! I bet it looks so cute at night," Skye murmured to herself, "How…how did I never know places like this existed in our cluster!" I have never seen Skye so silent and speechless. I bet the Middle and Inner Islands would make this look nothing, but I didn't care. The sight was beautiful, even for me.

I kept my eyes looking forwards but also told Skye, "Please don't run off again. I'm serious."

"Sorry, there is just so much here. We are free to do anything. I don't even know where to go! What about that place?" Skye pointed towards one of the first tall buildings on the right of the pathway. A few pink lights were outlining the bottom of the middle set of windows, illuminating the doorway. The crowd also looked like they had thinned out by that building too. This time, Skye stayed put. Instead, she said something that made me feel touched.

"Together?"

I nodded, and together we crossed over the bridge. It felt solid and didn't feel like it would collapse under our weight. We found ourselves standing at the foot of the building. We are one of the only people here. A couple of groups of people were digging through bags of shopping. They all seemed happy. Even so, I wondered why my parents said the people around here were dangerous. Sure, they were fighting and can be rude, but that isn't enough reason not to bring us here. I was still planning to be careful.

When we looked through the windows, we saw that the building was a place that sold food. Great! My stomach was starting to rumble. I let Skye push the door open, and we entered.

Many more people were inside, with stairs leading up to the next floor. The smell was similar to when my mum made fresh bread. Skye bounced on the spot, so I could tell she couldn't wait to see what they had.

A couple of minutes, we were up against the wooden counter. Skye was reading through a menu and making comments on food, and I just peered through a door than was behind the worker who was behind us. I could see large metal furnaces and a couple of people rushing about.

We have had most of the things on the menu before but still needed to do a few things. Of course, Skye ordered them as she wanted to try absolutely everything.

When we had our food, it took about twenty minutes; we had a choice of going upstairs or back outside. We agreed out would be the best as we had so many things we wanted to admire. I spotted a bench at the far side of the pathway, which I pointed out. Skye searched a little more but ultimately said the bench was the best location. It was slowly getting dark, but we weren't in any rush.

When we started eating, I finally saw what Skye had ordered. There was a packet of chips which had some brown sauce on it. I was expecting something else. There were also a couple of cakes in different colours and designs, but my favourite was the red one. Skye told me it was called red velvet. Switching between salty and hot chips to cold and sweet cakes was strange, but it was worth it. I was starting to see why Skye was so excited to leave.

Not having my parents nearby felt weird, but this was alright. Granted, we flew almost twenty minutes from home, but when we were home, we would return to farm work. Seeing Skye happy like this and finally starting her adventures was good. I hope she doesn't get addicted because I will not keep flying her everywhere.

We finished our food and decided to check a few tents and stalls. Skye promised not too to run off as she thought I was scared. Yeah, right; frightened she is going to get hurt more.

As we stood up, the food we had eaten hit us. Both of us felt sick and were ready to hurl at any moment. We then headed back over the bridge, taking another look at the lights between the buildings.

It felt like it was rapidly getting dark, so all the lights were getting brighter and brighter. The sky was turning sunset orange, and the shade of blue in the void got darker and darker. If anything, it made the place feel more magical. The number of people on the island with us was also dramatically reduced. I'm guessing everyone was going home. We should be leaving soon as well. It will take us a while to get back. I don't like the idea of flying in the dark. We didn't put lights on our skier so we wouldn't be very visible. Plus, the wind is stronger at night.

"Skye, I'd say give it half an hour, and then we need to leave. I don't want to leave it too late. Plus, Mum and Dad will be home soon," I told Skye. She was not too happy with the idea and tried to protest. This was one thing I wasn't going to let go so I stuck with the plan until she finally gave in.

We jumped from stall to stall, though many closed for the night. Skye was particularly interested in one booth that sold various stones and rocks.

The woman selling them told us stories of how they came from the void before the Skilands. I didn't believe her for a second; however, Skye did. She asked how I knew they weren't real. I couldn't give her an answer that made sense. She laughed as once again she one-upped me.

Skye dug out a few more coins and paid for several coloured crystals. She then danced over to another stall that was filled with books. Even I was interested in a few of them. We looked at it, and a couple of books caught our interest. I got Skye a couple of books and myself a book too. We also got ourselves bags as we were struggling to hold onto things. Then finally, we headed back to our skier.

We took our time on the way back, taking brief looks at various stalls, but the light rapidly disappeared. It would be dark by the time we got home. Eventually, we reached the parking zone. There were only so many skiers left. However, we searched around, but no matter how much we looked, we couldn't find ours.

"You left it here. I swear," Skye said, standing at the point where I thought we had left it.

"I did. It's gone!" We both started to panic as we quickly searched the area again, but we couldn't find our skier anywhere. We weren't sure what to do, so we thought we should return to the stalls and ask if anyone could help. We did that, but everyone either ignored us or couldn't help. Just when I thought things couldn't get worse, things got worse. I was speaking to another shop owner when I heard my sister scream. I spun and ran towards her sound. The screams became muffled. No one else seemed to bat an eye, but I was now sick and panicking. I shouted Skye's name and desperately scanned the island, but the place was almost pitch black. I had to rely on following the sound of her muffled screams.

Because of the lack of people now, I could see far and spotted Skye. She had two people grabbing and dragging her backwards a few stalls away. She was trying to fight them off, but it wasn't working. Straight away, I ran after them.

I wasn't sure what I would do when I got there. I ran and quickly caught them up. I was almost within reaching distance when Skye's screaming intensified. She looked like she was looking at me, but when I realised, she wasn't, it was too late. There was intense pain in the back of my head then everything went dark.

PART 5

I could feel vibrations and could hear the sound of wind blowing. Then the sound of an engine. I tried to open my eyes, but they were glued shut. My head had searing pain. Skye. Where was she? I had to see where I was first. With much effort, I opened my eyes and saw the night sky. My whole body hurt. I could barely move but lifted my head just enough to know I was in a skipper's back seat. That was all I was able to see before I blacked out again.

This time, I woke up and was a lot more awake. I still ached a lot. I couldn't move a single muscle. Looking around, I could see I was now in a building. The walls were painted brown, and the floor was cold, grey stone. Scraps of straw littered the ground as well, which at a glance, reminded me of one of our farm sheds.

Suddenly, one of the walls rattled and squeaked. It later opened, revealing blinding blue light and a man. He wore a leather waste coat and a white tunic underneath; a brown hat sat on his head. After entering my room, he slammed the door behind me and watched me.

"So, you're finally awake, huh," he said in a deep, authoritative voice, "how's the head."

He grabbed a belt around his waist, buried his thumbs next to the buckled and waited. I felt sick.

"Where...is Skye," I asked. I found out I was dehydrated, but all I wanted to know was where Skye was.

"You mean the girl? She is okay, don't worry. You will see a shack on a small island through the window behind you. She is there." I tried to move and turn my head but was paralysed. Nothing responded.

"Why can't I move," I questioned, but I could tell I was asking too many questions. The stranger's answer was, "That doesn't matter. You will

24

be able soon. Now, we have a few questions for you. We're asking the same questions to Skye…was it? If what you say doesn't match up, then someone will get hurt. We won't want that now, would we?" The man laughed and revealed yellow and brown teeth. I imagined his breath wouldn't be very pleasant after seeing those. My neck hair stood up and sent a shiver down my spine. This guy was starting to creep me out more.

Each minute that passed, I attempted to move my fingers. If I could move my fingers, then the rest would be easy. At least that is what I was thinking, but I couldn't move or feel anything that terrified me.

"So, you're the farmer's kids, yes?" It took a while to process what the man said. I was tempted to lie, but where would that get me? Also, would she get hurt if I lied and Skye told the truth? I had to tell them the truth. What harm could it do?

"Yes, we are. Why does that matter?"

"Your mother owes us a lot, and before she could pay us off, she ran away and married a farmer. I bet she would pay up if she knew her kids were in trouble."

My mum owed money to this guy? He was talking about before she was married to my dad. That was way before Skye and I was born. It must have been someone from her travels, but I didn't have time to ask questions.

"Tell me, has your mum ever told you about her travels to the Hurling Cluster?"

"The Hurling Cluster? Some of it, why?"

"So, you know about the object that she has from there?" I thought for a while. I tried to move my finger, and to my relief, I did it. All I had to do was work my way up my arm. The man then coughed loudly. I needed to answer the questions more quickly.

"An object? Describe it; I might be able to tell you." My train of thought was simple, buy some time until I could move properly. Then wrestle this guy and steal his skier or skipper, rescue Skye, and escape. I guess that is a lot easier said than done.

"It is a gold sphere that would fit perfectly in your palm. It is worth a lot of money," the stranger said, and right away, I knew what he was talking about. My mum has a lot of things up in the attic of our house from her travels. She never let us up there, but Skye and I used to sneak in and check everything out. I remember seeing a small sphere thing. We never paid too much attention to it as it was boring and needed more information written about it. What did this guy want with it?

"Who are you," I asked but instantly regretted asking.

"Who I am doesn't concern you. You know what I am talking about, don't you?"

"Whether I do or don't doesn't matter; I just wanna know who you are."

"Tell us what you know about the sphere," the man shouted, approaching me. He started to circle behind me and out of my field of view. For some reason, being unable to see him made my stomach lurch. I was vulnerable. I desperately tried to move my arm but couldn't. I knew I had to keep him happy, so I said, "I know nothing about it apart from the fact it is in my family's attic." I heard him laughing, and then I felt something hit my right arm. It didn't hurt. I cranked my head off the cold floor with more effort, but very slightly. I hoped that the man didn't notice. I tried to see what he had done to my arm but couldn't turn my head far enough without it falling back to the ground again.

Another shooting pain shot through my head.

Footsteps sounded behind me and then shuffled back in front of me. I saw the man once again who crouched next to my face. He crouched so close I could taste his breath. It stunk of mouldy fruit, which made me almost sick. He then whispered in my ear, "Excellent. Now, I will drop you off at your home, and you will get it for me. We are going to keep your sister until you do. Understand?"

Of course, they were holding Skye hostage. I had no idea who these guys were, but I was ready to hurt them however I could. I could feel my left arm stinging, the same arm I felt something hit me earlier. I assumed it was this man who hit me with something. Suddenly, something clicked in my head. I could feel my arm! The stinging was giving me a feeling which allowed me to move. I pinched my leg, and sure enough, I could feel that too. The effects had worn off enough now. Armed with this knowledge, I prepared myself. I wasn't sure what to do, but I was going to do something in the next couple of minutes.

"Okay, okay, but why not do it yourself? Surely if we both are hostage, my mum would just have to give you what you want," I said, now starting to push this guy's buttons. Judging by his reactions, I couldn't tell whether it was working. I needed him to get into a position where I could grab him properly, but he was just too far for me to reach. He crouched would have also been great, but he had just stood up again. He walked backwards, almost as if he knew my plan, then explained, "Well, why did I never think of that? Oh, wait, because I don't want to draw any attention to us, and you just simply going home and grabbing it would be great. And if you do as we say, your sister goes free. Simple."

"Do you think my parents aren't already wondering where we are," I asked, hoping he would come a bit closer? I could feel my arm throbbing and burning, but I resisted the urge to look. It felt wet, so I assumed it was most likely bleeding. I then felt another hit.

I ended up giving away the fact I could feel my body again because my body contracted and flinched to a burning swipe in the left side of my stomach. At first, I was lying on the floor in pain, but I saw the shock on the guy's face. I saw that he was holding a whip in his hand. I didn't know where he got it from, but I didn't fear it. I was ready to fight.

I sprung to my feet and speared the stranger. Together we tumbled to the floor and rolled a couple of times. I was on top of the man and threw several punches, but he was too strong. With ease, he pushed me off him and rose. He had an iron grip on the whip that he tried to hit me with again. I was ready and stepped aside. Once I heard the crack, I leapt forward and grappled the middle of the whip. I pulled as hard as possible and slammed my shoulder into his chest. He thumped into the wall that I found out was brittle.

The man and I fell through whilst wooden planks from the wall splinted. As swiftly as I could, I scrambled back to my feet and landed a solid kick to his face. I didn't stop. I was in pain, but my sister was in trouble. I kicked him again and again. Blood spurted out his nose, and he rolled about on the ground. A couple more kicks later, he wasn't moving, and I could finally get my bearings. My head was all over the place and whirling back and forth. I stumbled about before I was able to stabilise myself and focus.

The first thing I noticed was the hole in the wall of the building. I then observed that the island was just a tiny grass island with just one building. There were little bits of orange stone around the place too. I felt my arm stinging even more, which made me check it.

What I saw was way worse than I thought. My upper left arm had a massive bloody wound that was a few centimetres long and deep. I also saw dirt and mud mixed up with the blood.

"Great," I muttered to myself. I knew this meant it was likely to get infected. Whenever there was a gust of wind, my arm would sting even more. I had to cover it up, so I ripped some of the cleaner parts of my tunic and tied them as a temporary bandage.

Once it was secured, I scanned more of my island. I couldn't see any island anywhere on my side. I hopped over to the man I planned to check on in a minute and carefully headed to the other side of the building. There I saw a few more islands. Most of them were far away, but one, similar to mine, was pretty close. A few bits of stone had fallen off the bottom of the smaller island, making me question what my island's base looked like. Either way, that is where Skye was. I was also happy to locate a skier standing near the doorway. It was the one the stranger used to travel around.

The skier had black poles with read handlebars and red outlines around the thrusters. On the main body of the thruster was a red logo. It looked like a paw print with a circle around it. I could use the skier to get to Skye. Now I just had to hope that this man had the key. It would be stupid if he didn't.

I quickly bounded back to the stranger and searched him. I felt his pulse to make sure he wasn't dead, which he wasn't, and rifled through his pockets. Luckily, I found his key for the skier. It was a long red and black plastic key with the same symbol. I also found a pouch of money. I toyed with the idea of taking it and ended up doing it. I stuffed the pouch in my pocket, counted a couple of coins, and then doubled check for anything else. When I concluded nothing else was left to take, I strapped myself into the skier and powered it on. I probably shouldn't fly in my current state, but I didn't let that stay in my mind very long.

This skier felt a lot more like the ones I was used. It wasn't so sensitive and was an older model. It didn't matter. I kept my eyes locked on the other island and its building. I had to hope that Skye was in there. I approached the island and slowed right down. The island was empty outside, with no skiers or skippers anywhere. I prayed that meant no one was here. I wouldn't be able to win another fight unless I got lucky.

I found the door to the building and carefully tried to open it. It didn't budge. It was locked, so I resulted to kicking it down. I wouldn't care about breaking a door if Skye was in here. I took a couple of steps back and then ran. I brought my foot up, and suddenly there was a massive crash. The door flung off its hinges and hurtled to the floor after…silence.

I set foot in the room, holding my breath. I saw Skye lying on the floor, her eyes puffy from crying. When she saw the door break, she tried to back away as she was up against the wall, but he headed down. On the floor near my sister was sick, which I assumed resulted from what happened to Skye.

"Skye," I said, approaching her slowly. Her ears pricked up, and she lifted her head. When she saw me, she jumped to her feet and hugged me. The hug was so tight I could feel the air leaving my lungs. Bits of straw and hay fell out of her hair, and more was entangled.

"Y… you're okay? They t…told me tha…that you were k… killed," she stuttered, hyperventilating and crying. I hadn't seen her this hurt before, and even I wanted to cry. I had to stay strong for her.

"I am okay, just a few scrapes. What did they say to you?" I asked her, brushing straw out of her hair. She sniffed and let go of me, then wiped her eyes. Shakily, she answered, "Well, they asked about a gold sphere Mum stole from them. I told them I couldn't remember seeing it, and they left. When they returned, they said someone would keep hurting me until I answered their questions. I called out their bluff, and they…they showed me a video of them whipping you."

"A video," I asked, "I don't remember seeing a camera. It wasn't me, Skye." I figured she didn't want to be inside the shack anymore, so I led her back through the door.

"But I didn't know that! I kept telling them I didn't know, and they showed another video of them pushing you off the edge," Skye sobbed, her eyes watering again, though no tears fell. It ached my heart to see my sister this upset, but I remained as neutral and positive as possible.

"Either way, I am okay. I am here. There isn't another skier, but we can't stay here," I said, realising that our way off this island wouldn't be easy. Then Skye, for a moment, returned to her old self and laughed, saying, "Well then, someone is just going to have to hold on to the back until we get to those islands then. Your arm looks like it hurts, so you should fly. I will just hold on…."

"No," I interrupted, "you strap in and fly; I will be fine holding on. Besides, we want the better flier, flying with the extra weight." I knew that making her look better would make her happier and persuade her to do what I wanted. I used to use that to my advantage when we were younger. If I wanted the extra slice of cake, I would say that I was a fat person who needed it and that she was healthy. It wasn't until she turned eleven that she realised I was using her. But in times like this, it still works. Mostly because she and I both knew it was true anyway.

Skye thought momentarily, looking at the skier, then said, "Fine, but if you fall into the void, I will kill you!" There we go, the regular Skye was back, and almost as if she wanted to confirm it, Skye added, "If you tell anyone I cried, I will also kill you."

"Duly noted!"

After staring me down, she smirked and rushed to the skier. It was crazy. A moment ago, she was crying her eyes out, and now it was like nothing had even happened. She should be the older sibling because my mind still stewed on the people who attacked us. Skye wasn't too worried about them, but I had a feeling that they would be back. What if they attacked the home? Who were these people? What was the sphere? Now I had to get home. Home…where was home from here?

"Are you coming or not," Skye said, already strapped in. I couldn't believe I was about to do this, but I gripped the back of the skier and placed my feet on the back of the foot stand. Skye had moved her feet slightly further forward to allow room for me to stand. Once I was ready, she powered on the skier.

The initial launch felt precarious as the skier tipped backwards, but Skye used her knowledge to counter it. She described it as flying in upward winds. I thought I would be okay…then we left the island. Knowing I was one mistake from certain death didn't do the best for me.

Skye probably knew this and didn't even attempt to scare me; we were both aware of the significant risk that we were taking. Plus, she probably knew I was afraid, which would most likely amuse her. Instead, she flew as carefully as she could towards the silhouette of islands in the distance.

PART 6

"Where are we," I questioned aloud, but I didn't mean for it to have an actual answer. I already knew that Skye wouldn't know, but it didn't stop her from reminding me that she didn't have a clue. Her voice told me that she was apprehensive about our situation, despite her attempt to remain hyper and energetic. I kept holding on to the back of the skier and focused on spotting any potential building or landmark I would recognise, but I couldn't find anything. Everywhere was alien to me. Even as we approached the closest islands, the ground didn't look like anywhere I had seen. The islands we were stuck on must have been a few miles away as we flew for ages until we reached any new islands.

Orange and light golden dust covered a dark stone underground, and then now and then, the powdery dirt would blow off the island and create dust storms. They were a pain as the vents on the skier would clog up and make the skier unstable. It frightened me, but I could only hold on even harder and pray that my sister could keep us up. I will tell you now; this is not how I want to go out. I was about to hurl a few times, but I could hold it. I could feel my stomach contents sloshing about, which was highly uncomfortable.

Much to my relief, we found a place with a few people to land on. They gave us mixed reactions when they saw two strange kids, one clinging onto the back, touch down on their island.

"Excuse me," a deep-voiced woman asked. She had greasy threads of brown hair, starting to grey, in a ponytail, a dusty red shirt where the colour had begun to fade and short green cargo shorts. I later saw she was also wearing sandals with no socks on.

At the first chance I got, I hopped off the back of the skier and made a mental note never to do that again if I could avoid it. I let my heart rate lower as I helped Skye get off. The woman who greeted us folded her arms and stared us both down with confusion but concern.

"So, what are two kids doing flying about my island, huh," the woman asked, stepping closer to us. She noticed we were both scared; well, at least I was afraid and tried to be less intimidating. Skye seemed to be putting on a fierce face. I don't know why; we were in the wrong place.

Skye replied first, and her response was the complete opposite of the story her face was telling. She said, "We are lost! A couple of people kidnapped us at the Marhalm Cluster market, and we have no idea where we are. We have locked away on those couple of islands over there, and my brother was able to steal this skier from those guys. You're the first people we have seen." I was taken aback by her honesty and straight to the point, but I didn't say anything. Even if I wanted to, I only got a little choice.

The woman analysed us as Skye spoke and answered, "Let me guess, weird hat, tall, muscular guy, waste coat?"

"Yes, that's the guy. Who is he," I asked, slowly finding my words again. Her face dropped, almost scared.

"If you two are mixed up with that guy, then I am sorry, but there isn't anything I can do for you both but give you food, water, and a lift into the cluster's centre. I have no idea where Marhalm Cluster is, so I can't even give you any directions."

I gave Skye a fretted stare and then gazed down at the orange earth circling my feet. A blade of green grass, covered in orange stuff, poked out the ground in small groups and a bit further along was a small tree growing. It was leaning up against a fence that surrounded a house.

The house was painted white with dark red trimming going around the top. The flat roof created a box-shaped house with smaller boxes added to different sides and well-built windows in each area. Small, different coloured flowers lined the bottom of the building, alongside small cane holding up more trees of other coloured trees.

We were silent before I asked for any help that either of us could get. I was planning to ask the woman who the guy was, but we needed to ensure we were fed and had a drink. I was parched, and I am sure Skye was too. Besides, bringing up the waisted-coated man would cause problems neither Skye nor I were prepared to deal with.

Luckily, the woman agreed. She then told us to wait outside then, with giant strides, rushed into the house. A couple of seconds later, we had who I thought was a man with a trimmed dark beard staring at us through the window. He kept an eye on us, ensuring we were doing everything smoothly. He and I looked at each other just before Skye tugged my shirt. She leaned close and whispered, "We get this food and drink, and we're going, right? We can find out about that guy after we're further away. I have a bad feeling about this." I let out a sigh of relief.

Skye feeling wrong about this made me feel a little more confident in my gut instincts. I would want to leave right now. Something wasn't right. The man in the window hadn't stopped staring at me with narrow eyes, but he was speaking to someone. I assumed it was the woman. Skye was also eyeing up the man, then also at me. A few more moments later, I was feeling too uncomfortable to stay.

"Skye, get back on the skier now. We're leaving. I have money; I will get us something somewhere else." I didn't have to tell her twice. She backed towards the skier, keeping her eyes still on the man in the window, who had shifted at Skye's movement. Skye brushed off some dust that had built up in the vent with her feet and slipped the key into the key slot. The skier coughed into life, and Skye got on. She strapped herself in and was ready to take off; I was about to get on when I noticed the man was gone. I quickly searched to see if I could find it, which I couldn't. So, I was about to step onto the back of the skier like before, much to my dread, when the house door opened.

Skye and I swung our heads around and saw the woman with a couple of glasses, and the man stood behind her like a bodyguard. Now I could see him correctly and see he had tanned, oil-covered skin. He wore a black vest that was ready to rip. His body shape was the most muscular body I have ever seen. His biceps were bigger than my head, and his triangular body was as wide as Skye, and I side by side. The woman looked like a dwarf compared to him.

I gulped when I saw him but tried to remain polite. Skye had her hand on the rusted buckle of the skier strap, ready to release at any moment. Behind the house, the sun was setting, and the sky was turning into various shades of yellow, pink and orange, yet the void remained dark blue.

"Leaving already, are you," the woman asked, sounding offended. She approached us with devilish confidence, both hands holding a glass. I almost told Skye to leave, and ill grab on. We could get away quickly if we did. Yet here I was, frozen on the spot again, watching two people who freaked me out close the distance between us. We went silent, the only sound being the engine of the skier and the crunching of the people advancing towards us. Why couldn't I move? Why wasn't I saying anything?

"We were just making sure the vents weren't clogging up with all this dust," I heard Skye, noticing she had subtly unbuckled herself to support her story. She kicked the ground to emphasise what she was talking about and, with fake confidence, took a few strides to meet the pair. She then took hold of one of the offered glasses and held it, not taking a sip. Skye thanked the woman and gestured for me to do the same. Her actions allowed my body to move. I did as I was told, wanting to ensure Skye had planned everything. I, too, didn't sip my drink, but I did thank the woman. After I said thank you, I remained silent and prayed that Skye did have a plan.

Skye began to approach me, her eyes still staring at the woman. She was wearing a sad face but was also tense.

"So, you said you can give us directions to the cluster's centre," asked Skye, pretending to drink from the glass. I could see she wasn't letting the liquid get anywhere near her lips, but it was enough for the woman to smirk slightly. That was enough confirmation to know she had put something in the drink. I decided to do the same, so I casually raised my cup and tilted it. I let it splash against my lips but ensured they were closed. I wasn't about to drink anything from these people.

The man stood there, mute. His primary focus was me, which was unnerving. I could swear that he could read my mind. I felt he would be on me in seconds if I tried anything. For a brief moment, we locked eye contact, and his eyes narrowed. His greasy skin was more apparent now I was looking at him closely. His arms were massive; he had tattoos under his vest that slightly poked out.

Suddenly, I felt a body slam into me. My glass flew out of my hand and rolled off the island's edge. My body staggered back a few steps, and automatically, I grabbed whoever just hit me. When I regained my balance,

I saw it was Skye who had fallen into me. I saw her glass had smashed onto the floor just next to where we stood.

After I helped her up, Skye looked back at the woman and then at herself and said, "I am so sorry. I tripped on that stone. I don't suppose we could get another drink; I'll. Clean up this glass!"

"Ugh. Don't bother. Why don't you come inside with us," the woman asked, now agitated. I didn't want to be here anymore. I made the mistake of insisting that we stay outside, which gave away the fact that we wanted to leave.

"Marlo, will you please bring them in? We will keep them here until the Rogues get back." I had no idea who the Rogues were, but I wasn't planning to find out anytime soon. Skye and I backed away as the oily man grunted and stomped over to us. She stuck close to me, and I gently put myself between her and him. All I had to do was create enough time for Skye to escape.

The closer the man got, the closer to the edge of the island we were getting to the point it was rapidly becoming a concern. The skier was on the other side. I couldn't take this man alone, especially with a bad arm; even with Skye, I would struggle.

The wind picked up, and sand started getting into our eyes. Mine were glued together as a vast gust threw a stone that stung when that made contact with my skin. I shielded myself with my arm and saw the oiled man flinching. I took a deep breath and then threw myself towards him. Skye shouted my name, but I ignored her. I brought my knee up and into the crotch of the man. He yelped and bent over. I then turned and grabbed my sisters' hand and pulled her towards the skier.

I saw the woman attempting to grab me at the last minute, but I ducked. I told Skye to start the skier while I dealt with the woman. But I saw Marlo rising again and running back over to me. I gulped with fear. He wasn't about to let me do the same trick again.

I shoved the woman away from me and put as much space as I could between Marlo and me. However, it wasn't enough space. He reached out and grappled the top of my shirt and a handful of my skin. My first instinct was to grab his wrists and pull him off, but the oil made me constantly slip. Then I felt my feet leave the ground as I was picked up and thrown over his shoulders. No matter how much I batted at him, he wouldn't bunch.

Marlo then approached the Skier that Skye was desperately trying to start. She pushed the key in, and the engine revved several times. For a moment, I thought it wouldn't start, but a few clicks and creaks later, it did.

Skye had a couple of seconds to choose her next move, and after a sorry look, she got onto the skier and launched it off the island, just out of reach of Marlo's other hand. She then hovered on the spot, battling the wind that created a storm of sand. Marlo and the woman stood still, watching Skye and refusing to budge from my constant fighting. I was getting tired, so I chose to conserve my energy. When everyone was calm, the woman spoke up again.

"If you leave, it will most likely be the last time you see him, young lady. I suggest you come back down here." Skye didn't move. Marlo had the courtesy to turn himself so I could see her, but he could still. I waited for something else to happen. Anything to help me get out of the deadly grasp I was in.

"L…let him go. You will regret it if you don't," Skye shouted erratically, losing her focus slightly. The wind pushed Skye back further than she wanted, so she had to spend a minute correcting herself. Now, unless you were shouting, your voice would be inaudible.

I heard the woman next to me laughing.

"Kid, no one is coming to help you, and you can barely stay upright. Come down now, or your brother will…accidentally fall off the island. My fight came back, and I got desperate again. I pushed and fought as hard as possible whilst Marlo waddled over to the edge. Seconds later, I felt my body ragdoll, and I was flung back out in front of Marlo. My legs flopped downwards. When I looked down, all I saw was blue. He had me over the edge. There were a few rocks that stuck out with build-ups of orange sand. I paused once again, heart pounding. There was nothing I could do.

"Skye," I shouted, not knowing what I meant by it. Most of me were terrified and just wanted her to get back down. But if I were to die, I want to die knowing Skye got out safe. Therefore, I wanted her to fly as far away as possible.

"He only needs one of you," the woman informed, fixated on Skye. It was almost like I could see the gears in Skye's head working overtime. Her face was scared and also angry.

"I guess you made your choice then," the woman shouted, then nodded at Marlo. My body felt numb as Marlo's grip was released. I think Skye screamed, but I wasn't sure. The next few seconds felt like a lifetime.

As I fell, I saw the man holding me going up and then to the ground shortly after. My mind wandered to my parents. They would have no idea what happened to me. I would never see them again. Skye would watch me fall to my death. No, I wouldn't let her have that on her mind forever. I threw my arms out in an attempt to reach anything, anything to help me. I felt something, and my body jolted as I came to a sudden stop.

I felt around, not daring to move. When I looked to see what I was holding, I saw it was a rocky handhold from the bottom of the island. It was very crumbly, but it was something! I took care of my breathing as I was starting to hyperventilate. Next, I dared to look around. When I saw nothing below me, I was sick. The motion almost threw me off, but I refused to let go.

I searched for a more solid handhold, but there wasn't much choice. I wanted to find at least something to get my feet on. My arms were starting to burn, and I was losing grip. My whole right shoulder felt like it was tearing itself away from my body. The pain grew more, and I frantically looked for anything.

Then, I heard the engine of a skier. Skye! Skye was still flying and must have seen me. She lowered herself and spun around, revealing the back of the skier. I could see she was crying but trying to hold the tears back. My sister didn't have to tell me what to do. I used my other arm and grabbed hold of the back of the skier. Then I released my grip on the rock and felt the whole skier fall backwards. We almost tipped upside down, but I stood onto the side of the skier and placed a foot on the front footholds to weigh it forward. Working as a team, Skye and I stabilised the skier.

PART 7

She didn't waste any time and flew as far away from the island as possible. Skye flew towards the direction where there were a few taller buildings and where the islands were closer together. I was balanced precariously on the side of the skier and didn't dare move back around.

It was only a short time until we saw the most famous island I had ever seen. It had tonnes of buildings all over the place and people everywhere. All of them looked the same. Horizontal wooden planks made up the walls with flat roofs. They had windows about half a meter by half a meter dotted about the walls evenly. Underneath, the rocks and stones were bright oranges sticking out by a few meters. It was a vast, elongated pyramid with an almost flat, yellow top. I didn't care too much because I felt way too ill. I just needed a break. I told Skye to land on the big island, and with no hesitation, she did just that. We touched down in a skier parking lot, then hopped off onto land.

I was about to sit down on the floor to recover when Skye ran up to me and hugged me.

"Please never scare me again," she sobbed, trembling. It was a welcome stress release. I was in way too much pain and felt way too sick. The sky above was getting dark, and stars were becoming visible. In the distance, I could see the moon. It was huge tonight. Its light projected onto the many islands around us, allowing us to see. I pointed out the moon to Skye, who had let go. It was the first time I could stop and take a breather.

Her red dress was covered in mud; her hair was a mess. What kind of brother was I? I didn't even realise how rough we both looked and felt. I kept telling myself I had an excuse for being so wrong with Skye when no reason would be enough. I should be doing better looking after Skye and not almost dying on several occasions. By this point, our parents would have search parties out for us. There is no way they wouldn't just let us be gone this long. Hopefully, someone will find us so we can get back.

"Amp…" Skye said softly. She tugged on the side of my tunic to get my attention.

"Yeah?"

"They're watching us…." I followed her eye line and saw who she was talking about. A group of men and women, all with the same hat and waistcoat, similar to the man who kidnapped us, hovered together by the corner of a shop window. When we looked their way, they returned to their group and spoke amongst themselves, but as soon as they thought we weren't looking, they would look back up and watch us again. I felt shivers down my spine.

"You have got to be kidding me. Can't we catch a break," I muttered, feeling my eyes heavy. To make things worse, Skye tried turning on the rusty skier, but it didn't even make a sound. It was officially as reliable as it looked.

After several more attempts to start the skier, I said, "Let's head into the town. It is still light enough that we will have a lot of people. We're going to be fine." She agreed, and we got moving, pretending not to worry, but we checked behind us every other second.

The parking zone was a little small. It was a small flat gravely area with a few other skiers, a lot nicer than the one we stole. Everything was way more solid and better built than most places. Even the little trails around the island seemed to be regularly taken care of, the small spots of dark green grass being cut and then flowers dotted around.

As we reached the other end of the parking zone, Skye and I found a concrete pathway with lanterns lighting towards the central area. A few fences run on either side of the path, and both spread apart and into the sides of the first building.

"There are a lot of flowers here. I thought they were scarce," Skye said out loud, brushing her hand against a petal of a red flower. She paused for a second to smell them before we resumed. Most buildings had some form of flower, even if it didn't have any petals.

"I know, so did I. We only get to see grass and whatever crops we are growing. Marhalm barely has any flowers like these! You have a couple in your room, but they were expensive! Yet here, it seems like everyone

39

has them. We must be close to the middle islands, right," I answered, admitting that seeing various coloured plants was cool. Skye ran her hand through her hair, straightening it up after she took a closer look at the buildings around us.

Everywhere was tightly packed, with narrow walkways spreading around and between buildings. It was like nothing I had ever seen. If I tried, I could touch two buildings on either side of the street.

"Yep, I think we are near the middle islands, but wouldn't we still see some poor stuff," she asked, checking behind us again. I looked behind us and only saw a woman from the group tailing us. She didn't look away even when we made eye contact, which led me to conclude that they were following us. They wanted us to get the sphere for them.

"Well, we will see some later. We need to lose these people and get help. What's the betting that they'll talk to us nicely if we turn around and just speak to them," I questioned, paranoid of every corner we went around.

We found ourselves in a somewhat busy area with wooden archways over the path we were following. They connected to pillars on either side which were then integrated into the buildings. It looked so beautiful. White and green flowers weaved their way throughout the wooden archway and the pillars, breaking up the monotonous, light brown colour scheme. The shop windows all had glass which was rare to see for us. For us, if we opened our window covers, they wouldn't have drink underneath. These people were rich.

Skye suggested we try going into a shop and then leaving when there was a bigger group to blend in. However, I told her that our clothes would stand out too much. People around here had tops made out of cleaned wool and trousers made out of denim. A few even wore a shirt with a collar and held leather briefcases. This compared to my filthy tunic and Skye's dress; we would stick out like a sore thumb.

We both sped up our walk until we saw one of the men, who also struggled to fit in with the crowd, just a short distance from us. He was watching us too. I quickly checked behind us, and the woman was still tailing us as expected. I subtly pulled Skye in a different direction to avoid the man and the woman but saw yet another one. We were surrounded. I warned Skye, and both of us groaned at the fact tha we were unlikely to get away without yet another conflict. All these for a sphere. Why was it this important that they couldn't just get it themselves?

We upped our pace even more. It was now evident that we were trying to get away, but in every direction we turned, a new hat and waistcoat-wearing person would appear from around another corner. It got to a point where we had to stop. We spun in a circle, counting every single person. There were eight people, and now they were closing in. We prepared ourselves.

"Someone help," Skye shouted, and some people turned their heads. A man stopped and asked if we were okay, but as soon as we explained the people, his face turned from concern to fear. He then said sorry he couldn't help and scuttled away. Everyone seemed to run away from us like we were contaminated with a deadly virus. Silence fell after a few seconds, and we were the only people left. Only two people stood in a circle of people. We had to move, and we had to move now.

"Run," I ordered, grabbing Skye's hand again and aiming to go between two people. She was taken by surprise and was very close to being pulled over. Her first couple of steps were uneven, and she had to use her hand to brace herself off the ground. When she found her footing, the force required to move her eased off, and we both just about slipped between two aggressors. We would have been within their reach if we had waited a moment longer. The thought was repulsive, but I didn't let it slow me down.

We raced around the nearest corner, knowing we were being chased. The island felt deserted all of a sudden. No one was anywhere—just us and them.

Neither of us knew where to go, so we kept running. We had some close calls a few times, but our quick thinking allowed us to evade any attempts at stopping us. They knew these islands because they always came out in front of us. Knowing that our luck wouldn't last forever, we tried to find a way to escape again, but each time we thought we had an idea, it was rapidly shut down. Then, unexpectedly, Skye was grabbed and pulled in a completely different direction from how we were heading. The change of direction shook my entire arm.

"This way, and be quiet," a girl's voice whispered as we were led through a dark area between two large buildings. The light was fading again, and it was near impossible to see who this person was, but we didn't have a choice. She didn't sound like the attackers and seemed to know where she was going. We had to trust her.

About five minutes later, we slowed down. We hadn't seen anyone for a while, so I took the time to see who this mysterious helper was.

From my first impressions, apart from the hair colour, she looked almost identical to Skye. Hers was a chestnut brown, whereas Skye's was light brown. Even the dresses looked similar but the colour. Skye had a lighter red dress, and this other girl had a dark red dress. Both of them were similar in height and had hair in a similar style. From the minimal time she spoke, I could tell her voice was different, which was good because I didn't want to confuse my sister with a stranger.

"We're nearly there, come on," the girl uttered, keeping her focus on the direction we were going. I shrugged at Skye and followed her. So far, she hadn't led us astray. I was also starting to become conscious that we were still on the same island, which meant this place was huge! But we eventually emerged from a small gap between some wooden buildings with a path so tight we had to sidestep through. We picked up a lot of dirt and other things on our hands, but we didn't complain. We saw the island's edge and the void on the other side. It was officially dark.

A few more corners later, we approached a parked skipper. It was bright wine red and gleaming. Four black seats were without roofs; one heart was behind the wheel. It fits in perfectly with this place. It was exceptionally well built, just like everything else. The bottom part had sand and orange dust, barely noticeable compared to everything else. Much to my and Skye's surprise, our helper took out a key and told us to hop in. She then clambered in and pushed the key inside the slot.

The skipper whirled into life with a quiet hum. Not asking questions, I helped Skye scramble into the back before climbing into the front seat next to the girl. She then pulled back on the wheel, and we began to lift off the ground.

There were no vibrations, no loud noises; everything was quiet. As we hovered off the island, I could feel a cool breeze. I stared out into the distance, seeing the night sky once again. The stars twinkled brightly, the moon projecting its light onto the many islands. The gentle hum of the skipper allowed the whole experience to feel...peaceful.

For a moment, we flew in silence. I kept thinking about the people coming after us and the injuries Skye, and I had obtained in the last couple of days.

I looked at my arm that was hurt and saw my temporary bandage was grubby. Also, some blood had seeped through. It was a good job that dirt didn't get in my wound, although I am willing to bet it would still get infected.

I pealed the muddy dressing back slightly and looked at the cut underneath. It had started to blister, and bits of shredded skin stuck to the cloth peace. A clot was beginning to form, which was a good sign, so when my arm started to sting even more, I put the bandage back and left it alone. My next instinct was the girl.

I look over at her, curious. I studied her face more closely to find more differences between my sister and her. There weren't too many. I then decided that the least we should do was thank this girl as she had helped us escape.

"Um...thank you," I opened, wishing I knew what else to say. She turned her head and had a slight smile.

"You're welcome. I hate those guys. What did you do to get on their bad side? Not like you need much of a reason," she replied, sitting up in her chair.

"It isn't anything we did, more...what our mother did. Who are they? Why is everyone scared of them?"

"Where are you from? You aren't from around here. They're. The Red Rogues. Bandits who think they own everyone and everything. They're known for stealing, torturing, manipulating, even killing people, especially if you get on the wrong side, which you just so happen to be," she explained. The girl turned her head and looked at my arm, then nodded at it and said more.

"I'm guessing they did that, huh?"

I nodded.

"So why don't people just fight back? Surely, there is more of you than there is of them," I asked, wondering what her name was now.

"People do, and yet they're still not enough. The inner islanders don't seem to realise that this threat is growing bigger and bigger, and it won't take long till they have taken over everyone around us," she sighed with frustration, "anyway, what're your names?"

"Amphorn, though most people call me Amp. This is my younger sister Skye," I told her, checking on Skye. She looked ready to sleep, and her fiery spark was out. She had scrapes on her hand and dirt on her face.

"My name is Lily. Lily Azalea. You both look like you need rest. It would help if you had a proper bandage on that arm too. That thing is doing next to nothing on it now. We'll be at my home soon. The Rogues won't follow us, don't worry." Lily smiled again. She gently turned the wheel, and we lowered down. Lily said, "My home is those islands, just over there."

Lily pointed over two a few islands that took my breath away. They were large mountains of rocks in a circle shape. It was very dark, but we could still see that the centre was filled with bright-coloured flowers of every colour imaginable. Lanterns dotted several pathways through the flowery fields, which looked gorgeous. A small cave entrance looked like the way into the flowering haven.

The mountains looked like an extension of the rock underneath. They were just as jagged and dangerous and also just as beautiful. At the very bottom were several silver pipes in groups. They attached somewhere on the island and stretched into the void where the ends couldn't be seen. It was like nothing I had ever seen before. These were the sort of places Skye and I would talk about seeing one day after reading about them in books. And now...here we were.

The sight made Skye perk up a bit. She leant over the side, staring in awe.

"You...live here," she gasped, not taking her eyes off anything.

"Yep. It used to be my parents, but when they died, I took over. I now run and look after everything you can see, mostly alone. When we get down, I will set up a place for you both to stay and then give you a tour of the place tomorrow. We can also discuss the next steps when you have properly rested and cleared up." Lily kept smiling; this time, I imagine it was with pride.

Lily lowered the skipper and flew through the cave entrance I had seen earlier. It was a lot bigger up close. You could fit almost fifty skippers in the opening alone. A cave underneath the mountain went right through to the middle. A few doorways led off the cave and into the hill even deeper and were lit up by lanterns dangling down. The place was dark but light enough that Lily could see where she was going. It was also cold, which made me shiver.

Lily touched the skipper before one of the doors and turned off the engine. She then got out, as did Skye and me. Our footsteps echoed through the cave whilst we followed Lily to the nearest door. She pulled out some keys and unlocked them. It clucked open, and the three of us headed inside.

The temperature difference was the first thing I noticed. It was so warm. There were loads more plants all over the place. Green ferns and mini trees decorated the walls, which we painted in a lavender purple. Dark wooden beams lined the corners and the ceiling of the room. Everywhere was lit up by small candles. To the right was a fireplace with smouldering embers. Lily quickly chucked another log from a small pile of eight logs, neatly cut up, into the fire, and the flames rose again. A small grey sofa was placed in front of the fireplace, which Lily told us that one of us could sleep on. The other would sleep on a small bed in a room to the left.

Once she finished stoking the fire, Lily said, "The shower is around there. Turn the little tap, and you will get warm water. I will find you a proper bandage for your arm. Skye, you can wear one of my dresses. I have loads anyway. Amp...I don't think you would suit any dresses but would fit in some of my dad's clothes. I kept a lot of them."

"Amp would look so pretty in a dress, though. We could even decorate his hair," Skye laughed, placing her hand on my head. I flicked her off, but I saw Lily laughing.

"I have plenty of flowers if you want a crown to match the dress," Lily continued. Great, now both girls were talking about how they planned to dress me as a girl as if that would happen. I felt my cheeks blush as Lily stroked the side of my head to demonstrate how low the crown would sit. Her touch was so gentle and soft.

I groaned and replied, "If Lily can get us home, I will let you dress me however you like. Lily...did you say warm...water?" Skye looked as if she was already planning my outfit. However, Lily was taken by surprise by the question.

"Well…yeah, what else would I shower with," she asked, giving me a look that felt like she was slightly judging me.

"Well, isn't water, like, costly to get? Where we live, water is barely seen. We are lucky as we get water for our farms, but it is where most of our money goes. We use alcohol from some crops we grow to clean things. We also sell a lot. It isn't great, but it does the job," I explained to her. Lily led us into yet another room, which, too, had a lot of plants. This place looked like the kitchen, with a sink and a fridge. A stone oven was also carved into the side of the wall. It had black charcoal inside, which meant it had been used.

Lily seemed curious about our home. She asked, "So I am guessing you drink juice from all the plants too? I have water harvesters. I will show you them tomorrow. They allow me to do simple things like this." She then walked over to the tap and turned it. Almost right away, water poured out. Lily quickly grabbed a glass and held it under the water. It filled up and then repeated the same thing. She handed them both to Skye and me.

"Drink," she told us, which we did. We held the glasses to our lips and took a sip. The water felt so clean and cool. It was refreshing. I never appreciated how thirsty I was! My mouth was bone dry, so the water was exactly what we needed. It also made my stomach churn. I was starving!

I nervously asked for something to eat, to which Lily said, "Go get yourselves cleaned up, and I will prepare something for dinner." I didn't complain, and I did exactly as she spoke.

PART 8

I had never felt more rested in my life. I woke up from my sleep feeling full and happy. The fire in the fireplace had gone out, and there was a bright light. Above me was a small window that allowed light through from the side of the mountain. I didn't notice it last night as it was too dark, but considering the size, the light let through was enough to light the entire room. With my eyes shut, I lowered my head for a bit to get used to being awake.

I could hear someone scuttling about the place. So, I rubbed my eyes to stop them from being blurry and peered through into the kitchen. I saw Lily in the same red dress as last night. She twirled around the place like a dancer, so smooth and elegant. It sounded like she was humming a song. When I sat up, the sofa I was lying on creaked and caught Lily's attention. She spun around and then skipped over to me.

"Oh, hello, sleepyhead," she chuckled, placing a cup of tea beside me on the floor. I sat myself up and allowed her to sit next to me. She leaned against the left side of the sofa and held another cup of tea with both hands. Lily then stared at me with curiosity whilst I yawed and picked up the boiling cup off the floor. I took a sip and flinched. It scorched the inside of my mouth, much to Lily's amusement. Some of the tea spilt on the floor when I thrust the cup away. I apologised, but Lily didn't mind. Luckily, the bed was stone, so it was easy to clean up.

"So," Lily started, sinking back into the sofa, "how are you feeling today? How's the arm?" I caught her looking at my bare chest, but I was never one to be shy about my body. If I'm honest, I didn't care if anyone looked at me, though being shirtless in a room with a girl who looked like my sister's twin but wasn't her twin did feel slightly awkward. I was sure Lily was marginally older than Skye, but it couldn't be by much. She was

47

closer to my age. As much as I was tempted to ask her age, I was always taught that you never ask a girl their age. So, I didn't bother. Instead, I answered her question.

"My arm aches, but I am feeling pretty good. Thank you for letting us stay here!"

"You're both welcome to stay as long as you need, but we should try to get you two home as soon as possible. Speaking of your home, you never actually said where you're from."

"Marhalm cluster, it is the South-East of outer islands." Lily seemed to go into deep thought. The girl told me she didn't know exactly where it was but knew a few people who may. Afterwards, she suggested we see them later, but first, she had a few chores. I asked if I could help with anything, and she accepted instantly, saying, "Well, I usually have to do this on my own. No one else knows how to grow or care for crops, but being farmers, I imagine you both do?"

For a while, we exchanged knowledge of plants which she seemed infinitely more knowledgeable about! She promised to show us around and give us all a tour of her gardens, and I was genuinely excited. However, our conversation turned more serious quickly.

Lily switched the conversation topic and randomly said, "Amp, you need to prepare yourself." I asked what she meant, and she explained, "The Rogues that attacked you wanted something from your parents, right? They know where you live. Your family is in danger. I can get you back, but there is no guarantee that your life will not be the same. It'll be spent in debt until they get bored or you repay them." The seriousness was something I didn't want to hear, yet I needed to. Things would be different even if we got home. This whole time I was suppressed, but Lily was right. I needed to prepare myself.

"You also need to step up," she informed me, which confused me. I took a few sips from my tea, which I had had before but not often, and asked what she meant.

"With Skye. She is terrified and doesn't show it. You need to ask how she is, comfort, treat, anything., properly spend time because she is scared." That felt like a slap in the face—a slap in the face with another truth bomb. To give myself some slack, I haven't had much time, but that wasn't an excuse. I was meant to protect her and ensure she was happy, yet the only time she was happy was because of a stranger and a new island.

I replied, "I know. I just…I don't know how. I don't even know where we are. The only money I had was stolen from the guy who kidnapped us. We have no skipper. We…"

"Have met me! I can help you. Later, I will let you two have time to yourselves. I will also take you to the cluster centre. I will stay nearby, obviously, but I will give you time. The Rogues will probably be searching for you, so you need to change your appearance, but I doubt they will expect you to head into the centre again." I didn't want her to go out of her way to help me, but I needed all the help I could get. I thanked her.

We sat chatting for a while until Skye eventually woke up. She had messy hair and was wearing some of Lily's night clothes. We all had something to eat, and Skye and I got cleaned up and dressed differently.

The girls went out of their way to look even more similar by giving Lily a different red dress that brushed very lightly along the floor. There were a few differences, though. The most significant being the top half of Skye's dress was light red, and the bottom half was dark. Lily had white on the top and also white stitching.

Skye did a twirl with a smile, feeling cute. Lily gave Skye a small flower headband made of green leaves and white petalled flowers to add to her *cute and innocent* look. If there was one thing I knew about Skye, she is all girly and innocent looking until she wants to do something. Then she becomes a vicious beast if you don't follow it.

When we were ready, Lily said, "I need to go and pop into my shop first. It is normally closed today, but I have an important thing to take care of first. Don't worry. I will take you on tour after." I didn't imagine Lily owning a shop for some reason, yet it made so much sense. She has water, and from the small parts seen, she has many flowers. Both of which were rarities. She must earn a fortune!

The only thing I wore that was mine were my shoes. I wore a light brown leather jacket with a black tunic underneath. I had dark blue jeans. The clothes were slightly too big, but they fit well enough. I was just happy to feel clean again. Lily had put a proper bandage on my wound, which I planned to keep clean.

After we were ready, we followed Lily out of the underground home and back into the large cave. It was cold still but not as cold as last night. The sheer size still blew me away. We looked like ants compared to the stone walls. Now it was light, I could see that the ceiling was rougher and spikey than I realised. It didn't bother the echo, though. Every sound was amplified, including our footsteps. I could hear what sounded like running water, too, loads of it.

It reminded me of when I had read about large bodies of water in the old world; sometimes, it would lead to waterfalls. It was where the water would flow off the edge of a cliff or mountain. I didn't think they existed. It was way too unrealistic to believe that large bodies of water would exist naturally. These waterfalls were fantasies made up of fairy stories to look pretty and hold a secret base for superheroes. They were incredibly loud, too, which would make it off-putting.

Skye and I were led towards the inner part of the island. We finally came out of the other side of the cave, and when we did, Skye's and my jaw dropped. The mountains were in a large circle, leaving the entire middle open to the sky. There were fields and fields of flowers of every colour, shape, and size. Being down here made the scale that much more impressive!

Our small group followed were taken to a dusty party where Lily's mood changes. She hummed and skipped, happy. Very happy. She genuinely loved it here. I checked on Skye, who was fascinated with the bright colours and the smells of a small bush of pink and yellow plants that hung the path at waist height. Skye pushed her nose against them and inhaled, saying, "It is just...so...pretty! What are these plants called?"

"Zinnia," Lily informed, her face beaming and looking to the right side of the pathway. I, too, looked that way and thought I was hallucinating. I tapped Skye's shoulder to get her attention, and despite her frustration with me interrupting her, I knew she had to see what I was looking at. She stood back up and groaned at me. However, it was cut short when she saw what I was looking at—the source of the loud water sound.

There, about a hundred meters away, was a real-life waterfall! Glistening, blue, frothy water crashed down the side of the mountain, and spray was thrown all over the nearby plants. I couldn't see where the water was coming from as it disappeared over the huge rocks. A few birds were nestled in small coves beside the water. The waterfall was at least two hundred meters tall and landed into another water pool at the bottom. Now I was paying attention, I noticed the water pool was running through the grounds, under a bridge and into the other side of the mountain. I couldn't believe what I was seeing.

Skye squealed when she saw the bridge and rushed to it immediately. The bridge was a little small. Along the sides were railings that Skye leant on. She was lost in a trance, amazed at the running water. I joined her not long after and felt lost in the hypnotising flow of water. I was curious why it lapped over the sides but never flooded. When I asked Lily, she explained, "There are pipes at the other end of the stream that pumps the water and carries it back up to the top. It was engineered perfectly so the water would never go too low and yet wouldn't flood the fields. Naturally, the water goes down, but we have other ways of getting more. I will show you later. I need to get to my shop. We can come back after." I had to drag Skye away from the bridge and other plants she was smelling and asking about.

A few minutes of slow walking later, we came up to yet another cave, which looked a lot smaller. Lily went through first, then I pushed Skye through and came up from behind. A few seconds later, we were in a smaller mountain opening on the other side. It was a slight hill. A median-sized wooden building stood on the edge of a concrete area.

The concrete had a 'parking zone' painted on it. The building was only one floor high, but it had a massive tree behind it, making the house look taller. Hanging plant pots, weaved from willow, were out the front, near the door, and a large window was on the side. In the window were a surprise, surprise, flowers. Flowers in bunches. A sign was hammered into the ground, and it read:

Azalea Shop
Flowers, water, baskets
And more inside

So this was her shop. How many people came here? It was so out of the way of everything! How would anyone know it was here? Then again, it was the only place that sold these things. Lily opened up the front of the shop and headed inside.

It was a usual shop inside, but it was planted in various bunches, bottles and tanks of water, baskets, pots for plants, as well as a few bits of fruit and veg; the only thing I have seen sold in a shop before was the fruit and veg, as it was what we sold, everything else was completely different.

Skye was still obsessed with the flowers, but Lily told us we should stay around the back and off the shop floor for now. I was about to ask why but the sound of a skier engine interrupted us. It landed outside on the concrete, and Lily got a little tense.

"They're here early. Get to the back...now. Stay quiet! No questions," she said through gritted teeth. We did as she asked, and Lily shut the door behind us, but not before her face returned to her gentle smile as usual. But this time, it felt forced.

Skye and I stood with our ears pressed against the locked door and heard Lily speaking to a man or multiple. We needed to figure it out.

"Hey, how are you," Lily said. A man with a deep voice replied.

"We are fine, love. Do you have our delivery?"

"Yes, I have it behind the counter. I moved it here yesterday, ready for you," Lily answered. There was shuffling around and clunking of heavy boots on the wooden floor. They were muddy shows too.

After more silence, the man said, "Thank you. If you do something else for us, we can leave you alone longer." I heard Lily's breathing quiver after the boots sounded like they had gotten closer. I didn't like the sound of what was going on. Skye had narrowed her eyes too. She mouthed, "What is going on." I shrugged.

Then, Lily spoke again.

"I think our current deal is enough, Denny! Unless you want to cancel that deal." There was more silence. I assumed Denny was the man; whatever this deal was, Denny didn't want to lose it.

"Or we could take them ourselves and force you to do anything we want you to!"

"You don't know how to look after them properly. Also, good luck keeping the rare ones alive," Lily answered confidently. She had this guy right where she wanted.

The man grunted, and a few more clomps got further away.

"One more thing," he sneered with his deep voice.

"Hm," Lily replied.

"We are looking for two kids. One guy and one girl. They look like this." Some more noises could be heard. It sounded like the crunching of paper and more footsteps.

"Oh, she looks like me? I don't know them, unfortunately. What did they do," Lily asked with confidence. Two kids? One boy and one girl? Was that us? Was this man one of the Red Rogues who were chasing us?

"They assaulted one of our own and took something that was ours," Denny growled.

"You mean the things you think are yours because you stole them first," Lily chuckled. She was pushing his buttons. Denny inhaled with force, and his tone got even more profound.

"Watch your mouth, girl. You only have your freedom because of your knowledge...If you see these kids and tell us where they are, you will have your freedom permanently, and we won't bother you anymore."

The footsteps got further away this time, and Lily said goodbye. After the sound of a skier taking off and flying away, Lily opened the door again. Skye and I immediately fell into the shop floor but scrambled to our feet.

"He was one of them, wasn't he," Skye questioned, looking at a crumpled piece of paper with a sketch of Skye and me. Lily nodded.

"What is the deal you have them," I asked, trying not to assume anything. All three of us knew it was suspicious, so we waited for Lily to explain, which she did.

"These guys need my knowledge of the plants and flowers to keep them alive. They take them and sell them as they are worth a decent amount of money. Our deal, I let them take what they need if they leave me and my business alone. Some of them aren't bad people, but most of them are like Denny. Gross and rude." When she finished speaking, we stood in reticence. Lily was checking a few things around the shop to pass the time. Meanwhile, Skye and I were still thinking. What Lily said makes sense.

"So basically," Skye started, "because you have knowledge of the plants and flowers, even the rare ones, you have power over them. They need you, and you can keep them where you need them. Smart!"

Lily smiled, her green eyes twinkling, then said, "Exactly! They aren't so scary if you know how to manipulate them. Half of their boys love me, which makes it even easier." Her confidence was unmatched; I will give her that much. I would like to know how accurate the last part was. She was pretty, but she looked too close to my sister for my liking. Besides, I have only known her for a day. Still, her smile and presence did make me feel...happy.

"Ahem," I heard Skye cough, and I realised both girls were staring at me. I asked why, and Skye laughed. She could barely speak but said, "You were staring at Lily and didn't answer a few times! You think she is cute!" I felt my cheeks go red and saw that Lily was blushing too. She bit her lip and left through the front of the shop, telling us that she was done in there and was ready to lock up.

Skye kept grinning at me, and she kept disagreeing every time I denied that I liked her. I wasn't going to win, so I dropped it. When we were all out, Lily locked the front door and headed back towards the flower fields. She stopped for an instant and said, "Come, I'll give you a tour! There are a few things that you would love to see. I could also use help. Tonight I will take you over to my friend, who will be able to help get you two home. He doesn't finish his work until tonight, so we have time to kill!

"Who is this friend of yours?" You know the Rogues quite well," I questioned, sounding pretty intense. I didn't mean for it to come out so harshly, but I also felt slightly on edge again. Skye and I had been through way too much, so I felt like I was well in my right to be suspicious of Lily.

"His name is Mal-chin. If you want to know more about him, he can explain himself. You have to trust me because you don't have a choice, do you," Lily answered back, returning the sharpness that I used with her right back at me. She was now scaring me. She switched from cute and gentle this morning, and now she suddenly proves she can bite when needed. So that was another thing that made her very similar to Skye. Honestly, I could trust her purely based on that. Either way, I knew she was right, and so did Lily.

Lily waited for me to reply, but my silence was enough for her. She raised her eyes to prove even more that she was right, then moved back to the flower fields. Skye smirked, ran after Lily, and I followed from behind.

I watched birds flocking around the plants and landing on various areas on the rocks. They were all white or greys, the most common colour around the islands. However, I did see Skye pointing up at another bird. It was large and brown with black spots on its tail. Lily said it was some falcon!

Of course, she would have rare birds too. We didn't have mice or rats around our islands, so feeding them was hard. So they never stayed near us and instead flew away. They flew over to places like this. It makes sense. It was perfect for them!

Skye kept smelling more flowers along a different path. Lily took us down. It was parallel to the stream and closer to the waterfall. I was most excited to get closer because every step made it look taller and taller. I could feel the spray at one point, but not enough to get soaked. Lily stopped when the spray was the worst.

The crashing water roared so loudly I could just about hear Lily shout, "This waterfall is the only one for around hundreds of miles. Maybe a smaller one is closer, but this is certainly the tallest." We took a couple more minutes, staring in awe at its beauty and power. The spray made rainbows, which were also pretty cool!

Lily got us moving again, and we entered yet another hollow just to the right of the waterfall. It was a lot darker as there wasn't much lighting. However, it wasn't as deep. A black door blended in with the rocks, and Lily opened it. This whole place was starting to feel like a maze. Tunnels and caves everywhere!

Lily pushed the door inwards and invited us in. Initially, I didn't know what I was looking at. It looked like a gleaming machine that was pretty noisy. To the left were three large, silver metal barrels with a tap at the front and a pipe connected to the machine thing. The whole thing sounded like a pump, but I needed to figure it out. I asked Lily if my guess was correct, and her eyes sparkled. She nodded, her cute side returning once again. I preferred her this way.

"It is a pump. It is how I collect water. The large pipe you saw under the island is connected to this. It stretches into the void and collects water vapour from the clouds and the air nearby. A filter on the right purifies the water and is pumped into those barrels. I can then collect the water if and when I need it. The pumps running up there go to the top of the waterfall to keep it supplied with water as it eventually evaporates. Sometimes it makes mini clouds above here."

There was too much information to remember, but I was still fascinated. Right away, Skye kept asking about all the buttons and the void. Lily didn't know much about how the machine was made and said it was all made a long time before she was born.

We spent almost an hour just working out what goes where, and at some points, even Lily learnt something new. Eventually, we got to a point where we had to move.

Once again, we headed through yet another door behind the barrels. A small sign with a skull and crossbones was stuck on, which was ominous. However, the next room was Skye's dream room.

Books, everywhere! It was a vast library, two floors high, making my mum's one look like a garden shack. Having the library behind the water tank was weird, but I wasn't complaining.

"There is too much knowledge back here to let people in casually, so we marked the door and put it in a weird place so no one thinks about it. Amp, I hope this shows that you can genuinely trust me. You and Skye can read what you want, but only if you do me a favour. It could take you a while, though."

So this was a trust thing! I didn't say anything at first. Instead, I studied all the different books placed in front of me. Some books were old and tattered, and the names were faded. On some of the books, I couldn't read the title. Skye was already pulling out books from wooden shelves, followed by small puffs of dust.

"Fine," I said, watching Skye's excitement when she opened a new book, "I trust you! What would you like us to do?" Lily pointed at the shelves.

"All these need to be reorganised. They're in a weird order at the moment because my mum, before she passed away, kept changing them. Her mental problem made her go loopy and constantly fiddle with things, this place being the main thing. I never did it because coming in here upset me."

Her voice trembled and got quieter. She was opening up to us, which solidified my trust in her. I told her that we would do what we could.

"Thank you. If you don't mind, I need to do a few other things. I will return here in a few hours with something for lunch. Get whatever you can, done. Don't worry if you can't finish it. After, I will take you, Mal-chin."

As soon as she left, I had to explain what was happening to Skye because she was too busy reading and not paying much attention. Even when we started sorting through books, she would get distracted easily, making the task a nightmare.

PART 9

I didn't know the exact time, but I knew it had been at least four, maybe five hours since we started. Both my back and Skye's were beginning to hurt from the constant bending over. But we managed to get through most of the library, even when Skye stopped starting. I'll admit, I even had a read through a few books. They had so much knowledge and even pictures of the Inner Islands, and some showed what the old world used to look like.

The buildings and sceneries were beyond imagination! They had old temples and statues of famous people, apparently. Also, pictures of the ocean stretching so far that you couldn't see the other side. They would also ride on top of the water with floating things. It looked like so much fun! Skye and I kept coming up with theories about why that world no longer existed, and both of us thought maybe the islands were all once together, and the ocean broke them apart.

When Lily returned, she brought some fresh fruit and some bread that still felt warm. She was happy with our progress and thought we would get more distracted. We explained briefly how we organised the books into different genres and then into alphabetical order. Afterwards, the three of us sat on the floor and ate together, discussing theories and sharing knowledge.

Of course, Lily was just too clever. She already knew anything we knew about farming and could give tips and advice. It felt like one thing I knew I had over most was now so minuscule. Skye spoke about flying and exploring; again, Lily seemed to have travelled and seen a lot when she was younger. Nowadays, though, she has to look after her own island because her parents are no longer around to help do so.

When we finished eating, Lily helped finish the last bit of organising. Skye had to go toilet, and Lily showed her the closest bathroom. They were tubes that you do your business in, then it opens up and drops into the void. It's gross down in the void by this point though eventually, it will all decompose, right?

When Lily and I were left alone, she asked, "So, I gave you plenty of time alone. Did you ask her how she was?"

Shoot. I completely forgot about that. I mean, she sounded okay. I know I was feeling a lot safer. My arm still stung, and my muscles ached, but I felt okay.

"Of course, you didn't! You are useless, you know," Lily tutted, placing a book about space on the shelf. We were both crouched down side by side, each with a pile of books to put away. She continued.

"When we go into the centre, I will give you your time again. It won't be able to be too long, but it should be enough." I promised her that I would speak to Skye, and I have a feeling Lily was not about to let me forget again.

Skye returned just as we finished and headed out of the library. The light blinded me, but it didn't stop me from staring at the waterfall again. It was my favourite thing I had seen, and knowing there must be bigger ones somewhere, just excited me. I kind of didn't want to go home.

Lily grabbed a few things from her house, the cave she sleeps in, and I got my pouch filled with money that wasn't mine. After, we headed out to the red skipper in the vast tunnel. Once we had all got in, Lily took off and flew higher up. We looked closer at the tunnel's massive ceiling and saw its roughness and unevenness. Also, the colour wasn't just plain grey; it was a gradient of blacks, greys, and white dust.

After a few minutes of doodling, we were back over the void and leaving Lily's huge island behind. Seeing it from above in the day was way more impressive than I would have imagined. The multiple colours of flowers covered the middle of the island like a blanket, and the mountain hid the gem away. The waterfall still kept my attention as it slowly got further and further away.

I could feel my eyes getting heavy. I don't even know why I was getting tired. Another twenty minutes later, we returned to the orange, dusty islands again. Seeing rundown buildings and islands that looked so dirty felt almost weird. The skiers that whizzed around like flies looked awful, and that was after we spent only one night at Lily's.

We trundled past more islands, and I spent most of it watching Lily. She looked conflicted, trying to work out what she wanted to do. It's funny because your face gives so much away when you don't realise you're being watched. Like right now, I could see that Lily felt different from how she let on back on her island.

My first thought was maybe she was considering the offer the Rogue had given her. But indeed, she was more intelligent than that. From what she told us, they would never give her true freedom for handing us over. Then again, we don't mean anything to her, so it's an easy deal. She did share the library location with us, though. Skye and I read through a lot of stuff, and she told us it was a huge sign of trust.

I concluded that I trusted her still and turned my attention to our destination—the centre.

By the looks of things, we were close to the centre as the islands were closer together. I could see places that looked familiar and then remembered that it was where we had already been.

Lily touched down behind several wooden buildings with a few pink flowers dotted around the front.

"I'm guessing you sold them these flowers," Skye asked, seeing each flower like gold.

"Mhm," Lily replied in her usual sweet tone, switching off her engine. The gentle hum stopped and instead was replaced with distant voices and chatter from people on the island. As far as I could tell, we were the only skipper or skier and the only people, though there were people not too far away. Lily must like to keep her skipper away from everyone else, which I didn't blame her for.

We all scrambled out of the skipper then Lily closed the roof. A glass dome folded over the top of the skipper. We followed Lily between houses and shops, brushing off orange dust as we went along. The wind had picked up, so it kept twirling around our feet. It was getting chilly, almost icy winds today, but we powered on.

You would have thought it was early morning based on the fact it was so quiet. All the shops were open, including the tiny, crooked stalls with a single person slouched behind the counter. Just as we passed a bird store, Lily came to a stop.

"Okay, we're pretty much in the middle now. These buildings are the tallest around here, so it's a good beacon. I need to go and get some stuff quickly, but you guys are welcome to explore. Just be back here in about an hour," Lily said, rummaging through her small bag. Now she had brought it to our attention; I saw these buildings were four stories tall with tinted windows every meter apart. We could easily see these as they towered over the other buildings, making them significant landmarks.

"W... wait a second. I thought we were staying by you in case the Rogues come," Skye questioned, attempting to hide her concern. So she felt safe around Lily. Noted.

Lily smiled, almost ashamed, but she winked at me when Skye wasn't looking. That must be her way of telling me actually to talk to Skye.

Lily gave me a watch so I wouldn't lose track of time and said, "Sorry! I won't take too long. I promise. I will be nearby. If you run into any problems, then head down that alleyway. You will come out into a large open market area that usually has loads of people who know how to handle the Rogues. You'll be fine. Go explore for an hour."

"Skye, we barely look like ourselves. We can go an hour," I added, knowing why Lily was giving time. Reluctantly, Skye agreed. With that permission, Lily said goodbye and headed into a nearby alley, leaving Skye and me alone again.

We wandered into the bird shop, not knowing what we wanted to do. I wanted to wait a little longer before talking to Skye, so we studied the birds to kill time.

When we entered, the smell resembled the seeds we used to farm with. Birds tweeted away in various-sized cages. The building looks like it went for ages, despite looking pretty small on the outside. Skye was particularly fascinated with the kestrel in a cage that quickly took up two floors. A few dead mice were hidden on the bottom underneath a few leaves. There was a tree, and you could just about make out the kestrel between a few leaves. It was perched, head twitching and looking at the floor. Skye read through the small booklet about the kestrels she saw and complained that the information needed correcting. She recited several paragraphs from a previous book she had read and then said that the cage was way too small for a bird of its nature. I agreed so that we could move on.

Eventually, I was ready to ask how Skye was feeling. I pondered the idea for a while before asking, "Skye…."

"Yeah," she said back.

"Are you okay?"

Okay, I would have said something better, but I am not very good at this kind of thing, and I freaked out.

"Why wouldn't I be," Skye replied again, "Is this to do with what you and Lily are hiding from me?" She carried on browsing through bird leads. They were leads to keep your pet bird near you when training them.

"W…what do you mean?"

"Amp, I'm not stupid. You two have been having secret conversations whenever I am not here. What are you hiding from me?"

"I'm not hiding anything…." I stopped. Skye gave me a look my mum gave me when she could tell I was lying. She wouldn't believe me no matter what I said or did, so instead, I cut straight to the point.

"The last few days have been insane, Skye. How are you feeling? Scared, worried, okay?"

Her response, once again, completely surprised me. She was honest with me.

"Scared and sick."

"You feel sick?"

"Yeah. The stress, the lack of proper sleep. The right side of my ribs is sore. I am worried about Mum and Dad. And yet, here we are, browsing in a bird shop in a place we have no idea where and sleeping at a girl's house we have only just met, just after we were kidnapped and almost killed by a random gang. I want adventure, but this feels wrong." It took a moment to go through what she said as she sped up and sputtered. She was close to a panic attack, and my asking her about how she felt pushed her closer.

I didn't know what to say, nothing I could say would make a difference, so I grabbed her and pulled her to me. I then hugged her tightly. Now I felt a whole new feeling. I held my scared sister and felt a whole new level of protectiveness. She began to cry silently and again buried her head in my shoulder. I took a breath, held it for a couple of seconds and let it all out, imagining all my fear and problems.

"I'll tell you what," I said, letting Skye choose whether she wanted to end the hug or not, "When we get home and after we got yelled at or whatever from dad, I will take you to a bird shop and get you a bird." Skye sniffed and broke away. She neatened her dress, remembering we were still in a public place.

"I want a kestrel—or a parrot," she sniffled, slowly creeping back to her normal state. However, I could see through her more easily. I could tell she was putting on a tough face, and she did look sad.

"They are both very different," I chuckled, trying to light up the depressing mood. Skye frowned.

"And? I want one or the other." The sound of birds tweeting sounded like they only got louder when I became more aware of them. And also the smell too. The kestrel hopped onto a perch closer to the front so it was easier to see.

"We'll see, but for now, is there anything you wanna do? I thought this would take longer, but now we are just here for another forty minutes until Lily returns."

Skye took a sharp breath and said, "So it was Lily's idea for you to talk to me, hm? And there is me thinking you cared."

"I do care," I answered, my heartbeat rising. She actually thought I didn't care. Then I saw her face. She was holding back her laughter, and when we made eye contact, she burst out laughing.

"You're such an idiot! I know you care. You have a crush on Lily, and you still blush when her name is mentioned, which is just hilarious. Just so you know, you don't stand a chance with her."

I felt my cheeks burning. Skye always did this sort of thing when she was feeling in a hyper mood. She would play pranks and take the mick for the rest of the day.

I rolled my eyes at her, and after, she dragged me outside again. The wind struck first, sending a cold shiver down my spine.

"I want a weapon," Skye mentioned. She stopped and turned at me, bouncing on the spot. Everything froze, and I shook my head, thinking I had misheard her. But she repeated herself.

"If we're going to be followed by the Rogues, I want to be able to defend myself. There was a place that way; somewhere we could go to."

I wasn't sure if I liked the idea. I liked being armed to defend but buying a weapon meant that you were prepared to kill possibly. How would we react if we did take someone's life? Despite the mild pain, I played with my wounded arm and considered her idea. I answered, "I guess it wouldn't hurt to at least browse."

I didn't have much money, so that we couldn't get anything too fancy. Skye squealed. Yep, usual, Skye was back with genuine excitement and determination.

I had to run to keep up with her, and a couple of minutes later, we were at a one-story tall structure that had a green awning out the front and different coloured flowers that were browning in pots by the large window. We had to cross over a couple of smaller bridges to get here, but you would hardly notice they were bridges. It all felt like one big island.

We were in an area that was a lot busier too. Narrow pathways filled with crowds of people, all going about their day. No one would pay too much attention to us here as we looked like everyone else. We were obviously keeping an eye out for any Rogues, but neither of us spotted any.

Skye and I squinted through the glass to see if the shop was open, which it was, so we pushed open the green door and entered.

Inside was a lot of green and brown. The floor had a welcome mat to brush the dust off your shoes on entry. The walls were painted a dark green, and all the shelves and counters were dark brown. A couple of lanterns dangled from the roof with chains, causing flicking orange light and dancing shadows.

Shelves were stocked with things I had never seen or heard of before. There were blades of all sorts of shapes and sizes; one more noticeable was a silver star-shaped blade with a black handle in the middle. There were also a few guns; the cheaper ones looking like a spring were shoved inside a can and had scrap attached as a handle and a trigger that was about to fall off.

"That cannot be safe, surely," I murmured to Skye, but she was more interested in the knives. Suddenly, we heard a grunt.

"What do two kids need with weapons like these, hm," he grumbled, crossing his huge arms. His narrow eyes glared at us, analysing our movements. He hovered behind the counter, waiting for an answer. I figured it would be better if I responded, as I was the older one out of the two of us.

"Um, we have issues with rodents. Everywhere we go, we seem to run into them, so we want something that can deal with them quickly. Ya know, just in case." I could probably have said something smoother.

Even Skye looked over at me, probably thinking that I was useless. She wouldn't be wrong.

"Rodents, huh? What kind? You can buy poison in the verminator shop a few doors down.

Weapons like these aren't meant for rodents nor for kids." He eyeballed me, ignoring Skye, who was brushing her finger along a blade of a small, thin dagger.

"Um, these ones are pretty big, and they seem to end up with more and more each day," I stammered. I could tell he didn't believe a word I was saying.

"Okay, these rodents of yours, would they have happened to have two legs, two arms and a pawprint badge." Busted!

I was about to lie, but I realised that Skye and I looked at each other with desperation.

"They prefer to be in hand-to-hand combat, so keep your distance. I suggest a ranged weapon. Decent ones cost big money, and not only that, but ammo is also a regular cost. So, how much have you got to spend?"

I felt the pouch in my pocket. I didn't have much at all. Buying a weapon would almost certainly use all of it up, and we didn't have any experience in using anything like a bow or a long sword. We would have to settle for a small switchblade, and even that would cost most of the money we had.

"Not much," Skye answered, now walking over towards me, "my brother and I are being chased by them, and we figured that we would arm ourselves with something, just in case." It didn't come as a surprise to the man. He nodded his head at a poster. It was a sketch of Skye and me. We both looked at each other, concerned.

"Don't worry. I'm not in the market for handing kids over to the Rogues. But you guys need to be careful. Not everyone around here is like me. Most would hand you over so that they can get some form of freedom. Choose one of those smaller knives over there, one each. Then I suggest you two get as far away from here as you can. Don't worry about pay. You'll need every penny you can muster just so you don't starve to death."

It sounded like he was feeling sorry but, at the same time, pretty anxious to get rid of us. I understood. Us being here and him not turning us over would probably get him hurt if he is caught.

Skye and I had a brief scan over the smaller knives that the man pointed out. I chose a metallic switchblade with corrugated metal as a handle. Skye went for one of a similar design; however, it had a light wooden handle with dark outlines. We quickly thanked the man and scrambled out of the shop. For a few seconds, we hovered underneath the awning, folding our new weapons.

When we left, the sky had turned grey. It wasn't nighttime for a while, and I could still see some blue around the grey patch, but it was still grey above us. It looked like the white streaks in the void but grey. Skye and I took a moment to look at it and said it must have been a real-life cloud. As fascinating as it was, it got boring, and it was so bright we could barely see. It made my eyes water too, so it looked like I had been crying.

For the next ten minutes, we spent a while at a small market. It was the only thing around here that was actually smaller than home. We browsed a few places but settled on buying a couple of snacks which we ate on the way back to the meeting place. We headed in the direction of the tall buildings and, just as expected, ended up back where we started. Lily was already there, holding a white bag and sitting on a bench.

She saw us and said, "I didn't think you would actually take the whole hour." She looked at me.

"You two ready to head off? It's about an hour and a half flight to see Mal-Chin." Skye and I nodded, and together, the three of us headed back to the skipper. Lily put the bag in a storage compartment in the back of the skipper, and both Skye and I kept our new weapons in our pockets. Once we were all set in place, we set off.

PART 10

Surprisingly, the journey was pretty decent. Skye was sat in the front, and I was sat in the back. The girls chatted most of the way, occasionally laughing at me. I didn't do too much, just watched the world go by. I thought about Lily's friend, Mal-Chin, and what sort of person to expect. I was visualising a man with a strong accent, darker hair, and slim and tanned skin.

Mal-Chin, Lily's friend, was supposedly meant to help us get home. I wondered what his job could be and whether that was why he might be able to help.

Eventually, we got to a point where the skipper was being lowered down. I could see an island that would have been a big island compared to home; however, it looked tiny compared to what we have seen since.

This island was a hexagonal shape with rough edges. On top had a grassy hill and a tall wooden structure. There were wooden support beams holding up a platform with the structure on top, and as we got closer, I could see stairs spiral up the building. From what I could see, the rooms were all at the top, with huge windows overlooking the surrounding areas. They would easily be able to see us approaching.

"When we land, don't say anything. Just stick with me and stay quiet," Lily said, peering over the side whilst we approached. I didn't plan to say or go anywhere anyway. I wouldn't have a clue what to say, so it was a good thing that Lily would talk.

Finally, we landed in a flat, gravelly area next to a few skiers. They were jet black with a few dents and scratches. Then I noticed men standing by a gate, armed with guns. My stomach flipped.

I haven't seen a gun in person, not properly. I will tell you now, knowing there is someone with a gun near you really isn't the most reassuring thing ever. I didn't know where we were and told Skye to stand close to me. She rolled her eyes.

"Trust Lily, Amp, come on. They may be armed, but I'm trusting her," Skye answered back, dragging her feet. Lily had started talking to the men at the gate whilst I replied back to Skye.

"I trust her, but it doesn't mean I still can't feel queasy and cautious."

"Oh man, up! You're supposed to be older than me, and yet you're a wimp," Skye laughed, nudging my hurt arm. I winced. It still hurt a lot, and was starting to really ache. Skye apologised before we were called over by Lily. A guard opened up the gate and said that we could go through. Lily told us to come, and we did.

We had to climb stone stairs that were half buried up the hill, which was a lot steeper than I realised. My calves were burning when I got to the halfway point, and I was getting out of breath. It didn't help that the steps were big steps too. On both sides of the dirt path were dying bushes and trees with thorns. So every now and then, I would catch myself on a slightly overgrown plant. I just hoped none of them was poisonous. I could see the girls' dresses were also getting caught on branches which I just hoped weren't going to rip.

Eventually, we got to the top and stood at the bottom of the tall tower. It was taller than I thought, and I just prayed that I didn't need to walk up more stairs. But luck just wasn't with me. Another encounter with a few guards later, we were heading up the many, many metal steps.

"Why... didn't...they just...build...it on the floor," I exhaled. The higher we climbed, the colder I got. I saw the girls shivering and was going to offer my jacket, but then I knew I had to choose between my sister and Lily. Neither one would accept it anyway. Lily would want me to look after my sister, but Skye would say that I should be a gentleman and offer it to Lily. Being an older brother and a man sucked sometimes.

Three hundred and twenty-four steps later (yes, I was counting), we got to the top. My first thought was the fact that I knew I had to go back down those stairs. That didn't leave my mind for a while.

The room at the top was just as cold as the stairs. It turns out what I thought were windows were just open air and balconies overlooking the adjacent areas. It was so much wider at the top than it looked from both above and also below. About thirty people dressed in black uniforms and body armour hovered around at multiple stations. A central table had a large map on it, the majority of it being blue with green, orange and also brown.

Four men and two women leant over the middle table, looking at the map. They were speaking in turn intensely until the man at the end noticed us. Lily led us forwards, closely followed by Skye and then me cowering behind. I should have been at the front, being the man that I am, but honestly, it wouldn't make a difference where I was.

The dark-skinned man stood upright and placed his hands behind his back, and watched us three. A couple of seconds later, everyone around the table did the same. The man at the end then walked around the table, bowed at Lily then stood up again.

"It is a surprise to see you here, Lil. Who are these," he asked. His voice had a slight accent, and up close, he was pretty young. I would say my age. Perhaps even younger. For some reason, I felt my stomach lurch, and I took an immediate disliking to him.

Lily smiled, curtsying. I then caught Skye watching the man's every movement longingly. Great, she probably likes him.

"Mal, this is Skye and Amp. Guys, this is Mal-Chin," Lily said with genuine joy, "we came as we need your help." Mal-Chin bowed at us both; Skye blushed, and then he asked how he could help. After Lily explained our situation, he frowned. He gestured at the group around the table, who disbanded straight away and then told us to join him at the table. He took up his previous position, and the rest of us also leant over.

The map was huge!

There were so many labels. Almost every single island was labelled. There were hundreds of clusters, including a cluster of orange islands under Skye's fingers. Just over from it, two squares along was a tiny singular island labelled 'Lily's flowers.' That was Lily's Island, and that was tiny, especially compared to the islands in the middle of the map. They were virtually one big island with a lot, and I mean a lot, of white, greys and blacks.

"So, you need to get to Marhalm. That is over there, six squares above your hand, Amp," Mal-Chin, pointed to an extremely small cluster. I looked closer and saw that it was labelled 'Marhalm'. Then, just to the side, I saw another label. 'Aozora Farm'. Even our farm was labelled on here?

"U…um. How did you get a map this big," Skye asked, biting her lip and pretending not to stare at Mal-Chin. He kept a straight face.

"This here is hundreds of years' worth of research and mapping. You have found your home. I can have my men fly with you thirty squares, but we will not be able to stay. We need as many men as possible back here to help with the Rogues.

"I thought you guys had it handled," Lily questioned, concerned. She turned her head towards Mal-Chin and waited for an explanation. He looked at Skye and me, then said, "We have just lost thirty-six armed skiers and another three pilots in the Gruem Cluster. They were supposed to be the support for the attacks near the Cross Cluster, but no doubt we aren't going to be able to retreat in time without the extra support."

"What are you on about," I stuttered, trying to piece together the information being thrown about the place, "is there a full-scale war we don't know about?" Mal-Chin groaned with frustration. Clearly, he wasn't impressed with me.

"Lily, did you not tell this guy anything," Mal's chin said, frowning at me disappointedly. I hated this guy already.

"Well, I did say the Red Rogues were bandits who think they own everything and that they're not the nicest of people. Mal, I didn't realise how far they have spread!"

"Well, now you do know. They control virtually the whole southern side of the outer islands, and their numbers are growing quicker than we can keep up with. Our resources are growing thin, and the middle islanders don't seem to bat an eye." He slouched over the map again, his irritation obvious. I felt a cold shudder as the gusts of winds filled the eerie silence. All I wanted was to get Skye and me home, and yet I was stuck in the map room of some kind of military organisation. How did Lily even meet this guy?

"I can try to lend more money," Lily suggested, but Mal shut her down. He said that he is appreciative of all the support she has given them but that it just isn't enough anymore.

"Look, this guy's home is over there. I will spare a couple of men to get you through the rough parts, but after that, you'll have to be on your own. I'm sorry I can't help you more, but I just cannot lose more pilots."

"If you need pilots, I can help," Skye suddenly blurted out, standing up and facing Mal-Chin. She blushed at the sudden attention.

"Um, no, you can't, Skye. We are going home. This isn't our fight," I told her. I was not going to entertain the crazy idea. This time I would stand up and say no. Lily was surprised but nowhere near as much as I was. She said, "Skye, I think Amp is right. You can't get involved."

Skye didn't have it. She answered back, "We're already involved! If we go home, they're still going to come after us, so why not help?" There was silence. As much as I hated the idea, deep down, I knew she was right. The Red Rogues wanted the sphere thing that badly, so they would be back home already.

Mal-Chin laughed sarcastically and exclaimed, "Thanks, you can go work in the kitchen. Everyone needs food."

Skye scrambled up straight even more and replied back really quickly.

"No, I can fly! I can be a pilot for you!"

"I need people with experience already. We don't have time to train you up fully."

"I am experienced. I am really good, I swear!" For a brief moment, I saw Mal-Chin's expression flicker to curiosity.

"Really," he asked.

"She actually is! She always flew in the winds below the island and flew a rusted old skier with me on the back with no trouble," I uttered, hating the sudden change of attention. I didn't want Skye to join these people, but I did not want anyone to doubt her abilities to fly.

"Can you vouch for her," Mal asked Lily, who crossed her arms.

"Um, I don't really know. I know they escaped on a single Skier but I...I don't know." Lily went shy, and her body tried to turn itself inside out. I had a feeling we were entering a conversation that made her feel uncomfortable.

Mal-Chin stared at Skye, considering what was said. He looked at me but then straight back at her. He then inhaled sincerely, rubbed his dark eyes, then leant forward on the rugged table.

It looked like he hadn't slept in weeks. I did feel kind of bad for him, but I still didn't like him.

"I can set up a brief test for you. If you don't meet the requirements, you're going home. But listen, I don't like the idea of sending a young girl into a fight."

"I would be more scared for anyone who gets on her wrong side," I muttered under my breath. I didn't intend for anyone to hear, but Lily did. She actually chuckled a little and smirked. When Mal-Chin saw her, he scowled again. This guy was never happy, I swear.

"What," he questioned.

"Nothing," Lily answered quickly, still smirking. He wasn't impressed at all. Even Skye looked unimpressed. She was actually trying to look good for Mal.

Ignoring us, Mal turned to Skye and asked, "So, do you agree to our terms?" Skye eagerly nodded, but I stopped her.

"Skye! Come on! You cannot be serious! You're sixteen!"

"And I don't care! What do you need me to do? I'll do whatever you need me to," Skye asked, bouncing on her toes. For the first time, Mal-Chin let out a smile.

"You're really this eager? Trust me; it isn't anything to be excited about. I will get one of these guys to arrange a test and take you to our training islands. You're going to want to wear something else. We'll get you something." When he finished talking to Skye, Mal veered towards me expectingly. He stood tall, placed his arms behind his back and slowly walked over. He stopped less than a meter in front of me.

"Just so you know, I am only seventeen. Age means nothing. You... you're case and point. Older than all three of us, yet the only one not willing to join in the fight that could save hundreds, if not thousands, of people. We can still take you home if that is what you want, but it appears that your sister is going to be staying here with me," he said, squaring up at me. He was only seventeen, and yet he was acting like this? I hoped Lily would back me up, but she looked like she didn't want to be anywhere near this conversation.

"I just don't want my sister to get herself killed in a pointless feat!"

"Saving people from the terror that is the Red Rogues isn't pointless! Besides, I try not to get anyone killed, including you and also your sister," Mal-Chin argued.

"Fine…I will join your little group. But only because I want to protect my sister." Mal-Chin Laughed.

"You have to earn the position. Take the test with your sister. If you pass as well, only then can you pass. If you don't, well…there is always cleaning up after the pilots. That will keep you busy and close to Skye."

Argh, what would I do to this guy if I wasn't surrounded by armed people? Mal and I glared at each other. Neither one wanted to break eye contact.

"Oh, both of you, please stop! If you think you look tough right now, then you're wrong. You're acting like children, and it's so pathetic," Lily yelled, standing between us. Her fresh flowery smell was enough to distract me, and I found myself looking at her. Her ashamed face still looked pretty and was addicting to study. Her skin still had a lot of flaws, but they added to her beauty. Her dress perfectly complimented her skin tone and also her hair colour.

Lily held her hands up, one at me and one at Mal, who hadn't stopped glaring at me.

"Amp, I think you should let Skye make her own choice. She clearly wants to go, and Mal will look after her. Maybe it'll be good for you too. Go with Mal, both you and Skye. Train and help fight. I'll always be close by too. Ya know if that is any motivation for you."

Ugh! Lily knew that would get me. She knew that I liked her. Yet I denied it constantly. I haven't known her that long so why would use that as an argument work? The worst part, it actually was working. If I did go home, I would most likely never see Lily again, which felt like I was leaving something more behind. I wasn't prepared to say goodbye.

"Fine, lead the way, *sir*," I told Mal.

PART 11

Mal-Chin spoke to a woman in uniform and body armour and gave a few orders before summoning a couple of men to follow us. The woman began to dish out orders and took Mal's place. Mal then guided us back to the entrance, staying behind all of us. Skye stayed next to him and initiated a conversation, which he willingly carried on with. She asked a bunch of questions about the training, the skiers and also the organisation. I overheard him call themselves 'the O.I.D,' which stood for, 'Outer Island Defence."

I hovered next to Lily, following the guards assigned to us. I wanted to start a conversation with her, but I didn't know what to say. She seemed sad, which was even more reason for me to say something.

"Do you want my jacket? You're freezing," I asked, marching down the never-ending stairs. She gave me the, *really*, look but crossed her arms to keep herself warm. I didn't wait for her answer and took off my jacket. Straight away, the cold breeze hit me. I never realised how much the jacket was keeping me warm. I wrapped it around Lily and resumed my walk.

"Thank you. Amp…why did you agree," she questioned, keeping her focus on the steps. The bottom was slowly getting closer, much to my relief.

"What do you mean," I asked, knowing full well what she meant.

"Why did you agree to join Mal-Chin," she asked again bluntly, yet so delicately.

"I don't want to leave Skye," I answered simply. I was at least telling half the truth; no one can deny that.

"Oh, right. Obviously," she said with a little laugh. Seconds later, things were back to an awkward silence again. I held back the urge to shiver because every step got warmer and warmer. I only had to last about five more steps.

Four, three, two and one.

Finally, our group reached the bottom of the never-ending flight of stairs.

We wormed our way through the overgrown path; Mal-chin asked if Lily was going to come with us or leave us with him. She thought for a bit, and looked at me, then said that she would tag along.

"In which case, he can go with you. Skye, would you like to fly with me," he resumed, pointing at me cynically. I rolled my eyes, and then again, when Skye agreed to go with him. Lily promised we would stay close. The guards that were with us were ordered to fly in skiers by our sides, which I later found out were heavily armed and customised for aerial combat. They had extra flaps to help turn quicker and gun barrels underneath the handlebars.

Mal-Chin informed us that we were running out of light time and that we had a thirty-minute flight. As a result, we all split into the appropriate modes of transport and embarked on our next trip.

I sat next to Lily as she took off, tailing Mal-Chin's skipper. From what I could see, he was still in conversation with Skye.

"I get that you don't want Skye to get hurt, but I would vouch for Mal-Chin's word any day. He comes across as tough-skinned, but I promise you, Amp, he is going to look after her every way that he can."

"She likes him too much," I told her, letting built-up anger out. Lily tittered.

"What are you laughing at?"

"Amp, she has a little crush. It isn't the end of the world."

"But I..."

"But nothing, Amp! She is okay. Trust me!" Lily giggled.

"Oh, now what are you giggling at!"

"You," she told me.

"What did I do?"

She shrugged, but she wore a devilish smile. It is scary how quickly she can switch moods. One minute she would be all serious, and the next, she would be playful and giggly, like right now.

"Lily?"

"Yes?"

"What did I do?"

"Nothing."

"Well, I must have done something because you are laughing at me."

"You really don't get it, too, do you?"

"Get what," I asked. I was so confused. I hadn't done anything. Lily let out a long, smiley breath.

"You're cute when you're frustrated."

"Uh, thanks?"

"No, you're *really* cute," she said. I blushed, and she went into hysterical laughter. Barely audible, she said, "You can't even take a compliment without blushing. You're adorable!" Straight away, she changed mood yet again, but this time I could tell she was joking around. At least, I thought that she was. She scowled at me.

"You haven't complimented me yet!"

"Uh... you're hair looks pretty," I mumbled, not knowing what was going on.

"Wow, such a creative way to woo a girl. Amp, you can do better than that!"

"You are actually the worst," I mentioned, not falling for her pouty ways.

"Is that why you like me?"

"Oi, I don't like...ugh!"

Lily laughed again. The fact she was teasing me this much was really annoying.

"I hate you," I exclaimed.

"No, you don't!"

"Yes, I do."

I felt her eyes watching me.

"Stop!"

"Why? Are you getting nervous," she asked.

"No! It's just weird!"

"Because you like me!"

"Ugh, you're insufferable!" Lily kept laughing, and even I couldn't help but join her. This was just ridiculous.

When we settled down, I wanted her to ask her more serious things.

I asked, "So, what's the story with you and Mal-Chin? Why didn't you tell me he was military?"

She answered, "He saved me. Next question."

"You didn't answer why you didn't tell me he was military."

Once again, I was pushing it, and I could tell she wasn't happily talking about it. She hollered frustratingly, "Would you have come if I did tell you? You wouldn't because you would want to look after Skye, and you'd know that this exact thing would happen. She would want to join the fight."

"Well…I don't know. I probably would have still gone anyway."

"I don't want to talk about it, please, Amp." Lily rested her right elbow against the door of the skipper and planted her head on her palm. She kept one hand on the steering wheel, and her eyes were fixed forwards.

As we flew, the light levels gradually depleted the longer we flew. It got pretty chilly, so Lily shut the glass roof. We were completely sealed in. It felt weirdly quiet now. The hum of the engine couldn't be heard, and nor could the sound of the wind or other skiers and skippers. It was now just pure silence, with Lily and I sitting alone.

"Have you been to this place we're going to," I tried to say, struggling to break the silence. Lily nodded wearily. She looked so tired. Or was it mad? I couldn't tell.

We passed through a tiny cluster that consisted of only a few islands, which I didn't think even counted as a cluster, but it was. Lily told me it was the Dorlow Cluster and was one of the smallest clusters ever. I asked what the other small ones were, and I was told that there was one island that was considered a cluster as it technically was broken into multiple islands but was held together by supports. It didn't seem like much of a cluster as most islands were like that, but hey, whatever floats your island, I guess.

I noticed we were passing over a lot more green islands and that most of these islands didn't have any buildings on them. They were lower than most islands and had a lot of short grass.

"Why don't people use these to grow flowers on? I mean, the grass must be good enough to grow things on, or it'll wither and go dry," I asked, amazed by the untouched islands.

Each of them floated above the void, with birds pecking away and settling in little hovels in the ground. Again, Lily shared her knowledge and perked up a bit.

"You can always try, but they'll be either eaten by birds, grow too quick and die without the right nutrients, or get destroyed by the strong winds down here."

"How strong are the winds if no one has even bothered to touch this area," I asked, intrigued.

"Well, people have tried a lot. But anything they build barely lasts a night. I'm sure with the right materials, you could build here, but no one in these parts has that kind of money, so why bother."

"Yeah," I carried on, "but if we're nearly at this training base, surely, the O.I.D could utilise it for something."

"They do. They use the winds for flight training. People never really land, but they certainly fly low to the island."

"Wouldn't that be dangerous, considering the wind is strong enough to knock over buildings?"

"Yeah, it is, but at the same time, the experience you gain from it far outweighs the danger. When people go off to fight, their ability to control skiers in strong winds could mean life and death."

"Do you think Skye would need to fly in it," I anxiously replied. Why did everything dangerous feel like something Skye would like? It was really getting on my nerves now. As expected, Lily said that she probably would have to at some point, but she isn't fully aware of how things work.

We chose to drop the topic and resumed the talk about the plants growing right the way until we could see a complex of buildings. These were by far the most impressive buildings I had seen yet, but they still stuck with slightly polished scrap metal.

They had a fence and a few towers, which I assumed were watch towers. I also spotted a lot of thick, silver rods disappearing into the rock below the island. The rocks were large rocks and created a very thick underground for the rods to attach to.

Buzzing about the complex were men and women in skiers, all completing various tasks. Some were carrying things with special attachments on the skiers, and others were just flying about from island to island.

Lily followed Mal-Chin and our escorts to the left, where a tower and a smaller oval-shaped building stood. The tower was slightly smaller than the one we met Mal-Chin in, but the oval building was still even smaller, easily being dwarfed by the surrounding areas.

"Where is this," I asked Lily, knowing that Skye would be freaking out with excitement.

"It is the headquarters for the O.I.D.," Lily answered, seemingly not really knowing, "I have only been here a couple of times when I was a lot younger. Not a whole bunch nowadays." I had already learnt not to push it by asking any more questions, so I kept watching as we got closer.

We were guided down towards landing bay fourteen by a man on a radio that I didn't even know Lily had. Mal-Chin and Skye were taken to another bay around the other side of the oval building. As I lost sight of their skipper, I felt a sudden feeling of isolation and the need to find Skye. Lily had already figured that I would be worried, so she reassured me that Skye was in safe hands once again. There wasn't much I could do, so I forced myself to relax and stick by Lily.

Our landing bay was in a small opening of the oval building, which was still pretty spacious. You could fit about three skippers in the bay and still have enough room to move about with ease.

Once we landed, Skye opened the glass roof again. Noise flooded in. Sounds of machines blasted around the landing bay, which felt more like an oversized shed. The wind rustled through our hair, and occasionally, you'd hear it whistle.

We were greeted by a man in a body warmer who waited for us to hop out of the skipper. He had a receding hairline and yellow ear mufflers on. On the left ear it had a small device sticking out, which he was speaking through. Lily told me it was a microphone and that it was treated like a portable radio. I guessed that was what the guy on my test used to talk to me. It's all radios and microphones.

Standing in the landing bay was cold. There were a bunch of tools and shelves around the walls and on the floor, placed in an organised mess. Tins of fuel, paint and other various liquids and objects dotted the shelves, some half open and most sealed shut.

On the far side of the garage was a double glass door leading into an open area. I couldn't quite see what was through the doors, but I guessed it was where we were going to head through at some point. That was unless we went back out the large missing wall that led outside to a really busy area where a ton of skiers were hurtling about.

"Well, you guys, you're with Mal-Chin, correct?"

It took me a moment to realise the balding man was talking to us. We nodded, and he asked us to follow him. As predicted, we were taken through the double doors where another person was waiting for us.

She was in a fancy suit outfit, with a long black skirt that was tightly wrapped around her legs. Her hair was shiny and black and reached her lower back. I placed her age around thirty, and the heels she wore made her look even taller as well.

"Amphorn and Lily, welcome to the O.I.D. Please…this way," the woman said, gesturing towards her right. We stood in a corridor that looked like it circled around. It had been painted a cream colour with a dark violet strip that wrapped around the wall about a quarter of the way down. The floor was a complete contrast in colour. It was a dark grey stone, polished and shiny.

The corridor was a lot warmer and quieter, the sounds from the landing bay sounding like a distance echo now. Along the wall were more doors. Which were spaced equally apart and, I assumed, went into more landing places. They had black numbers painted above the door, counting down. Above ours had the number fourteen painted on top, and each door had the next number down.

On the other side of the corridor, the inner wall of the circle was yet a few more doors, but most signs and telepads projected adverts for joining the cause and welcoming people to the O.I.D.

Our footsteps bounced down the corridor whilst Lily and I tried to keep up with the woman. Her heels clomped every step, filling the uneasy silence.

"Uh… what's your name," I asked breathlessly. My question was answered quietly. I looked over at Lily, who gave me a look that told me she, too, was just as confused as to why the woman was remaining mute. However, I had a feeling she knew who this woman was because she was way more comfortable around this stranger than I was.

No one spoke a word until we arrived at bay two.

"Wait here!"

We were commanded by the stranger, who proceeded to knock on the door leading into bay two to stand up against the inner wall. A few seconds later, the entranceway opened, and a woman dressed similarly to the man in our bay was standing at the door. She nodded and then moved aside. Mal-Chin and Skye clambered out from behind and met us in the corridor. Mal bowed his head at myself and Lily and asked us to follow him.

"Amphorn…Skye told me that you had passed your flying license, correct," Mal-Chin questioned, keeping his head forwards. He took over, leading us through the corridor, and the other woman tailed behind us, still mute.

"Uh…yeah," I said back, glad that we were talking again. We paused next to a huge sign that was about upgrading your skier. Besides, it was a door that Mal opened. We crowded through the door.

"Excellent. Less work for us," Mal answered, guiding us through the next room. This room was a lot more open and was about three of our houses large. It was an oval shape, as I expected.

Inside had carpeted blue floor and at least fifty chairs placed side by side, rows of five, all facing forward. At the front was a huge telepad showing one of the black skiers that Mal-Chins army people used. It had "welcome to the O.I.D" above it.

"So this is the intro room," Skye mentioned, a beaming smile on her face."

"Indeed it is," Mal started, "Just like I told you on the way here, you and Amphorn will be sat in here and go through the introduction. It'll give you an idea of what we are about here. I have made arrangements for you to be kept together when it comes to accommodation, but when it comes to tests and training, it's likely you'll both be separated."

I felt sick and lost and made a point to stand close to Skye. I was not letting her out of my sight any time soon. I watched as a few more nervous people were guided in. They all seemed older than us and certainly more clued up on what they were getting themselves into. They took their seats straight away, which I assumed would be us in the next couple of minutes.

As it would be, I was correct. We were invited to take a seat after Mal spoke to someone at the front. He came back and told us good luck and that he would love to carry on with the conversation he had with Skye later.

PART 12

Lily left with Mal, whispering to me that we'll be okay on the way out. Skye was excited, but both of us were apprehensive. Even for Skye, the reality of what we were doing was starting to dawn on her. And yet, we carried on.

The seats around us filled up until only a handful of chairs were free. After a few more minutes of muttering, the place fell into silence. A guy with a white collared shirt stood at the front, and the area plunged into darkness. The only light left was the telepad next to the collared man. I wasn't even sure how they lit the place up anyway; my only guess was that the roof had windows that I didn't notice. If that was the case, they were blocked now.

"Hello, everyone. My name is Daisuke," the man started, capturing everyone's attention. His accent was similar to Mal-Chin's, just slightly different. He was easily in his fifties, his dark hair receding and ageing.

"Welcome…to the O.I.D! I am sure you all know what it is the O.I.D. does. Otherwise, you wouldn't be here. However, I will still go over everything for those who may still be unsure. O.I.D. stands for Outer Island Defence. It is the strongest armed force in the outer islands. We mostly operate in the southern regions, yet our ever-growing force allows us to branch further northern, western, and eastern."

I took a moment to watch everyone else; they were all glued to the telepad screen. It now showed a map of the entire south side of the ring, with a few arrows explaining where the O.I.D were. I tried to find a home, but instead of being labelled, it was just a tiny cluster. We were nothing, yet I thought we were large my whole life. From what I could see, most islands were bigger than our whole cluster. No wonder why no one had actually heard of us. I carried on listening to the man when the screen flicked to a picture of the oval building we were in.

"In this building, you will be briefed and split into various training groups. You will be taken to your accommodation and main training site from there. Please be aware these places may change. Speaking of your groups, there are many sectors you may be stationed at. These could be the Skier Squad, some form of the ground team, or just a cook or cleaner. Either way, you'll be trained appropriately."

Knowing my luck, I'd be a cleaner for Mal-Chin's squad just so he could annoy me. I watched as a list of faces appeared on the screen. They all seemed to be smiling but also looked like they had power.

"These people are who you will be working under. Each group has its own leader, training regime, and the team below them. They'll be one of the first people you meet, so learn the faces and learn to respect and follow any orders they give you."

Daisuke went through eight different people, their names, a little background information on them and finally, what they were in charge of. Eventually, though, we reached the end of this introduction and were directed to the right side, where eight people lined up. They each stood by a doorway.

"These are the people who will take you to the next area. When they call your name, please collect your things, and stand by them," Daisuke finished. It wasn't long till names were being called.

"Are we sure that Mal said that we're going to stay together," I whispered to Skye, feeling dread. I didn't want to be here at all.

"Yes, I asked him to ensure we weren't separated. I heard him on the way here talking to people to confirm," my sister answered. I felt anxious watching people peeling away, and finally, our names were called. We were told to go to a line of people at the far end. As we rose, with no bags or anything, everyone watched us. It took every single brain cell to make sure I didn't fall over or look like an idiot. Luckily, we did make it without any incidents.

A few girls studied me and started chatting with each quietly, and a group of guys just lingered about, waiting for our next instructions. Skye and I awkwardly stood at the back, watching as the final few people were called to their group.

Once we were all in our respective groups, the group were instructed to follow our leader. I don't know where the other groups went, but ours were taken through a wooden door that was tucked behind the telepad. We were back in the corridor that looked the same as the one earlier. I guessed it must have circled the whole way around the building. There were more landing bay doors, and we were at landing bay thirty-one.

This bay was a lot wider and longer. It had two men working in this one, both of which were chatting with each other about a clipboard the guy on the right was holding in front of them. Right in the middle, instead of a usual skipper, was a long, rusty green, open-aired vehicle. It would easily hold up to at least fifty people on it. It reminded me of a bus in the old world, except this had no roof and could hover.

As soon as the men saw us, the man without the board hopped into the driver's seat and switched on the engine. The entire bus kicked itself alive with a puff of black smoke, a clunk and finally, a loud groan. It was just below deafening.

The other dude came over to us and proceeded to read out names from the board. Each name that was called was allowed to get into the bus through one of the three doors on either side of it. People had to shout to be heard over the bus's engine. Its rattling could be felt in my head and didn't improve when we were finally seated on a couple of seats.

Skye sat next to me, saying it was just an adventure, but it didn't stop me from feeling awful. I missed home so much. Have I mentioned how much I didn't want us to be here?

After we were all on board, the clipboard man stood clear and waved a green flag. That was the signal for us to take off.

We didn't rise very high, only about half a meter off the ground. We also didn't move that fast. We moved slowly, and every meter felt sluggish. Despite that, the view we got was like nothing I had ever seen.

We left the oval building, where we were travelling above ground. A huge, flat piece of ground that had concrete and tarmac on the floor. Lines were painted white in various ways. Alongside the tarmac were a lot of grass and some tiny, white flowers that broke up the monotonous green.

Above us were a lot of skiers, all buzzing about into various landing platforms and bays scattered over the insanely large island. Occasionally, we would come across the edge of an island, but almost right away was the edge of another. It was almost as if it had been split in half before and was attached together again very loosely. Either way, we sored over the top of them with ease.

We trundled passed another bus that was empty except for the driver. It was weird seeing something so long flying by us, and it made me realise how silly we must have looked, though it did seem really practical. I wondered if this was just an O.I.D. thing or whether it was available to the public in various areas. I don't see why they wouldn't if they had the money to maintain it. It'll solve a ton of travel issues my cluster has, that's for sure. Some people probably don't even need a flying license if they have buses available.

Finally, we approached a really tall building. I counted at least ten stories tall. It was on the outside of the island, visible from the oval building, but it didn't look anywhere near as tall as it did when you stood right below it.

We were dropped off at the front entrance of the large building, which we were told was accommodation. Each of us was split into groups of four, these groups being the people we were to share our rooms with. I didn't sign up for this, and Skye knew exactly was I was thinking.

"Amp, it's only temporary. Just think how much good we will be able to do. A bit of training, help fight…" she started, but I stopped her talking.

"Skye, I know you're trying to help, but right now, I just wish I could tell Mum and Dad exactly where we are. I wouldn't mind being here if I had a choice, but if I return home, tell Mum and Dad I left you, that wouldn't go down too well." Her eyes widened and then narrowed.

"Excuse me, but Mal gave you a choice to leave. You chose to stay for Lily; it wasn't even for me. Don't you dare try to turn this against me, Amp!"

"I chose to stay for you and her. I'm not blaming you. I just don't understand how you're so okay with this. This isn't right!" She didn't appear to be happy with me. She shook her head and said, "You're unbelievable, Amp." Right after, she turned her back towards me and listened to find out who our roommates would be. It didn't take long at all.

"Amphorn and Skye Aozora, Tyler Flynn, and Darcy Wilkins, you are on floor D and room Twelve. Please take your stuff and head that way. Make sure you find your papers. These will be what will give you your next instructions. You'll find them in your room already." The leader of the group gave us each a key card that had the number twelve on it. As we hobbled towards the stairs, a boy about my age and a girl also similar age appeared from the crowd.

"I'm guessing you're the siblings, huh," the boy said. He had a very crisp accent. I couldn't tell where he was from. He introduced himself as Tyler, and then Darcy introduced herself with a simple nod and silence.

Tyler had light blonde hair and wore a green canvas jacket. He pulled a small bag with wheels and carried another one over his shoulder.

Darcy had short hair. It was jet black and only went down to her shoulders. She had an attitude about her, and yet she was very quiet. She only carried one rucksack and a bottle of juice that was attached to the side.

Together, the four of us trotted up the stairs, each level having the floor letter painted onto the wall. When we reached floor D, we crumpled into the next part of the building. It was a red carpeted floor in another corridor. It had large windows that overlooked the complex of tarmac we were just at. Directly in front had a black sign with white writing. It had '1 – 15' pointing one way and then '16 - 30' in the other direction. We were in twelve, so we headed left and, a few seconds later, saw our door.

"After you," I said to Tyler, who took out his key card. He swiped it against a black card reader on the door, and a small green light flashed. There was then a quick beep before a click. Tyler opened the door and stepped inside.

Tyler fumbled about until he found a switch on the wall. Bright white lights flickered on and lit up our new home. The four of us entered and took our first look around.

"Whoa, we...get to live here," Skye questioned. I felt the same. We stood in a room the size of our house. It had a sofa that was bent around a corner and a telepad on a small cupboard. There was a small round table near a black kitchen counter. Five rooms extended off the main space; I guessed they were four bedrooms and a bathroom.

Darcy didn't say anything. Instead, she just pushed open one of the side doors, and that was the last time I saw her for a while. She entered it and shut the door behind her.

"Uh...I guess that means those are for us to choose," Tyler chuckled, pointing to the other few doors. Skye gently nudged open another door that was near her, which turned out to be a bathroom with grey stone flooring and walls.

"So that's where that is; good to know," Tyler said again. I could tell he was just trying to make conversation, but I really wanted him to be quiet.

"I want this one, Amp; you can take the one next to me, Skye answered, skipping over to yet another door. Tyler and I agreed it was fine, so we split into our individual rooms.

My room was pretty small, literally a grey bed, wardrobe, and a chest of drawers. Regardless, it was still mine, for now, a place for me to sit alone and think. There was a small window behind the drawers where light pushed through and illuminated the rest of the space.

I didn't have any belongings, so I convened with my thoughts on my bed. It was firm but softer than my usual bed. As I sat, I saw a bit of paper with a bunch of writing and drawings. I grabbed it.

I scanned over it and realised it was a map of the entire building. It also had times when places were open. It turns out only a few floors were for people to live in. This building had entire areas for shops, clothes, food; you name it, this place had it. I did want some new clothes to wear, so I planned on visiting them at some point in the future.

After a few minutes of half studying the map and blanking out, I sunk back and leaned against the pillows on my bed. I kicked off my shoes, which were gross, and heaved my legs onto the bed. Right after, I shut my eyes and let out a huge sigh. It made me feel sleepy, and I ended up yawning. I didn't want to open my eyes. They felt like glue was holding my eyelids shut.

PART 13

I must have fallen asleep because when I woke up, I was lying in a pool of my own sweat on top of my covers. I had a horrible taste in my mouth, and my eyes felt really puffy. I was also really thirsty, which gave me a pulsing headache.

I rubbed my eyes to clear my blurred vision and ran my fingers through my hair. The place was really dark now. Only moonlight lit the room, and even that wasn't enough to see anything. Only really dark silhouettes that blended in with the blackness behind them could be seen. What even was the time? I know it was dark when we got here, but it was now really dark. It must have been midnight.

I heard rustling outside, so I made an effort to go see who it was. When I reached the door, I pushed it open as quietly as I could, as I didn't want to wake anyone else up if they were asleep.

Outside the room was Darcy. She sat on the sofa, her legs crossed. It looked like she was playing with a telepad that showed a bunch of islands and small skiers flying around them. Darcy would grab one of the holographic skiers and physically move them to another area, which would then carry on. I'd never seen anyone move the display on a telepad before.

"Whoa," I said in amazement, alerting Darcy to my presence. As quickly as she could turn her head, the telepad switched off.

"Oh, um, sorry. I didn't want to interrupt," I told her, feeling guilty that I bothered her. I approached her cautiously. She stared at me like a scared animal. I stopped. If I got any closer, I felt like she would swipe at me or something.

"So, um, Darcy, was it? Are you okay?" I wasn't sure how to talk to her. She looked like she didn't want to be here, at least with me anyway. She fiddled around the bottom of her top, sinking back into the sofa and turning back away from me. She pulled out another telepad and placed it in front of her. It lit up right away, with glowing blue lights protruding from the small cube. I waited for them to form into a shape, but the lights didn't. They were just shining in the dark, lighting Darcy's face. It flickered slightly. Darcy then turned to me again and waved me over without speaking.

Confused but curious, I shuffled over, and the lights split and formed a screen. On the screen had writing.

Darcy then pulled out something from her bag. It looked like a small radio with buttons on it. Upon further inspection, it had letters on them. As she pushed them, the screen started to show the letters. She was typing something. I waited for her to finish before reading the sentence.

"I can't speak," she wrote on the screen. I read out loud so that she knew I was finished. Darcy then carried on. This time, it was a long sentence.

"If we're going to be living together, you may as well know. My name is Darcy, and I don't have a tongue anymore." I had to reread it multiple times before I made sense of it. Darcy didn't have a tongue. I asked her to show me, but she shook her head quickly and became timid and nervous. The attitude returned, and she typed again quickly.

"Sorry, I need to go to sleep." She waited till I had finished again, and as soon as I did, the telepad switched off, and she sprung up and rushed into her room. The door slammed behind her, and I was left perplexed. Why would someone start explaining and then leave? I was more curious than ever, but I knew better than to knock on her door and pry. Maybe in her own time, she would say more.

Suddenly, another door opened behind me. Tyler came out, dressed in bedclothes. He looked half asleep. The guy didn't see me at first and waddled towards the toilet, but he stopped and did a double take.

"You have a strange sleep schedule, man," he yawed, squinting to see me.

"What time is it," I questioned. Tyler laughed tiredly and shrugged

"Not a clue, but it's late, and we gotta be up early tomorrow," Tyler explained, yawning again. He made me yawn, and I felt sleepy again.

"What do you mean, up early? How do you know," I asked, leaning on the back of the sofa? Tyler leant up against a wall and explained that whilst

I was asleep, he and Skye had found the timetables for us and a map for how to get there. He pointed to the kitchen counter, and I saw the paper. He then said he was going to go toilet and go back to sleep. I didn't blame the guy. I felt myself feeling sleepy again, and I'd just woken up.

I figured it was probably a good idea to check what I was actually meant to do tomorrow, as honestly, I had no idea. I didn't really know how I ended up here. Everything has just happened way too quickly. I've just rolled with it. I don't have much of choice anymore. Skye wanted to do this, and I wasn't about to leave her.

I took the paper and skimmed through it. My eyes were blurry now, but I forced myself to focus on the words. It had Tyler and Amphorn written at the top and a bunch of things underneath.

At Eight o clock, I was supposed to have my first assessment at the Foundational Skier Building, or F.S.B. for short. More acronyms to remember. That was supposed to last most of the day. At least I would be with Tyler. Speaking of which, he shuffled by again, and just before he closed his bedroom door, he told me, "Oh, I know you don't have an alarm, so I'll wake you up tomorrow as you're with me all day. Night."

I didn't even think about that. I had no way to wake myself up in the mornings, so I made a mental note to buy myself some form of alarm thing. I had no money, but I'll figure something out. For now, I was appreciative that Tyler had even thought about that. I headed back to bed, trying to mentally prepare myself for the following day.

I woke up to the sound of Tyler rocking me and saying my name.

"Amp buddy, you gotta get up now," he softly said in his crisp accent. I rolled onto my back and felt his let go as a figure stood up. After quickly focusing, Tyler was hovering by the door.

"We've been given clothes to wear. They arrived this morning. I've left yours at the end of your bed. Oh, and before you ask or worry, Skye left with Darcy this morning. The show-offs in the advanced group have to wake up really early." He didn't wait for a response. He shut the door and left me alone once again. It was still dark, but the light was creeping in. I let myself lay for a few more minutes before forcing myself up. I saw the outfit I was meant to put on, folded neatly on my bed.

It was dark green, and after picking it up, I saw it was a one piece. There was a black stripe right the way down the side, shoulder to feet. The chest area had a silhouette of a skier as a logo.

When I put it on, it was a bit tight and felt like I was exposed, but I wasn't too bothered. The costume felt incredibly mobile and surprisingly warm too. I left my own stuff on my bed, which I couldn't be bothered to make back up. I guess I was making myself at home after all.

The living room and kitchen were just as alien as ever. Tyler was sitting on the sofa, learning the map.

"Hey, about time. I'm gonna go grab food before we head over there. If we head up a few floors, we'll be at the shop," he explained. This guy spoke a lot, probably trying to break the ice. I agreed to join him anyway.

Before we left, I gave my shoes a quick clean. I made sure I had my map with me so we didn't get lost, and Tyler made sure he had his money. Then, together, we left.

We stayed quiet, but the footsteps bounced through the corridor. We quickly found the stairs again, and both stopped.

"Okay. So we need to find, uh, floor...ha you know what, why don't you find it. A challenge for you," Tyler laughed, passing me a map. I gave him a weird look. I'm pretty sure he couldn't read properly, which is probably why he wanted me to find the place. I didn't care, though.

I took his copy of the map, not telling him I had my own.

"We want floor J, right the way up to the top," I told him, pointing to it on the map, "at least that is where a food shop and a canteen are."

"Ugh. Trust it to be all the way at the top," Tyler groaned, "the food had better be worth it." We started up the stairs together; this time, Tyler was talking.

"So, where are you and Skye from again?"

"The Marhalm Cluster, it's, um, pretty far from here. What about you?"

"Oh me, I am from way out. The Terahelix Cluster."

"Terahelix Cluster? Isn't that the place where the islands form a spiral? One of the five places that have unnatural formations of islands?"

"You've heard of it? How? We aren't even that big," Tyler said.

"I read a lot," I answered back, "besides, it's a weird formation, so it's bound to come up at some point," Tyler grunted with amusement.

"Well, I never realised how famous we were," he said as we reached another floor, "Ugh, why are there so many stairs." I wasn't about to complain out loud, but even I was starting to get annoyed. Just in the last few days, I have climbed so many stairs. The muscles in my leg will most likely be bigger than my head by the time Skye, and I eventually get home.

Several minutes of panting up steps later, we finally arrived at the top floor. I ached, and I felt gross, so I hoped a drink and food would give me a boost.

I followed Tyler to the canteen, which was pretty hectic. A huge glass wall overlooked both the rows of silver-coloured tables and benches but also the entire complex. The walls were plain white with bright white lights integrated into the roof. To the left were a line of people in similar outfits to mine and Tyler's, a dark green suit with a black stripe. A hole had been cut out of a wall where a couple of ladies were serving up steaming hot food on blue trays. Most of the benches were full, but there were a few places free. Tyler and I quickly joined the line, and he prepared to pay for both of us. I was going to owe him a lot more than I wanted to. He and also Lily.

I hadn't really had time to think about her, but now, she was stuck in my head. Even when I had my toast, I kept wondering where she was now. Had she gone home? She must have done. What reason would she have to stay here? Plus, she had a shop to run, so why would she *not* go home? I came to the conclusion she must have gone back to her island, and yet so much of me longed for her to show up later and say hi, ask how I am settling in and tell me what I should be doing. I quickly shook my head. What was I doing, thinking about Lily? I barely know the girl. I can't just miss her.

"Um, we gotta go soon, dude, and you've barely started eating," Tyler explained, nudging me. I looked down at my food, not hungry anymore. I took a couple of bites. The toast was okay, nothing compared to the homemade bread at home. The O.I.D toast felt grainy, mass-produced and cheap. Perhaps I could strike a deal with these guys when I get home and convince them to buy from our farm.

I redirected my focus to the conversation that Tyler was having with a couple of girls who were sitting opposite us. They looked a couple of years older than us, and both had two silver star badges over the top of the logo. Also, they did not appear to be interested in what Tyler was telling them.

"Tyler, I don't think they care about what you're saying," I informed them, making the blonde girl smirk a little. She looked at her table, embarrassed. Tyler paused and glared at me. When he tried to speak, the black-haired girl interrupted him.

"Yeah…no, sorry, we really aren't interested. We have to get going, rookie, and if you take much longer, you'll be late for your first day. You do not want that, that's for sure." They both very quickly grabbed their trays and were gone within a few seconds. Tyler was mad.

"I had them hooked, and you killed my chances, man," he complained, huffing.

"You really didn't have them hooked. They weren't listening. Also, we really do need to go now. It is from ten to eight. We have ten minutes, and it'll take us that long to get down those stairs again. Tyler grunted again but stood up. We quickly chucked our rubbish away and placed our trays on the pile that everyone else had put theirs on. We just assumed that was the right this to do. Once we were ready, we raced back down the stairs.

PART 14

If I hadn't studied the map and remembered it as well as I did, we would have been extremely late. Luckily, there was a taxi available, and the man was able to take us straight to the building we had to get to. Again, we got lucky.

The F.S.B. was a small, black-stone building just behind our building. It was close to the edge of the main island, with a Skier parking area under a shelter just to the right of it. I felt almost at home again, seeing the void. It felt very strange, knowing how long it had been since I had actually been this close to the edge of an island.

Tyler gave money to the taxi man, whose skipper was made of a similar rusted green that the bus was made out of yesterday. We quickly hopped out and headed to the main entrance, assuming that was the way to go. There were two large glass windows on either side of the main door, which seemed pretty small compared to the rest of the building. We both stumbled through and were met with a small reception deck. Inside reminded me of the test centre back in Marhalm.

Behind the small wooden deck was the woman with the clipboard that greeted Lily and me when we arrived there. She was in a similar outfit, and her face was still as stern as before. She held her clipboard again, too, just as if it were the same day as when we first met her.

"Uh, we're here for our first day of training," Tyler explained as politely as he could, "Tyler Flynn and Amp, uh, what was your last name again?"

"Aozora, Amphorn Aozora." The woman looked down at her board, then her watch.

"Cutting close, aren't we," she said. Usually, I'd think I was being told off, but I was surprised when she sounded friendly.

Still, I felt my cheeks go red.

"Right through there, you'll see the rest of the group. There are still a fair few to arrive, though, so consider yourselves lucky," the woman told us, gesturing towards a small corridor. From what I saw, at the end was a huge open place.

We followed our instructions and made our way towards the open area. At least a dozen people were huddled together, which I assumed was our group. Everyone looked like they had a conversation going, chatting and waiting for something to happen.

The space we were in was somewhat big, though smaller than I had originally thought. A fair few skiers were at the front, green with a red stripe down the middle. There were also platforms, ranging in height, dotted all over the place. Each was made of a black rubber brick of some kind.

As I took in my surroundings, a couple of other people joined the group until a man called us to attention. He had a dark beard on, and his clothes looked like cloth had been strung together quickly with a fancy green coat that brushed the floor.

"Good morning, everyone," he bellowed, his voice echoing, "Please may I have your attention!" The chatting fell silent.

"Welcome to your first day of training. My name is Henry Avery. I am the head of the foundation Skier programme. My job role here is to get you guys up to the standard level of Skier and Skipper training level three, where you will be eligible to take the test for advanced level one. Each level requires you to pass a test before you can progress. You're all starting on Skipper and Skier level one, or S.S.L one for short. Don't worry. All today is going to be, is a brief assessment so we can gain an understanding of your current skill level for both skippers and skiers. From there, we will split you into your various levels."

I was probably meant to listen to how the assessment works, but I was too busy thinking about Henry's name. Henry Avery was a pirate in the old world. According to myths, Henry Avery sailed vast stretches of water on boats, where he would attack and pillage other boats. It sounded kind of similar to the Rogues. All this thinking had just made me question whether or not the guy in charge of my training was a secret pirate or just a coincidental name. It was a weird thought, but it was short-lived when people started to move, and I had no clue what was going on.

I chose to go where the main crowd was, which was by the skiers I had seen earlier. As I got closer, I saw a couple of skippers, too, also green with a red stripe going horizontally.

"These are the Skiers and Skippers you will be training with. The red stripe shows you are a foundation-level learner. When you reach advanced, you will have a yellow stripe. Then after that, the colour right is based on whatever regiment or squad you are placed in. Now, you are all wearing your uniform, which is great. At the moment, you are wearing the basic uniform. As you progress, you will be given various badges, and the colour strip will change." There was a lot of talking, but I remained focused as best as I could.

"A black stripe is the basic uniform for both foundation and advanced level. After that, the stripe you have will be based on your squad, the same as the skier and skipper too. You will, however, see various badges. These are to do with rank within your level. If you see bronze star badges on a logo, that means they are foundation-level but are team leaders. These only go to the ones who prove they are ready to lead a basic squad on minor duties if the occasion should arise. If you see silver stars, then that means they are advanced group team leaders and can give basic commands to foundation groups."

I tried my best to remember everything. Henry Avery asked if anyone had any questions so far. So far, he seemed like an okay guy.

"Excuse me, sir, I've seen people will multiply stars. What does that mean," a random girl asked. Henry was happy to answer.

"Good question! Multiple stars mean they have proven themselves in a genuine assignment as a team leader. Any other questions?"

"How do we tell who superiors are," another person asked, and again, Henry was happy to answer.

"I assume you mean after the advanced level? Anyone with a different colour stripe is your superior, and you must answer to them. However, golden pins on the badges mean they are captains of a full squad."

The ranking system made sense. I didn't plan to stay around long enough to get to all these full squad groups, but it was information worth having anyway.

After Henry had explained the ranking system and answered a few more questions, he introduced us to two other men, both of which were trainers and assessors. Apparently, they were the guys who decided whether or not we were ready to move up.

"Okay, time to get started. We are going to split into three groups, and each group will go with one of us three," explained Henry, showing off the other two men.

The bearded man started to read out names, and once again, we were split up.

I was with Henry's group, which I'd wanted anyway. We were brought to the skiers, and the leader put his hand on one of them and faced us.

"So, the first thing I'll be testing you guys on is your skill with a skier. There aren't many of you, six in each group. Once we have done all three assessments, we are able to finish early. Let's get this done as soon as possible, huh." The six of us nodded, everyone, looking pretty nervous. I should be fine with a skier.

"Three volunteers, please," Henry insisted. No, put their hand up.

"Anyone," he asked again, raising an eyebrow. I thought for a second and then stepped forwards.

"I'll go," I tried to say with as much fake confidence as I could fake. This would be my second skier assessment this week, and pretty much nothing to show for it. I was thanked by Henry, and then two other people apprehensively volunteered.

We took our places on our skiers and were given commands such as turning on the skier. Once the basics were over, we could finally start actually flying. The test was very basic.

"Lift up and hover at about two metres for me," Henry ordered. It was easy. I simply pulled back on the skier handles, and I was up. I then straightened up and waited for the other two, who took their time. I'd just assumed we were setting up to start the assessment, but this was the assessment. How low was the foundation level skill level if this is what I have to work with?

Eventually, the others joined me, a little unstable. We were then asked to land again, which again seemed basic, but the others took ages to stabilise themselves.

The next task was to land on a platform that was five meters tall. I did it with ease. I gently placed my skier down, this whole time, watching the other two. The girl with brown hair seemed to be able to get up to the right height but was shakey when approaching and landing next to me. The boy appeared to be scared. He slowly crept up, Henry giving out encouragement.

"Come on. Hold it still. That's it," I explained to him, "now, very lightly, bring it forward. Not that much, just tiny movements. There we go. Okay, now, bring it down. Again, small movements." The landing feet touched the ground, and there we cheered.

"Thank you," the boy said, looking like he was ready to be sick. The brown-haired girl smirked at him and then frowned at me. I don't know what her problem was, but it didn't bother me. At this rate, I'd be in the next rank anyway.

Half a minute later, we were asked to perform various manoeuvres, such as hovering and spinning on the spot. I easily managed it. The sensitivity on this skier felt very slow, which meant I had a lot of control. It felt way too easy but way too heavy for my taste. Anyhow, the assessment itself took about half an hour, and the others stood watched.

Eventually, we were done, and we were asked to land roughly where we had started. The boy improved slightly, though he still looked like the colour had been drained from his face. The girl, well... she adapted somewhat well and seemed to be rather proud of herself. Henry noted a few final things before he repeated the same assessment on the last three. Watching these guys confirmed that this level was way too basic for the things I had for real above the void.

The other three were eventually done, and after a ten-minute waiting period, all three groups swapped stations. We were brought over to the skippers. Now I felt my stomach lurch. I had next to no experience with these. The brown-haired girl seemed to be more confident, which made me angry. Luckily, Henry said the three that went last would go first on this one. It gave me a chance to see what was going on.

I made a point to watch every detail, even how to turn on the skipper, which all three struggled with. They rose up in the air, only a couple of metres off the ground. It turns out the test was pretty similar to the skier one, just in a skipper. All I needed was to know how to move up, down, forward, and back. How hard could it be?

It was my turn soon enough, and I hopped in. I switched on the engine my second time. Of course, the brown-haired girl did it in her first. And then…we were off.

Controlling a skipper was like controlling a really heavy skier with a lot more blind spots. To control the amount of thrust and lift you had, you used pedals by the feet, which felt awkward at first, but I got the hang of it pretty easily. I ended up nailing the test and was now ready for the next test. This one took about half an hour to do as well.

"Final assessment, we're smashing this out, so well done," Henry shouted, trying to sound as positive as possible. It took a while for everyone else to finish their assessments, but eventually, we got to the last station. I had no clue what to expect for this one. There was just a door and a back room.

"So this one will take a little longer as we need to go individually. However, this assessment is simply going to be basic repairs and problem-solving on skiers and skippers. Any volunteers to go first?" I stepped forwards. I wanted to get this over with. I know how to put skiers together, so I should nail this too. I was starting to feel like this whole thing was an insult to me.

I was asked to come into the back room and was met with a skier that had no panels on it. I could already tell what was wrong and what needed to be fixed, and as soon as I got the green light, I began.

The main repairs were easy. Tightening things and screwing things. It was simple enough. I was then asked to take the repairs apart and ready for the next people. It was a little annoying, undoing all my work, but it was only a couple of minutes worth. I felt Henry's gaze staring at me whilst I twisted my screwdriver, but as off-putting as it was, I managed. When I was done, I asked if there was anything else. Henry gave me a sheet that had a diagram of a skier.

"I need you to write down the names of each part that has an arrow pointing to it. There is also a skipper on the other side, though I imagine for you, this will also be an easy task." I guessed that meant he realised I had been finding this too easy.

I had the sheet filled out within two minutes and handed it back. I was thanked and let back out to rejoin the group, where Henry called the next person in. I wasn't sure what to do, so I just waited with the group. A couple of people asked me what I had to do, but I said that it was simple and that they'll see.

Suddenly, I heard a voice I recognised instantly.

"How's your first day," Lily asked, tapping me on my shoulder. I felt my cheeks go red and my pulse rate increase. I thought she had gone home, but she was actually here.

I tried to say, "It's easy." However, it came out as gibberish. Lily laughed and asked me to repeat what I had just said, and this time I said it a lot slower, and it made sense.

"If it really is too easy, you'll be moved up pretty quickly. They won't keep you at this level if you're too good," she explained, studying the rest of the room.

"How come you're here," I said out loud. I wanted to keep that question in my head, but obviously, I didn't. That didn't stop Lily from saying, "For you, obviously. Besides, this is my second home. I have pretty much access everywhere. I do provide a big chunk of funding for the O.I.D., so it's only fair that I see where the money goes."

"Wait, you fund the O.I.D? How much money do you even have?"

"Well, that's a very forward question." Although she said sternly, I knew she was being sarcastic.

"Sorry, I didn't mean it in a blunt way." Lily tried to hold back a smile, but no matter how hard she tried, she couldn't stay serious.

"Well, having a water harvester and selling flowers do have a very solid income," she explained, folding her arms. I noticed that Lily and I were being watched by the other members of my group. They appeared to be more curious about who Lily was than anything. I tried not to pay attention to them and tried to reply to Lily.

"Where do you sleep when you're here? Also, who watches your shop?" Lily suddenly seemed to be distracted, looking at my group.

"Uh, hello," I asked, trying to follow where she was looking at or who she was looking at.

"Huh? Sorry," she said back. I repeated myself, and she said, "Oh, the shop will be fine for a few days. The flowers should be okay too. I have an automated system that spreads water. And I stay in a random room that's free." We had a brief discussion about what her water system was like as the final people finished their assessment.

Finally, Henry came out and asked for silence. He saw Lily, who waved and greeted each other. They clearly knew each other.

"So, that is everyone, yes," Henry asked the group. After a few exchanges of looks, we all nodded.

"Fantastic! That means you guys are all free to go! If you guys could all meet back here tomorrow at the same time as you did today, we can put you guys into your new groups and hand out your official timetables. Good work today!" Henry said goodbye, and everyone started to pour out the exit and mingled with the other groups who had also finished.

"Mister Aozora, could you stay for a moment, please," Henry asked whilst putting paper into a blue plastic folder. I was uneasy but waited, glad Lily was with me too. She gave me confidence for some reason.

"You probably did so well. They wanna promote you already," Lily whispered. She was so close to my ear that it made my neck hairs stick up. I blushed just as Henry approached.

Once again, he greeted Lily properly and then turned to me, saying, "Amphorn. You performed exceptionally well today. I feel like foundation is way too easy for you. However, instead of pushing you to the advanced level. I want to train you to be a team leader. For the first few training sessions, you'll be with the rest of the group, but we will start to take you aside for extra sessions."

Lily grinned at me. I was too busy trying to work out what he meant and also making my face return back to a normal colour. I could feel Lily brushing against my arm, and I found it hard to focus.

"That's uh…that's gr…great," I managed to get out. Henry clapped his hands.

"Where did you learn stuff so well," he asked curiously, the other two assessors joining us. They remained silent, and I explained my family's farm, books, and my dad teaching us.

"Oh. You are *that* Aozora family," a balding man had said, looking like he had worked something out, "so that must mean your mother's name is Isla Somerled?"

"Uh… it's Isla Aozora now, but yes. That's my mother. How do you know her exactly?" My voice reverberated around the room now that it was empty.

The other two assessors put their papers in a folder, too, just like Henry said as the man replied, "Well, she travelled a lot, right? She stopped here a few times. Reminds me of young Lily here. It's good to see you again, by the way, Miss Azalea." Why am I not surprised that this guy knew my mum and Lily? After a little more talking, I was finally allowed to leave.

"Do you want to go find something to eat? I know a good place a few islands away from here," Lily suggested on the way out, "my skipper is just around the corner."

"I should probably let Skye or Tyler know," I answered.

"Skye won't be finishing for a couple more hours yet. I assume Tyler is one of your housemates.?"

"Oh, well, hopefully, she'll be okay. And yes, Tyler is."

"What are your housemates like?"

"Well, Tyler is very loud, and Darcy is very quiet. You know Skye and me."

"Yeah, Skye is fun, cute and sarcastic, and you're the paranoid big brother." I scowled at her.

"Hey, that's just mean," I said back, "I'm not that paranoid." She raised her eyebrows at me.

I knew she was right. I was really paranoid, despite how much I denied it.

We were at Lily's skipper within a minute of leaving the F.S.B. Lily told me tha after we had eaten, she'll show me where I could find work in the O.I.D so I could start getting some money to my name.

PART 15

It was good to get fresh air and get away from the O.I.D. Plus, being alone with Lily felt normal now. She and Skye were as close to home as I was going to get.

Lily started up her shiny red skipper, which purred itself awake. I was tired but relaxed. As Lily lifted off, she said, "So I was speaking to Mal-Chin about you and Skye."

"Hm?"

"About getting you guys home."

"Oh?"

"The Rogue's presence has more than doubled in the last few days around Marhalm and the nearby clusters. It's near impossible to get close without losing a lot of people in the process," Lily informed, now serious. My insides turned themselves inside out. Lily apologised, and I told her not to. It wasn't her fault.

"Mal thought the news would be better coming from me than from him."

"Well, he was right. Any news on my parents, do you know?" Her head lowered, and she paused for a few seconds before she said, "Um…well, a lot of islands had been raided or destroyed. Way worse than their usual behaviour. They burned and destroyed a lot…including…."

I didn't want her to finish, but she did.

"Including most of the farming islands. Mal's team aren't sure whether your parents are okay or not, nor what house is exactly yours, but they know farming islands were destroyed, which means your home can't be too far from the fighting."

I wanted to be sick. I had to tell Skye this, too, which would ruin her.

"Did they say what they wanted," I asked, having a feeling I knew what it was already?

"A gold sphere," Lily stated, "that's about all they know. Do you know what or where it is? Skye mentioned it before, and Mal-Chin picked up on that." I told her I didn't know what it was, but I knew where it was.

"It's at home. Is there a library or something around the O.I.D.? This place must have something about the sphere if it's *that* important. At least then, we could find out what it does and what the Rogues want with it so badly. My mum apparently stole it from them, so perhaps she stole it for a reason. If we find her, she can tell us!"

"There is a place that has information, so I can show you and Skye that tonight. But Amp, you won't be able to get home and ask your mum. Not anytime soon. The Rogues are just…." Lily started.

"Too strong, I get it. But maybe we could send a smaller group. We won't get seen as easily, and it will cost fewer resources. Plus, half of the team will be Skye and me anyway. We aren't just pushovers. We can handle ourselves." I felt myself buzzing. I wasn't sure if it was the fact I was too stressed and panicked at the moment or the fact I genuinely thought we could get home.

Lily didn't seem convinced, but she watched me, thinking. We had officially passed over the edge of the main island and were heading to a few buildings about a mile away.

I peered into the void, thinking about seeing Mum and Dad. I bet when we told Skye, she would be all for going. For once, I was glad she was getting close to Mal-Chin. She might be able to convince him between her and Lily. That was if I could convince Lily.

"Okay, what if it was a voluntary thing? We asked people if they would want to go. Keep a small group," I suggested, but Lily still seemed like she was disagreeing. She looked like she was ready to cry. We flew in silence for a minute. I was still looking out into the void. A few birds were flying about in triangle formations. I wondered where they were flying too.

The two of us weaved between a few tiny rocky islands, where we finally approached a few buildings. They were made from the same black stone as the O.I.D. Even the windows had flowers planted out in front of them, giving colour to the monotony.

Lily parked us down in a skier parking zone, where she switched off her engine. Neither of us moved. I gazed at her, the way she had her hair over her shoulder. The curls make it look fluffy. Then I saw the outfit she was wearing. She wasn't in her usual dress anymore. She had a white shirt on, with a red scarf wrapped around her neck. She then had a red and black chequered cardigan over the top. It complimented her black skirt that hung just under her knees really well. Despite any of that, I couldn't help but focus on the fact Lily was upset.

"Are you alright," I asked her, placing my hand on her shoulder. She bit her lip, shut her eyes then looked down. Then she nodded, but I didn't believe her. I asked if she was sure, and this time she didn't nod. Instead, she blurted out, "I don't want you to get hurt, Amp!" It took me by surprise.

"What," I asked, stuck for words. A few tears formed in her eye.

"I don't want you to get hurt. Plus, say we did get you home. Say you were able to find this golden sphere and fix all these issues. You would stay at home with your family, and I won't get to see you, probably ever again!" Now I could definitely tell she was holding back tears. I wasn't expecting this to happen. My first instinct was to wrap my hand around her shoulders, and she buried her head into me.

"But you haven't known me that long. You have friends like Mal-Chin here. I bet you'll be glad to be rid of me," I told her, not knowing what I meant to say. I did get a muffled chuckle from her.

"What about me would you miss?" I figured that would be the wrong question to ask, but apparently, Lily didn't care. She answered back, "Well, I know I haven't known you for long. Hey, I don't even know that much about you. You're just. I don't know, dumb." I laughed but was shocked.

"Uh, excuse me," I asked, confused, "Did you just say I was…dumb?" Lily lifted her head and looked at me with a devilish smile. She nodded and giggled. I couldn't help but laugh back.

"I'm hungry, come on," Lily said, jumping out of the skipper with newfound energy. I hopped out too. I was barely standing upright when Lily grabbed my hand excitedly and pulled me towards the buildings. She was really reminding me of Skye, the way her attitude has just changed that quickly.

Lily dragged me down a pathway where people minded their own business. In the distance, I could see tall wind turbines with wires stretching right across the void.

The wires then spread about the small town, connecting to posts with lights at the top. The lights decorated the pathways, with benches and small flower beds placed in between. Lily told me that the seeds came from her, and after teaching them how to look after the seeds, they blossomed into the beautiful colours we can see now.

After a while of Lily explaining the history of the small town and an explanation of how it was technically a part of the O.I.D., we finally arrived at the restaurant that Lily told me about. A woman greeted us and showed us to a table for two. The table was right next to a window that had a view of the void, the small rocky islands, and the wind turbines. The sun beams create a slight yellow haze to break up the blue.

"See, this is pretty," said Lily, also looking out the window. A few skiers were flying about in the distance. It did look pretty. I let my mind meander from reality to see where it would go.

The first thing it went to was my skier test. I pictured what it would be like if I had just stayed at home with my parents. I'd have told them I had passed. My mum said she would cook us something fancy for dinner to celebrate. My first trip alone would be to Marhalm Centre. I would be doing shopping runs and working at the shop full time.

My attention then drifted to Lily. What would happen when I get home? It's way too far to just casually meet up, and staying in contact would be pretty hard. We would just say goodbye, and that would be that. The thought made me upset. I didn't want to say goodbye to Lily. We have only just started getting closer and being friends. Why would I want to stop?

"I'll go with you," Lily said, breaking me out of my dreamy state.

"Huh?" I shook my head so I was alert, and Lily repeated herself.

"Go with me where?"

"To your family, your parents. If you want to do this mission, then I will go with you." I felt myself blushing.

"Yeah, but what about," I tried to say, but Lily interrupted with, "Mal? Approval? My shop? They'll be fine." Before I could say anything, a lady came to us and asked what we wanted to order. I hadn't even looked at the menu, so I picked the first thing I saw. A salad of some kind. That would do, I guess.

"I was going to say, what about when we get there? Then what would you do?" I gave Lily my full attention, sitting opposite her. Her eyes had a determined sparkle which made her face look like it was glowing.

Lily said, "I guess we will cross that island when we get to it. But the main thing that matters is getting you home. I said I would help you, so that is what I am going to do. I will speak to Mal-Chin and see if we can get any support and if he has any ideas."

"Are you sure you want to do this," I asked, feeling hopeful, "you do realise the risks. If the Rogues are that bad, then you're risking a lot. I doubt your leverage will help you this time, Lily." She took my hand and looked me dead in the eye.

"I promise, I am sure." She broke away again and then carried on.

"When we get back, train with these skiers, and try to find information on the sphere. If we have enough information and you feel comfortable enough, we can prepare to leave and get you guys home." I felt a flame spark into life. Lily really was determined, and it was inspiring. I wouldn't want to get on the other side of her. I had to think for a second before agreeing.

PART 16

The next couple of weeks were the same each day. Skye and I had settled in well. Despite being too good for them, I was put in the leading group for the foundation class. Skye was middle-tier for advanced flying and was lacking on the skipper front, but we both expected that. Neither of us was very experienced with skippers, but we both learnt and adapted very quickly.

Lily had shown us where the library was, which didn't disappoint. It wasn't too far from their apartment, and we spent most of our time outside of training there.

The floor was polished wood, with a red-carpet pathway spreading between the several shelves of books. There was also a small café out the back, which was always empty, so it was perfect for us to get lunch. Even though we were meant to search for the golden sphere, we got distracted by many other things. We had spent so much time there that the librarians asked if we would like a job just helping out. We were paid on a weekly basis.

Almost every category had books about the floating islands and even more about what could be in the void. It sparked so many conversations and theories that we almost forgot what we were looking for. That was until I found a picture of a golden sphere in one of the books I was reading. I looked closer and realised it was the same one in our attic.

"Uh, Skye...look," I said, allowing Skye to come around. She was getting us juice, so I had to wait a few minutes. I took those few minutes to try and briefly read up on what it was.

'The Sphere Mechanism'. It's the key component to a larger machine that has the ability to drop any island into the void. Hundreds of years ago, the machine was kept in the Inner Islands and used to keep power. But eventually, *the sphere mechanism was stolen by rebels and hidden so the machine couldn't be used anymore. It has been lost ever since.'*

The book didn't give any more information, not even what the old device did, but if it destroyed islands, then that couldn't be a good thing.

I thought to myself. The sphere wasn't lost at all. It was stuck in our attic, and somehow my mum has got possession of it. That was if it was the real thing and not a fake. If I was hiding something this strong, I would make fakes to throw people off the trail. Or just throw it in the void. Who is going to go down there and find it?

Skye finally joined me and put two glasses of freshly made juice on the table. We were both wearing our uniforms which we had finally gotten used to. Skye tended to have her hair up in some form of a ponytail, so her overall look now looked a lot older and mature. She got a lot more attention from boys, who I had to keep away from her. I've even caught Tyler checking her out sometimes, which really annoyed both Skye and me.

The only person she seemed to have her eye on was Mal-Chin. They had got to hang out a few times, though I could never tell if he liked her or not. I did, however, know that if he hurt her, I'd hurt him.

I showed Skye what I had found, but she was a little suspicious. She didn't like the fact it was only one book and insisted we checked out the books on machines in an attempt to find it. Now we knew roughly what we were searching for; it would narrow our search even more.

"But surely, this would be a good start to give to Mal. He has been getting on my nerves, constantly asking me if we have found anything. You know he won't let us go anywhere unless we provide him with any information. If we give him this, we can finally leave for home. He has his own team who can research," I explained. I have been itching to leave for a while. Tyler has been asking questions as to why we are out so much, and Darcy, I barely see. She just stays in her room and only leaves with Skye for training.

"But surely it is better if we know more about the sphere ourselves? What if we aren't told any more about it and are kept in the dark? We came from nowhere, and suddenly we were planning this big adventure home. We won't have another chance to research properly."

"We can find out more when we are back home! Mum obviously knew what the sphere was. She will tell us." Skye looked down in shame.

"I know, Amp, but aren't you even slightly curious to learn more," Skye answered back. I could tell that she was torn. Two of her favourite things were adventures and knowledge, and I was essentially asking her to choose between one or the other. I thought for a moment, trying to think of a way I could persuade her.

"Mum knows what the sphere is. She must know more details about it, or she wouldn't have it. We could ask her when we reach her." I was winning her over. Skye longingly gazed back at the rows of books in the library, probably trying to absorb their contents just by looking at them.

"But what if she doesn't know, and it's just a fluke?"

"There is a library at home. If in doubt, we can ask Lily about her library."

"Lily's is too far to just casually travel to and from," Skye said, now sounding like she was trying to convince herself that staying here a little longer was a good idea. I raised my eyebrows at her.

"Skye…come on. We have another way to gain knowledge. What we don't have, is time. The longer we wait here, the less chance we have to see Mum and Dad again, to see home again.

"Fine. I will tell Mal, and you can go and tell your girlfriend," Skye chuckled, sipping more from her juice and laying back in her chair.

"Lily isn't my girlfriend!"

"*Really*, Amp, I have seen you both sneaking off to your *private* lunches."

"It's just lunch. There isn't anything else going on!"

"Yeah, just lunch…alone, just you two." Skye took another sip, wearing her usual rascally smile. She had lost the young girl look she used to have, but having her hair up made her look scarier. Skye didn't look like someone you would want to mess with. Although, some guys I know would like a girl like that. Personally, I would rather have a girl like Lily. Clever and funny, it isn't a pain in the butt. I felt myself blushing, so I forced Lily out of my mind. But it couldn't be kept out for long.

"Why are you blushing," Skye asked, smirking," you're thinking about Lily. Don't worry. We have the whole journey with her. She does seem like a good sister. We can talk about girly stuff. Hair, flowers, dresses…."

"Ahem!" I stopped her and waited for her to stop smiling before I said what I wanted to.

"Let's finish our drinks and go and see Mal-Chin together. We'll explain what we have found out. No doubt Captain Miserable will tell us our next orders."

"Amp, Mal isn't miserable. It's just you he is like that with. You're both just as bad as each other."

"Yeah, yeah, whatever. Anyway, we said we would get volunteers. Just us and Lily?"

"Who else is going to be crazy enough to risk their lives for us," Skye questioned, "We don't know anyone here. Apart from Tyler and Darcy." We both took a moment to think about what I am guessing was the same thing. Would Darcy and Tyler come? Would Mal-Chin let them? I told Skye that we could always ask them after we spoke to Mal. She agreed, and we quickly finished our drinks.

Since I was technically a leader of the foundation group, I was allowed my own skier. Skye was allowed to rent one being in the advanced group. It didn't make much sense to us, but either way, it was finally our chance at freedom. We had our own money coming in and our own skiers. It felt like home…at least what home could be. Unfortunately, this is just a small snippet, and in reality, things looked a lot bleak.

We got onto our skiers, which were parked out front of the library. Our skiers were green with a yellow stripe. Technically, that meant I was using an advance level skier, but no one asked questions.

The building itself looked smaller from the outside, still made of the same black stone that the other buildings were made from. The library was on its own tiny island, connected to the main one by a small wooden bridge.

We took our skiers and stuck close together. It was weird flying on a skier that was at a good standard and without any form of pressure. Despite the layers of rules the O.I.D. had, it was freeing. My arm was almost healed, and my sister and I were happy.

We finally got to our destination. It was a little way off the main island and was a four-story building with a glass dome at the top of the black stones. I made a mental note to ask Lily where and why the whole O.I.D complex was made of the same stone. Skye had been here many times. She got *special privileges* because she *knew* Mal-Chin. Skye doesn't even tell me what they even do, not that I want to know anyway.

We parked outside. I followed Skye's lead. The entranceway had a couple of patches of browning grass with a pathway splitting them up. The path leads up to the glass door.

Inside had a wooden floor, with two white, cuboid porcelain vases on either side of the door. A grey carpet leads forward to a front desk.

"Hey Megan," Skye said, "Is Mal around?" A girl, slightly older than me with long blond hair, sat up over the desk.

"Oh...Hey Skye. He's upstairs as usual. You caught him just in time, though. His squad are going to depart on a mission soon." Skye seemed shocked.

"A mission? Where too?"

"Sorry, you know I can't tell you, Skye." Megan seemed to notice I was there and smiled at me.

"This must be your brother you talk about," exclaimed Megan, "Amphorn, correct?" She stood up and reached over to shake my hand. I nodded and shook her hand. Megan told us she would buzz Mal-Chin for us, and afterwards, she studied me again.

"So Skye tells me you're dating Lily. You're a lucky guy. Lily is extremely clever and kind. Plus, she can make really good bread too." I felt my cheeks go warm, and I glared at Skye, who was smirking by a staircase.

"I'm not...." I tried to stay but was cut off.

"Skye, a pleasure as always," said Mal-Chin, emerging from the stairs that Skye was standing by. He then noticed me, and his smile rapidly straightened.

"Amp, good to see you well." He nodded, almost in a bow, and I did the same.

He spoke to both of us, saying, "I hope this visit is worth my time. I don't mean to be rude, but I haven't got much time. I need to prepare my squad to depart within the next couple of hours."

"We found out some key information about the sphere," Skye informed, "we thought you would want to know." We were invited upstairs. This guy must have some really strong legs because he seemed to always be at the top of a huge set of stairs.

On the way up, Skye was asking questions about getting back home. We were told, and by we, I mean Skye - I was just trailing behind and ignored – that Mal couldn't afford to lose equipment or people's lives.

His echoing voice said, "Getting you home is a personal thing. I have spoken to the higher-ups, and they agree that we can't afford to lose anything over this. I can allow you to take your own skiers and basic provision but that I it. I am sorry...for both of you." I could tell he genuinely seemed distressed that he couldn't help, and I didn't blame him for anything.

Many more steps later, we reached the top and were taken through an office-looking area. It was similar to the lookout tower where we first met Mal-Chin in. Except for this time, there was a glass dome instead of open air. There was a large map in the centre and desks with equipment all over them. Some I could tell were for communication. Others had telepads that portrayed islands with various buildings.

We were asked to take a seat then I explained what we found.

"The sphere, it's called the sphere mechanism. It's part of a larger machine that is capable of destroying islands. At least...that is all we know." We were joined by a man who had a telepad and wrote down everything we said.

"The Rogues want it for power, then? They're looking for a sphere which I assume is separate from the machine?" Skye and I nodded, and I explained about the rebels keeping the sphere away from the capital.

Mal-Chin spoke to the man writing notes and held his chin for a while.

"Is that everything?" Once again, we nodded.

"Thank you. Your research will prove most valuable. I will have a team to carry on the research. Here, take these. They will help you get the provisions you will need for your trip home. You're both free to leave whenever you feel fit."

We were handed a telepad each. We opened them up, and a letter was shown in blue light. It was giving us a list of things we were allowed for free, signed by multiple people I didn't recognise.

"Skye, you will want this too," Mal informed, passing over a second telepad. We gave each other a confused look as she took it. When she opened it, her eyes lit up.

"Wait...Mal...are you serious? This is...an actual skier license." Skye was ready to explode with excitement. She got her license this easily, and yet I nearly died.

"You have proven yourself on a skier. Now I suggest you both get going. We'll let Lily know you're ready whilst you collect provisions."

We were dismissed right after. After a very quick goodbye, Skye and I were on our way back down the huge flight of stairs.

Skye complained, "Is that really all I got? I thought we were closer than that, and yet he dismisses me like we're going to be home by dinner!" I couldn't help but smile a little bit. Finally, we went home.

I told her that perhaps he wasn't thinking too straight and that he was probably just thinking about too many things at once. She grunted the whole way down, and soon enough, we were back on our skiers.

PART 17

"Oh, come on, spill the beans. Where are you two going," Tyler questioned after noticing Skye, and I had packed a couple of bags. Even Darcy was sitting on the couch, listening to our conversation. I never did find out what happened to her tongue, and I probably never will.

"We're going home," Skye beamed, "we're just waiting for our friend, and we're going to be off." There was a tiny moment of panic from Tyler, who scowled.

"Home? What? Why?"

"Well, Tyler, our home is being attacked by Rogues, and our parents are there. We want to get back," Skye explained, with what I think was a hint of sarcasm. She didn't seem too eager to talk to him. I think she just wanted to get going. Skye was fiddling with her bag, constantly making sure she got everything.

Darcy was tapping away at her keypad, writing on her telepad quickly, and when she stopped, she waved me over. I did as she asked, and Darcy pointed to her telepad. I read aloud.

"The Rogues have swarmed your home cluster. But if you get to the cluster at about six p.m., their reinforcements won't be as strong. You're better coming in from the southeast side as that is where there is minimal resistance." I frowned at her. Her dark eyes felt like they were piercing through me.

"H…how do you know that," I asked, aware that Tyler was trying to persuade Skye to say more. Darcy swiped, and the previous words vanished. She then typed up more.

"I…like…to work out…plans. I have seen the maps of the Rogue's movement and…make a point to…work out their patterns." I have seen Darcy playing with her telepad a few times, but she always hides it as if it wasn't allowed. This whole time, she was working out strategies.

114

"You do realise you can join a squad that trains in that," I mentioned, still slightly confused. Darcy looked like she thought she didn't think about that. It took her a while before she quickly typed again.

"Who would I talk to about it," she wrote. I couldn't help but smile at the talk part. Darcy noticed my smile, and she, too, let out a slight grin, shaking her head.

"Talk, write, you know what I mean," she quickly typed again, frowning at me sarcastically. It was the first time I had seen her show any other emotion, and I was honoured it was because of me.

After the initial smiles had gone, I mentioned that perhaps she could talk to whoever was in charge of her training. Darcy shrugged and wiped the last text.

"I guess. You never know; I might be able to help organise a team to take back your home cluster." Darcy now seemed excited and hopeful, which felt more concerning than anything. She barely spoke or showed any emotion, and yet she seemed positive. What was the catch here? I felt doubt when I know I shouldn't.

Suddenly, there was a knock on our door. Tyler answered it, and Skye looked relieved that Tyler had stopped talking to her. As soon as Tyler saw Lily, he beamed and looked at me.

"You must be Lily," he said, stepping aside and letting her in. Lily had her hair in a bun and another dress that was frilly at the bottom, and it fell just above her knees. It was purple and black, which dashes of red stitching around her torso. Lily also had a black cardigan on too, which complimented her outfit perfectly.

"And you must be Tyler," Lily answered back, faking a smile. Her eyes were telling me that she was screaming, "Leave me alone", and yet she was way too polite to say so. The poor boy seemed to have taken to Lily straight away, as he was now switching between Skye and Lily constantly but nervously.

After the introductions, Skye and I were ready to leave.

"So, I have a map of the areas we will be crossing through and marked areas where Rogues are most active. We also need to account for the fact your faces are on posters all over the place. Luckily, you both look very different to them now, so we shouldn't have too big of an issue." Lily thought for a split second, then carried on, making sure we were listening.

"We need to head west from here. It's still morning which is great for us as we will have plenty of time for light. There is a place that will let us stay the night, several hours' flight from here. They're aware we are coming." I hadn't even thought about the fact that it would take more than one day to get home. It would take us a few days to get home. I was grateful Lily had thought about that.

"So if you fly ahead, Amp and I will follow behind. We don't have too many things with us, only a bag each," Skye said, nodding her head towards our bags that were near the front door. Lily saw them and answered, "They should fit in the back of my skipper, so you won't need to worry about strapping them onto your skiers."

"I guess we should get going then. No point wasting any more time," I said to both of the girls. A quick bag check and a few goodbyes later, we were at our skiers. Lily obviously knew where our skiers were, as her shiny, red skipper wasn't too far away from us. We placed our bags in a small compartment in the back of her skipper, including our spare food. We did one more final check, and finally, we were off.

There was something very nerve-racking, flying away from the O.I.D. We barely saw the void anymore, so I did get a small case of voiphobia, the fear of the void. It was even worse when we were flying over an area where we couldn't see any island anywhere. Our only sense of direction was the sun.

It was pretty windy and very chilly. If it wasn't for my jacket, I would be frozen. I checked on Skye, and she seemed to be staring into the void. We'd both chosen to put on the ear mufflers, which were like headphones. They did have combination devices in them, but we couldn't be bothered to set them up.

It was probably wise to do that when we got a chance, though. The ear mufflers helped reduce the noise that the skiers and wind made, but I was using them for the extra warmth. The noise reduction made things feel peaceful also. We were free to go anywhere and do anything.

I pondered what Skye was thinking right now. She was probably half tempted to just fly into the void right now. It has always been one of her biggest dreams.

My thoughts turned to the skipper ahead of us. I saw the back of Lily's head and, again, wondering what she was thinking. Did she regret coming out? Did she think about her home and her shop? It can't have been easy for her, surely. I couldn't help but question…what would it be like if Lily and I dated? Would I want to stay in Marhalm, or would I move and be closer? Would Lily and I even work? We hadn't known each other for too long, and it was clear we liked each other. Well, at least I thought it was clear. Skye seemed to think Lily liked me too, and Lily does get emotional thinking about saying bye. The thought made my chest feel tight. She really would miss me when I got home. Now I just felt guilty she was coming all this way for us. She'd have to come all the way back again on her own.

We were in the endless void for about an hour and a half until we saw silhouettes of some islands. The sun was directly above us, so it was good that we now had another point of interest to fly towards. We would have had an hour or so flying almost blindly in the direction we thought was west.

We flew closer, and I got a proper look at the islands. For some reason, I had assumed I would recognise the islands as it was between home and the O.I.D. But we obviously haven't been past these ones, as they seemed scarily peaceful.

Every island was covered in coarse, rough dirt and gravel. It felt a little similar to home, but the dirt was a lot drier. The houses were also very similar. They were all made from the same scrap metal and wood that created windshields with no insulation that we called buildings. There wasn't a single building higher than two stories. The islands were also spaced apart similarly. The centre could clearly be seen from the outer islands of the cluster, easily a ten-to-fifteen-minute flight.

A few rusted bridges linked islands together that arched over voids of space. The rocks and stones underneath the islands looked like they were puzzle pieces, each bulbous part seeming like I could fit into the crevasse of another island. The islands that were attached together with posts both looked like they had cracks on the surface. I could tell some of the islands looked so crumbly; they could fall at any moment.

A quick glance over to Skye told me she was thinking the same thing. She flew a little lower and towards an island that had a rusted pole protruding from the side. The other side of the pole stretched into empty space. Apart from a small clump of stone, it seemed like there used to be an island, but it had fallen. A closer inspection of the still remaining island showed us that the rock felt like a fine powder.

Skye and I gave each other a confused and concerned look and then quickly caught up with Lily. She had noticed us flying on a detour and was just hovering above us. She was studying the islands, and when we finally got next to her, Lily pointed at a wide but short building a couple of islands away.

That was the direction we headed, and within minutes, we were landing next to the construction. Just like the rest, the island was covered in the same dirty gravel.

Two other skiers occupied part of the island space, so it was a squeeze to fit all of ours on too. It was even harder fitting Lily's Skipper on. I felt like I was either going to knock a skier off or fall over the edge myself, but despite that, I worked my way to the empty space where Skye, Lily and I reconvened.

It was still pretty tight even when we manoeuvred our way to the entrance, which was decorated with an off-white fence. It was the only bright colour around, aside from the red skipper that was Lily's. A gentle breeze swept through our hair, and I felt a strange feeling when I saw how Lily's just fluttered about. It was messy yet, so…perfect. She opened the door, and we clambered through.

At least when we were inside, I didn't have the constant feeling that I was going to trip over a pebble and end up seeing what was in the void. The place was very plain and incredibly uninteresting. There was a very dark and dull colour scheme everywhere, with only two doors. One was left, and one was on the right.

"Uh, which door," Skye asked Lily. Lily went straight to the door on the left and knocked three times. We waited in silence, but it was long until it opened. The woman who answered was miserable. She had choppy brown hair and was wearing a white shirt and blue jeans. Behind her, in the room, I saw an office and a chubby man sitting in the office chair.

"Oh, it's you," the woman moaned, her voice sounding like a squeaking dog toy which was extremely unnerving.

"Bernie, it's that flower girl again. The one who booked the room earlier." The woman faced the man in the back. He was a large man in a shirt three sizes too small. His head was bald and reflected a lamp of some kind that was obviously behind the door. It looked like he had rolled his eyes and then dove into a drawer. The wood looked rotten, and the office was a mess, and yet he somehow found what he was looking for. It was a key which he handed to the woman, and then she passed it to Lily.

"Have a nice day," she said before slamming the door in Lily's face. We all stood still, trying to let that event run through our heads.

"Well, they were pleasant. Come," Lily sarcastically laughed, though I could tell she felt just as unnerved as Skye and I. Lily held the key, not very willingly, and unlocked the door on the right, and together we crammed ourselves in.

The place was run down and very dirty. The was one excuse of a bed and a window with a crack in it. An old curtain hung by the window, but it was stained, ripped, and covered in dust.

"You said you arranged places to stay," I asked, disgusted. I was surprised when I couldn't smell anything bad. It just smelt normal.

"Hey, I didn't say it was going to be pretty. We are in the outer islands. The options aren't exactly grand," Lily defended, stepping further into the room.

"Um, right. And you know there is only one bed. All three of us can't sleep on there," Skye pointed out, hesitantly sitting on it. It was plain white covers. They appeared clean, but I didn't blame Skye for being careful.

"Well, I guess someone will have to sleep on the floor then," Lily explained. I was hoping it was another joke to keep us motivated, but we knew she was not joking. I looked down at the wooden floorboard. I may as well be sleeping on gravel.

"Well, I will sleep on the floor. Amp, who should sleep on the bed with Lily," Skye suggested. It felt like my stomach had been hit. Even Lily was taken by surprise as she went just as red as I did."

"Skye, come on! We are queens, and if Amp was a real gentleman, he would take the floor, and we have the honour of the comfy bed." Both girls looked at me expectantly. I groaned, "I can't possibly let you ruin your precious hair now, could I." There wasn't much discussion needed. I had a feeling it was assumed that I would let the girls have the bed, so I didn't argue. I also volunteered to collect bags we might need from Lily's skipper.

PART 18

I couldn't sleep all night. The wind must have picked up during the night because I could hear it howling through tiny gaps. The floor was extremely uncomfortable, and I am pretty sure I was being eaten alive by bugs that lived in the cracks of the floorboards. I attempted to look through the window and saw dawn was slowly breaking. There wasn't any point trying to get sleep anymore, as Lily's alarm would be waking us soon anyway.

I wondered how well the girls slept. They seemed peaceful and relaxed, but the bed seemed to be a very thin sponge with a sheet over it.

Lily was on my side of the bed, but her head was turned towards the centre. I studied her and felt my heart beating. She was so pure. I kept replaying when she told me she would miss me if I stayed with my family. I wished she would stay, but I know she wouldn't. Why would Lily give up her flowers and her island? The idea of never seeing each other again felt like a storm cloud was lingering.

I was lying there for about ten more minutes when I caught Lily stirring. Her alarm hadn't gone off, yet she was waking up. It took a little while to wake up properly, but she eventually lifted her head and looked about. Lily didn't notice I was awake, too, until I said, "Do all queens wake up with their hair in a mess?" I must have startled her as she flinched, but she quickly turned into a tired smile.

"Do all courtiers wake up with bugs on their faces and dirt on their clothes? Seriously, did you roll around in a field or something?" Her exhausted chuckle made my heart melt. It was so cute.

"So I'm just the assistance, hm?" Lily turned and faced me as I sat and leaned up against the wall.

"Would you rather be a peasant serving boy? I'm sure Skye would love that."

"I mean…"

"Or maybe even a slave." I didn't even bother to respond, and instead, I raised my eyebrows and rolled my eyes, which I guess could be taken as a response.

"So that's a no to slave but a maybe to a servant?"

"Yeah, sure. Nothing but a servant," I muttered, having a stretch.

"Does that mean you will do anything I ask of you," she asked curiously. She sat up slowly so she didn't wake Skye, who appeared sound asleep still. Lily then got herself out of bed and stretched herself.

"Do I even have a choice with you two," I answered back, and Lily took that as a yes.

"Okay, serving boy, grab my dress from my bag," Lily sarcastically said, imitating a well-spoken queen. I crossed my arms and stared at her as she stared back. She stood in between the bag and me, so I knew she was doing it on purpose.

"Do you want to be a slave," she asked again, pretty harshly, "go grab my dress!" She stepped aside, revealing her bag more clearly. I decided to play along and hauled myself up, and headed over to her dress. However, as I passed her, she poked my lower back playfully. It sent a shock through my whole body, and my body uncontrollably did a weird action before quickly resuming back to normal.

"Really?" I asked, but I couldn't help but grin at her, trying not to laugh. "Dress?"

I slowly backed towards her dress, poised in case she tried poking me again. I kept watching her watch me and kept going back until my foot touched the bag. That's when she tried it again, but this time, I grabbed her wrist and pulled her towards me. Next, I did the first thing that came to mind and tickled her. She burst out laughing to the point she was practically crying. During the process of grabbing her, we both fell, but I was able to keep her pinned as she desperately tried poking me. But I kept tickling her.

"Guys, seriously? Get a room that doesn't have me in it, please!" Both Lily and I stopped, breathing heavily with huge grins on our faces. Skye was sat up in the bed, her eyes barely open. She yawned as she switched between Lily on the floor and me next to her. I took that time to quickly grab Lily's dress and hold it up.

"Here, your highness," I said mockingly, causing one last laugh between Lily and me.

"Oh, why thank you, serving boy."

Lily's alarm finally went off at the same time as us getting dressed. Despite the room, we were in pretty high spirits.

"I'm just gonna go grab some food from the skier, and then we can head off. We have a fairly long journey today, so make sure you are ready."

When the door was closed, Skye beamed at me.

"You guys are so cute together! You have to kiss her! Can I be a bridesmaid at the wedding? I guess that is her choice. Oh, Aunty Skye. I'm going to be a great aunt."

"Shut up!"

Skye frowned at me.

"Is someone embarrassed?"

"No, I mean it, shut up. I hear talking outside!"

Our room fell into silence as we listened to some muffled voices through the wall.

"It is definitely the two! We'll get a huge reward if we hand them over," a woman said. I guessed it was the woman who gave us the key.

Now mental alarm bells were ringing, and after seeing Skye's reaction, I knew she was thinking the same thing.

"So, how do we keep them here long enough? They're ready to leave, and we're going to lose our chance, a man answered, who I guessed was the man in the office.

"That pretty flower girl is outside. They won't leave without her. She what if we…kept her in here. By the time those two notice, it'll be too late."

It took a few seconds for it to sink in, but I suddenly felt sick.

"Speaking of the girl…." The voices went silent. Suddenly, there was a scream, and I could only guess it was Lily's. Skye and I burst through the door, but no one was there. Then we saw the door on the left was slightly ajar, but as we got to it, it was slammed shut. I pounded on the door, but it was locked.

"Skye, get our things on the skippers. Make sure they're ready to leave!"

"What are you going to do exactly," cried Skye, but I ignored her. She hesitated but did as I asked as quickly as she could. I started trying to shoulder barge the door, but it was still not getting through. All I needed was a little bit more force. These doors were not strong at all.

Skye carried the last few bags out as I stepped back. I pressed my back against the wall opposite the door to get as big of a run-up as I could get. Then I charged.

The door splintered everywhere, and I found myself stumbled up from under the wooden desk. The woman yelped and flailed her arms about and backed towards the far wall of the room, which was wide but short. The man had his arm around Lily's neck. She was clawing at this arm that was clearly choking her, but it didn't seem to make any difference.

Skye had finished moving things and came in next to me. I felt a sense of relief, having her with me, but I couldn't risk her getting hurt. I couldn't risk Lily either. One wrong move and the man would crush Lily's throat.

"The Rogues are going to be a few minutes. Once they're here and we get paid, I will let her go. But I won't hesitate." I had to think quickly. I studied them both. I could easily take the woman. Hey, Skye could take her. The man didn't seem to be much of a threat either. But he had Lily.

"Hurting her would be a mistake. The Rogues need her. She is very important," I quickly spurted out, attempting to maintain my seriousness and not panic. I had got a reaction out of them, and the woman stammered, "How? How is she important?" She was in the same clothes as yesterday, and the fact her voice was so weird made this conversation a million times harder.

"Important enough that if they find out she is hurt, you will pay with your lives." I tried to put as much power behind my voice as I could. I took two steps forward towards them, closing the gap even more. They were only a metre away now. A step and a reach, and I would be on them. Skye was fairly close behind me, and I trusted her reaction times to help me if and when I needed it. Lily stopped struggling now and was now listening to what I was saying.

"Who is this flower girl to the Rogues? They'll be here and second anyway," the woman carried on. I knew she was right. If I was going to act, I needed to act soon. I couldn't see an opening on the man. He had Lily pretty much shielding him. The only part exposed was his face, which I couldn't reach. The only person who could be Lily.

Suddenly, a lightbulb lit up in my head. I had a plan, and now I had to hope Lily would get my signal. Plus, I did have my knife that was tucked in my back pocket. I'm pretty sure that Skye has hers, too, though both of us agreed not to use them unless absolutely necessary.

"Give me a second. I think some dirt got in my eye. How do you not get anything in your eyes." I admit the way I came out with that was random, and I could have said something way better. However, Lily's face lit up. I knew she got the idea.

"Anyway, we need to get going now. I am sorry for this."

Lily took that as her sign and thrust her thumb into the man's eyes as hard as she could. As expected, he screamed and let go, giving me enough time to pull Lily towards me. The woman tried to grab her, but Skye was quicker and shoved herself into the panicking woman. Just as I had predicted, Skye was easily able to overwhelm her and was able to retreat back to the door. I let the girls get out first.

"Get yourself to the skiers and keep an eye out for the Rogues. I will keep these guys busy." The girls listened and ran out the door.

The man had gotten over his shock, and when he came charging at me, I could see his eye was watering. He tried to grab my shirt, but he was really slow, and I effortlessly stepped aside. The woman didn't even try to attack me and instead had her back against her wall, which I had only now realised was plastered with notes ripped out from a book. I didn't bother with her and turned to the man.

This time, I attacked first. I rushed the man and got a hold of his top before I guided him towards the wall. His head crashed against it with a thump. He turned around and aimlessly swung his fist at me. He let out a bellow when he couldn't connect to anything. I took the chance and punched his throat. I don't know why I did it, but I hoped it would slow him down. But it did something I didn't expect.

Almost instantly, he slumped to the floor and was motionless. I didn't have time to think about what had happened as I heard a scream behind me. The woman raced over, and I prepared to fight. But instead, she ignored me and checked the man. Her water-logged eyes glared at me as I backed out the main door.

"Amp, we have company," Skye yelled. She was in her skier, already strapped in, and Lily was in her skipper, hovering just off the island. Skye pointed up, and I saw four skiers rapidly approaching the island.

I quickly analysed them as I strapped myself in. None of the skiers had weapons, so we could lose them by flying. The main issue would be Lily. Her skipper couldn't reach anywhere near the same speed we could on our skiers.

"Lily, get out of here. Meet us at those buildings. Skye, you, and I need to distract and lose them." I prayed Lily wouldn't protest. She looked back at me, and I could tell she was putting a lot of trust in me. She did as I said and ignored the approaching enemies. Skye had already zoomed off and attracted two of the four. One had peeled off the group and followed Lily, and the last one came towards me.

I took off as quickly as I could. Maybe a little too quick, but these skiers were way more stable than any I had flown before.

The other skier was almost onto me, but I was able to swerve out of the way. I swerved a little too much, and for a couple of seconds, I plummeted towards the void, but I stayed calm and readjusted. I could see the Rogues had a hook on the end of a pole and that they were using them to try and latch onto us. I'm guessing we were wanted alive and not dead, so that was a reassuring thought.

I had already lost track of Skye, but I didn't want to think about that. I saw Lily in the distance, barely staying out of the way of the other skier's hook. I knew I had to get them off her, so I put my skier into full throttle and raced over to her. My heart was beating as I knew that I was closely pursued. I had no idea how I was meant to get their attention, nor how I was going to lose these guys. All I knew was that I had to get creative.

As I was closing the gap, I started thinking of weaknesses. The guys couldn't have been trained properly, right? The Rogues were so big and always moving about the islands. So they wouldn't have the most trained pilots because they didn't have the time. That would be their main weakness. Plus, they had less stable skiers. I knew that as I had flown one already and knew what they felt like.

I formulated my plan as I whizzed between the narrow hook of a skier and Lily's skipper. I didn't know what I was doing, but an idea was forming. Despite the temporary distraction, the man following Lily carried on pursuing her, and I was still being followed. What would happen if I was caught? If I was flying fast, I would be yanked the wrong way. It would put me off. That was it. That was my attack.

I zoomed about a few islands, narrowly missing sticking-out pipes and other civilian skiers. I even flew under a bridge that had two kids on and probably gave them a heart attack. I was able to gain a little lead and found a large space with no islands where. I stopped and turned to face the man following me.

As I thought, he was flying right at me. I prepared myself and flew straight back at him. I had obviously confused him as he tried to swerve to the side, but I reached and grabbed his pole. My whole arm yanked to the side, and I felt a pain jar my body.

Not only did I have a scar on that arm forming, but I had probably torn half my ligaments. Either way, both skiers had been pulled in a circle and thrown off balance. I felt the force of the pole stop, and I was suddenly drifting away from the other skier, who I could see was really struggling to keep his skier still. I had his pole in my arm, but I was now upside down once again, getting lower into the void than I had ever been before.

PART 19

I didn't realise how much danger or pain I was actually in until my initial shock passed. I saw the other skier smoking from one of his thrusters and snaking side to side in an attempt to right himself. Everything was white with a few hints of blue. I couldn't see any islands above me or to the side.

I held onto the pole whilst I desperately pulled the handles towards me. I heard a clunk, and suddenly there was a huge force flipping me around. My insides swirled about, and I threw up. For a little while, everything was spinning, but then I realised I was hovering. I figured that the skiers had self-righting equipment. That was handy to know.

I wiped my mouth, and I looked about to find the fate of the smoking Rogue, seeing someone spinning about below me. He was almost upright, but the engine looked like it was damaged. For a moment, I was going to fly up, but I couldn't bare leaving him to fall. So I plunged down after him.

I caught up quickly and extended the poll. Extending it made me realise how badly my arm hurt, but I gritted my teeth. I was able to latch on to his skier and was able to maintain my stability whilst stopping him from spinning and rotating. The Rogue took off his brown goggles and looked up to see what had happened. I saw he was younger, easily in his late twenties or early thirties.

"Why are you helping me," he growled, but he didn't resist much. I didn't answer and instead just flew up. It was a lot of work, and I felt my skier struggling to lift, but I slowly rose. The islands were just shadows, and the wind was cold. I felt wet, and the air around me was moist. It was also freezing too, which made everything just way more uncomfortable. I just kept going closer to the shadows.

It took a few minutes, but the shadows came into colour. My arm holding the other skier was burning, which left me with a grand total of zero healthy arms now. Despite that, I was able to lug the damaged skier to the nearest island and unlatched it.

"Thank you," the man said, his voice getting distant. I didn't wait and instead flew towards the building I told Lily to meet us at. I had to find her or Skye. They had to be around somewhere. The whiteness had faded now I was back on the islands. I peered down into the void below and saw the usual blue had large white streaks. They were so far down that they seemed tiny, but I figured that was where I just was. I was that far down in the void. I didn't want to think about that and kept focused on finding Lily.

The buildings on these islands looked like rusted ruins. Everything was broken, buildings and the islands alike. Most of the islands had clumps of rock and stone on a pole that was on the edge of another island.

I scanned the islands and saw there were still a lot of people living there. Most remaining islands had old skiers parked outside. It reminded me a little of home but way more run down. I had a horrid thought that Marhalm would end up just like this when The Rogues were done with it. Perhaps, if they actually found the sphere, even middle island clusters would look like this.

I saw a few glints of red, but they were just old cans of water or a painted fence. I tried to find any signs of skiers in a chase too. Dealing with one skier was hard enough, but Skye had to lose two. I had no choice but to hope she would be fine and kept searching.

I was able to wedge the pole on my skier, so I was able to rest my arms whilst flying. I wished I had my goggles because dusty and dirty debris kept flying in my eyes. There were a few birds that flew next to me, probably curious about what I was looking for.

I had to result to asking some locals, which was probably a risk. However, a nice woman said they saw a red skipper and pointed in the general direction. I followed when she said, desperate now.

I approached the highest parts of the cluster, and I spotted Lily's skipper still flying around. I couldn't see the other skier, so I took precautions as I flew to her. My relief was unmatched when I found no one nearby.

"Oh, thank the void your safe," Lily cried as I hovered next to her. We landed on a small island with nothing but a singular dead tree and mostly rocky top.

"What happened to the guy chasing you," I exclaimed, now looking for Skye. I didn't even unstrap myself, and Lily didn't get out her skipper.

"I don't know. No longer after you flew off, they ignored me and flew away. I caught a glimpse of Skye around here, and she still had two chasing her. What about your guy?" I grimaced as I recalled the events that happened. Even Lily felt sick for me.

"That doesn't matter now. We have to find Skye!" Lily nodded and joined me as we carefully flew through the cluster again. We didn't dare separate.

I kept trying to remain optimistic, but my optimism was starting to dwindle as we approached late morning. It had been at least two hours since we started looking for Skye and couldn't find anything.

Lily told me, "She can't be here. If she was, we would have found her by now. I'm running low on fuel, so we need to start looking for somewhere to find that soon." I hadn't checked my fuel levels, but I knew I would be low too. I hated to admit it, but we had to stop looking for Skye and find a place to stop.

The closest place we could find was about half an hour from the cluster. A lot further away than what I wanted to be, but we had no choice. When we landed, I checked my fuel levels and realised I was running on empty.

"It's a miracle you managed to get here," the man who owns the shop laughed as he started filling our things up. He was small with a white goatee and no hair. He wore an oil-stained white shirt underneath black overalls. His station was simply a wooden shelter with larger metal tanks in a fenced-off section. Two hoses came out attached to the pump that fuels the skiers.

The fuel that skiers run on is an artificial oil that is made from a rare type of plant called the harp flower, and it can only be found in certain parts of the Middle Islands. They require a lot of hydration and maintenance, which meant most outer islanders couldn't provide the right care, and inner islanders were too rich and lazy to care. Lily said that she was dying to get her hands on them, but finding a source was near impossible as those who had access to it often never sold a single petal as everything was worth a lot of money.

The flowers came in various colours, but the most common was a brilliant blue version. The stem was also very thick at the bottom compared to ordinary plants. The most distinct part about it was the fact that the petals formed a crescent moon shape and had very thin parts of the stem that grew between the top and bottom part of the crescent, thus making it look like harp strings.

I'm not too sure about the oil-making process, but from what I had read before, they grind them up, and the sap in the stem mixed with some properties in the petals create a thick substance. A few other things are added, and then it is left for a while. It's then shipped out to fuel places like here. Fuel wasn't expensive, but it was hard to come by if there wasn't a place nearby that was listed as an official fuel station by the inner islanders.

I sat on a bench near the edge of the island, under a tree with no leaves. Its roots came out of the side of the island and then back into the ground again. I guessed it was around thirty years old as it wasn't the thickest tree around. So once upon a time, there must have been water around these parts, or it was planted here and grown elsewhere.

I kept looking in the distance, scanning every little island and rock. Lily sat next to me, handing me a roll.

"You haven't eaten," she mentioned, taking a bite out of her own roll. Since losing Skye, I have lost my appetite. I declined the roll, but Lily insisted.

"I know you want to find Skye, but that doesn't mean you can't eat. You had dinner early yesterday and nothing at all today."

"I'm not hungry," I snapped back. Lily faltered but rewrapped the roll. We sat in silence.

"You haven't failed, ya know." Lily broke the peace.

"Huh," I asked.

"You're thinking about how you failed as a brother again, aren't you? Well, you haven't."

"Yes…I have. I told her to distract the other two. I should have told her to escape." Lily rolled her eyes.

"Really, Amp? Do you really think the Rogues would have just focused on you and let her go? Even if Skye had tried to escape, they would still chase her. We would be in the same situation. What if she was the one with me right now? She would be sitting here wishing the exact same thing."

I knew she was right. Lily placed her hand on mine and kept going.

"You put trust in Skye and let her make her own choices for a reason. She is still out there! And we are going to find each other.

She is smart. She knows where we are going, and my guess is she'll need fuel too. There aren't too many around here, so my guess is she just happens to be at one of the other ones." That put my mind at ease. It was Skye, and I had put trust in her as I knew she was capable. Now I had a mission. Search the other fuel stations and find which one Skye was at.

I had a new spark light up, and Lily smiled at me softly.

"Let's go get your sister, serving boy." That got me. Her calling me serving boy made my heart skip a beat, and so much of me wanted to grab her and kiss her. The temptation was overpowering, and yet I took a breath, and as quick as it had come, the moment was over. I paid the man and took off, flying closely to Lily. I didn't want to let her out of my sight.

We flew a little while and soon reached the next closest fuel station. This was a scrap metal building with a single tanker. We barely spotted it. I landed as if it was just a rock, only one skier to fit on. Over a tiny bridge, a woman waited. I asked about Skye, and she shook her head and told me she didn't know her. We were given directions to the next closest one.

The next station was another forty minutes away, and it was quite busy. There were skiers everywhere, and the station had a building with a shop inside. We followed the flying lane rules until we were next in line. For a brief moment, we had to separate as Lily was in a skipper. I wasn't happy about leaving her, but it was only for a few minutes.

I parked up in the parking zone and rushed to the front entrance. It was very noisy with the amount of thruster noise about and fuelling noises. There was a huge metal canopy, with twelve pipes dangling down a pillar each. I followed the hoses and saw the four huge tanks on their own island.

On the main island was the shop made of scrap iron, but it was polished and seemed well put together. On the other side, I saw the landing zone for the skippers. I couldn't see Lily's, but I knew she was around there somewhere.

I was as quick as I could be, rushing to the front entrance. Lily also didn't seem to wait around, and I saw her running towards me.

Together we entered the shop. I held out hope that Skye was either here or they had seen her.

The man in the shop wasn't very useful. He had a black beard that he kept fiddling with whilst he spoke. He told us he saw hundreds of people come in and out, so I would have to narrow it down for him.

Between us, Lily and I described what she was wearing, her hair colour and even how she had it up. He kept shaking his head.

"You're describing half the people I see here. I'm sorry. Now you're holding up my line. You may as well ask those guys over there. Rogues know everything and everyone."

We were dismissed pretty quickly, but the mention of Rogues made the hairs on my neck stand up. Lily had also clocked onto that, so we both found ourselves scouring around. There were two men in tatty waistcoats who were hovering next to a shelf that had cans of vegetables. The logo was printed on their chest, out for all to see. The men appeared middle-aged, well built and had a strong presence about them. The way they held themselves showed others that they had power and that they were in control.

I didn't like the idea of talking to the Rogues at all, even more when it was about finding my sister, who was being chased by them right after I was just chased by them. It's an unpleasant chain of events that didn't need expanding.

"Should we," Lily asked. She actually sounded like it was a thing to consider.

"Uh, no. We have other stations we can check out first without drawing more attention." I lowered my head and left the station building, Lily doing a double take towards the two men before joining me.

PART 20

"This is our last one. If she hasn't been here, then what will we do? It's already approaching dusk, and we have gone miles off course," Lily informed, lingering outside another small metal shack. I unstrapped myself from my skier and then rubbed dirt out of my eyes. I wish I had my goggles so badly, as my eyes kept watering. The last thing I wanted was for Lily to see and think I was getting emotional and crying about our situation.

"Let's just ask this woman; if not, we will go over our next point of call." You'd have thought that Skye was Lily's sister. The fact that it was getting close to dusk already should have me worried, but I wasn't fazed. The truth was, I had been conducting another plan in preparation for when asking the fuel stations didn't work.

As expected, the owner knew nothing about Skye. Lily was the one who let out a long panicky breath.

"We will find her," Lily said again, but I felt like she was talking to herself more than she was talking to me. I felt numb, as I was hoping that plan would work. But I had to result to my next one.

I slumped to the island's ground and dangled my legs over the edge. The void was turning dark blue, and the white streaks looked greyer. The wind rustled through my hair, and I sat in silence. Lily joined me.

"So, what now," she said, gazing up at the couple of stars that dimly came into view.

"Well, we get some rest…and carry on to Marhalm in the morning." Lily was shocked but remained silent. I took this as a chance to explain the plan.

"Skye will be thinking about us. So what will she do? She would assume that we were looking for her and would try to think how we would.

133

So, she'd know we would need fuel. Perhaps she tried them all like us. Maybe she is at the last one we checked."

"Get to the point, Amp. Why go Marhalm if she is so close?"

"There is no guarantee that we would search for her at the stations. However, she knows that we would still go to Marhalm. So I think Skye would start heading there as she knows where we would need to head eventually."

Saying it out loud confirmed my faith in Skye.

She was smart. She knows the rough direction we need to go and knows it's still a couple more days flying from here.

"And if she isn't heading home," Lily asked. I looked at her with confidence.

"She'll be heading somewhere we know, either home or O.I.D. Either way, she won't be lost."

Silence fell again. Only the wind made noises and rattled a broken metal fence with a screw loose. Suddenly I had a thought.

"Hey! Aren't you meant to be the one with optimism? Ya know, being a queen and all that. I'm just a serving boy," I said. I got a muffled chuckle. Lily shook her head again, embarrassed.

"Someone needs to balance us out. Someone must point out the downsides if you're the one with the plan. Usually, that'll be you, but hey, things happen."

"Well, it's getting dark again. We need to find somewhere to sleep. You know any places?" I was hoping Lily would say yes, a nice comfy bed in her castle that happens to be just over there. But nope. She admitted that she wasn't knowledgeable in these areas. We asked the woman inside the fuel station, and she said she had nowhere to recommend either.

Lily wasn't bothered. If anything, she seemed excited.

"Well, we have that island over there. It's a warm enough night to sleep outside. If not, sleep in my skipper." My heartbeat rose rapidly. She wanted me to sleep outside with her? I lost focus over something so silly.

"Are you okay," Lily asked, and I realised I was jiggling my leg up and down, "It isn't that bad of an idea, is it?"

"Um, no. It's a good idea. Let's do it." Lily was still unsure if I wanted to actually sleep outside, but she got in her skipper anyway, and we headed to a small island.

It had no man-made things on it. There was a dead tree, a bunch of dirt and gravel, and nothing to stop you from rolling off the edge.

"So, under the stars or the glass?" Lily asked, stepping out of her skipper. I stared at the ground that crunched when we moved. It was really dry and looked very pointy and painful. I then looked at the red skipper, which wasn't looking so shiny anymore. It had dust littering it, making it look similar to other rusted skippers around.

"The floor looks painful, and I don't want to fall off."

"Well, I have a few blankets. If we put my skipper there and your skier there, we shouldn't' roll off. They'll stop us." I didn't bother arguing. I wasn't even that tired, but now I was looking; Lily was exhausted. I wondered if she had actually got any sleep last night. I should have been way more tired than I was, considering the fact that I didn't sleep well, but it didn't feel right sleeping when I knew Skye was still alone.

We set out the blankets, and I moved my skier. Then Lily took out some food from her skipper. We sat in silence as the night bloomed bright and brighter. The air was cool, and the wind slowed. It was peaceful. Every now and then, you'd see a flock of birds migrating somewhere, probably getting ready to roost up in the night.

"They are so pretty, aren't they," Lily said softly. She laid back and gazed into the sky. I joined her. My head hit the bags we were using, and instantly, the lack of sleep caught up with me. My eyes grew dreary, and before I knew it, I was asleep.

In my dream, I was running. I don't know where I was as the island seemed to go on forever. There was no sign of the void, and the ground was grassy.

I ran and checked behind me, seeing four Rogues. One was the man with the whip, and the other three had a metal crowbar, a pipe-looking thing. I couldn't work out what they were, but I didn't stick around to find out. Suddenly, a wall was in front of me, and I collided with it. I turned at the grass was now bright yellow, and the trees were on fire. The Rogues approached slowly.

"Come with us, and she'll be released," the whip man growled, now holding onto the weapon as if he was ready to attack at the first chance he got. I tried to back away, expecting the wall to be there, but I kept moving. I turned to see where the wall was, but there was nothing. Instead, a dirt path forged its way down between two huge hills. I didn't think twice and ran again. I felt my lungs burning and knew I couldn't keep it up. And yet, my legs carried me down the path.

A few bushes brushed my face as I ran, the pathway getting narrower and narrower. The hills closed on either side of me until I reached yet another dead end.

I turned to face my pursuers, but there weren't any. There weren't even any hills or bushes. Instead, there was just a large stone building. It looked like a castle I had read about in a book, and the front gate was enticing me to come inside. So I did.

I walked in, and the gate slammed shut behind me. All the doorways were blocked off by white gas, leaving one hall. There was a girl on the other side, slumped on the stone floor. Between us was a red carpet. I carefully approached the girl and knelt down. It was Skye.

Her face was blotchy and red, and her clothes looked burnt. I called her name, but she wasn't waking. Then I heard footsteps echoing behind me.

"Is this really your sister? Or is she a fake?" A familiar voice growled. The whip guy was back, and there was another person with him. A girl. Skye! There were now two of them. After that, the gates opened up again and revealed a sheer drop into the void and a man holding onto yet another girl dangling over the edge. A third Skye.

"One of these is your sister, and the others are just illusions. Pick one to save, and the other will die!"

My body didn't do as I wanted, and I couldn't control my voice.

"Her. The one you are holding," my voice croaked. I sounded rough, and talking hurt my throat. I didn't get a chance to see the other Skye, who was dangling over the void.

The man grumbled with laughter, and he threw Skye towards me. I went to catch her, but her image dissolved. There was a scream, and the Skye lying down raised her head just as an arrow flew from the gas rooms. It struck her in the back, and she, too, dissolved. The last one was real. My body kicked into motion as I ran and dived for the last Skye. However, I was too late. Her body was cut loose, and she fell. Her body didn't dissolve as it faded into the void.

I awoke with a jump. I was sweaty and felt clammy. I took a second to compose myself and sat up. It was still dark, and the stars were still bright. Lily appeared to be asleep still, but I noticed her feet moving.

"I know you are awake, Lil," I said quietly. A groan later, Lily opened her eyes and looked at me. She was so pretty. I wasn't even going to try and deny it now. I have fallen for her, and I have fallen hard.

"You had a nightmare," Lily pointed out, still covering herself under a blanket.

"How did you," I started, but Lily told me she heard me.

"You kept asking where she was and shouted her name. I wanted to wake you, but you need sleep too. Then you were shaking, and it scared me." Her voice was so gentle, even with the trembles as she spoke.

"I'm okay now, I promise," I replied. I felt numb, replaying the dream in my head. I explained what had happened to Lily. She listened to every word.

"Just please, don't scare me again," Lily cried. She didn't even ask when she shuffled closer and laid her head on my shoulder. I cradled her, getting flashbacks to when we did this last. I kept thinking, staring into nothingness, when I noticed Lily was looking at me.

I looked back and felt my heart pumping. Her eyes were still watery. Temptation pulled me towards her as I kissed her. She felt warm, delicate and soft. My body exploded internally as she pulled away with an embarrassed grin. She shyly hid her face. No doubt it was blushing and burning like mine.

We both laughed nervously.

"Serving boys aren't meant to kiss their queen," she managed to say. Leave it to Lily to turn this into a joke.

"I was just testing to make sure you were prepared for the future. I may have to try another test later, though," I answered back, not really knowing where I was going with it.

"Prepared for who, hm?"

"Um…I don't know."

"Well, you have permission to kiss me whenever you want."

I wanted to kiss her again so badly. I bet she was hoping I would. But I didn't. I wanted to let the moment sink in without overdoing it. I was addicted to the feeling of wanting but not doing. I craved being near her, and it drove me crazy, but it was crazy. I wanted it all the time.

"So…I…um… won't be able to sleep now," I mentioned to Lily, who was snuggled up to me. She again nervously laughed.

"Your heart is beating really fast right now," she mumbled, her head pressed on my chest. I was embarrassed, but I didn't move.

"Skye would be making a joke or screaming *about time,* something like that," I said.

"Or tell us to get a room…despite the fact that we are sleeping outside." There was more giggling.

We cuddled for another half an hour, and I managed not to kiss Lily again, though there was a moment when I nearly did. There was a small glimmer of sunlight which Lily took a sign as the morning.

Lily sat upright and said, "We should eat and then get going. It's early, but we'll be able to cover more distance."

I knew she was right. We lost a lot of time yesterday, and that meant that we delayed the journey even more. So we finished off the bread we started last night and strapped ourselves in for an early flight. As it was still fairly dark, Lily switched on her lights and guided the way.

Below us, we could see the void with a glimpse of yellow light weaving its way through the white parts. The sun was rising, and a new day was ahead of us.

PART 21

The sunrise was stunning and was even more impressive when we flew over the large empty spaces. It was almost enough to distract me from the fact that the islands we were just at were now so far away they were distance silhouettes. Once again, I found myself in deep thought, thinking about Lily. I had actually kissed her! And she liked it! It was my first kiss too. I wondered if Lily had ever kissed someone before. Who was I kidding, miss' I own flowers' over there in her shiny red skipper? Of course, she has kissed someone before. I stopped before I got jealous of someone else who may not even exist.

We flew past several clusters, each being similar to the last. Both of us obviously kept an eye out for Skye, though we wanted to focus mostly on making up for the lost time. It did get pretty challenging, though, as local law enforcement had dissipated, and Rogue's presence became a lot more noticeable. Every other island had a logo on it or a couple of members who were lingering about outside shops. People weren't exactly acknowledging them, nor were they ignoring them. It was pretty weird to see the power they really had. They looked more like they were restricting people from going to certain areas.

In some places, I saw a few armed skiers, which made things feel even worse. We were approaching dangerous territory for us now. Skye would probably be better on her own. It was by far the easier option. A bright red skipper and a skier following behind wasn't the most inconspicuous thing. It's even worse when the skier has their enemy design on it. To our luck, though, we didn't need to stop and didn't draw any attention. We simply followed the flying lanes past recycled, rusted metal bridges and buildings. Some were occasionally wooden, but they were few and far between.

It was when we were approaching what I believed to be the Desmiter Cluster that the scale of the Rogues really dawned on me. There was a lot of violence going on, and random skiers were being pulled over and searched. Lily noticed and signalled to follow. I didn't really have any other plans, but still, I followed her anyway.

We went low. So now that we weren't far off from the white gases. I felt my clothes getting damp, but at least we were avoiding the Rogues. At least, that is what I thought we were doing.

In the distance was another island. It was fairly big and yet so low down no one would ever know it was even there. Lily headed straight for it, and if I was honest, I was curious to see who was living this low down. My first thought was maybe it was Rogues, but then I figured Lily wouldn't lead us straight into them. Maybe someone she knew?

The island was a decent size, though you could still see the other side of the island when standing at one edge. On approach, I noticed huge metal pipes straight into the void that emerged through gaps in the island rocks. They seemed rusted but still fictional.

I landed next to Lily as usual and only then realised my eyes were still stinging. The amount of dust in the air was becoming a huge issue. I have never felt so jealous of people with the big goofy eye protection more than now. It also doesn't help that the wind kind of stung too.

I rubbed out all the dirt and dust and brushed my clothes. They were also pretty mucky, and I have only just realised. Then again, I just looked like I was at home again, with dust-stained clothes.

"So I figured we could use a stop. Plus, these people could have some information to avoid the Rogues. You might recognise a few names here, and I am pretty sure they're in a similar situation to me, in case they have something the Rogues need them for," started Lily. I wondered what names I would recognise, so I looked about. Something might jog my memory.

This island was green. The grass was very prominent, and there were a few flower beds with multiple colours littering them. I kept looking, and behind the main house was a medium tree, leaves blooming over the island and creating patches of shade. How I hadn't noticed it before, I wasn't sure, but here we are. I then laid my eyes on a sign on the island.

"White's Water," I read out loud, tracing the dark wooden frame of the sign. The name felt really familiar and rattled in my brain as I desperately searched my memory. Lily watched me with a slight smile, only for me to realise I had my tongue out when I thought. I must have looked like an idiot. Suddenly, the name clicked.

"These guys sell water to Marhalm!" Lily nodded.

"Which means," Lily asked.

"That means we aren't that far from home," I excitedly worked out, "What Cluster is this? I don't remember seeing any of those islands."

"The Fronston Cluster. We are close to Marhalm but still have a solid day ahead of us. White's Water has multiple islands with water pumps around here, and I am fairly certain that they're the only ones nearby that do. There isn't any near my island, and I think White's would be the next closest. That shows how much they're spread about."

The thought was pretty impressive. These guys supply water to this whole section of the outer islands. They must have had people working with them, as there was no way they could cover that much distance on their own.

Almost as if she was reading my thoughts, Lily said, "I think they have about eight islands, each with two workers. This one is the closest to the O.I.D. They're smaller pumps and by no means supply anywhere near the amount my island does. However, the fact there are multiple makes it easier to keep up with demand." I sensed a slightly smug tone in Lily's voice as if she was proud to have the better water. I would be too if I was her, but the fact it was just her was also a downfall. One woman doing all that work on her own must have been really tiresome. Now I actually thought about it, Lily must have been so busy making sure everything was okay. Now, her island was on its own.

"Lil," I asked, "when you aren't home, who watches your stuff? You have flowers, the river, the waterfall, and the water pumps. Surely, they need some kind of maintenance on a daily basis?" Lily went silent, hovering by the entrance of the building. It was made of brick and metal, poorly put together.

"Lily?"

"Someone helps. You don't need to know who. Amp, please, don't talk about it."

"But why?"

"If I say, then they will get hurt. So please... don't ask." I guess that made sense. Lily controls a lot and has knowledge that not many have around here. If the Rogues found out someone else had the same knowledge, one of them won't be needed anymore. I didn't push Lily anymore and followed her inside.

It was pretty empty inside but was also loud. The floor was plain concrete. To the left was where the water pumps. A large machine rumbled and groaned, and the sound of swishing water washed about in the various tubes. There were a few glowing lights, green ones, flashing. I followed the machine and saw six large barrels that stood upright. They each had pipes going into the top and taps at the bottom.

In the back right was a corner counter with two girls slightly older than us. They had a white top with blue dungarees. One was a dirty blonde, and the other was a brunette, but both had their hair up in a messy bun. The blonde girl had blue eyes that sparkled with her smile. She caught my attention first as they introduced themselves.

"Hey, welcome to White's Wa...ter. Lily! Oh my Islands," the brunette shouted, "You've grown so much!" Lily beamed.

"Hey Lucy, hey Megan," Lily replied. The girls hugged, leaving me confused and awkwardly stood in the doorway. When Lily broke away, she laughed at my awkwardness and said, "Oh. Did I not tell you that I knew these girls?"

"Um...no...you didn't."

"Oh, Lily, who's the cutie," the blond girl interrupted, eyeing me up. Lily blushed.

"Shut up! Amp, this is Lucy and Megan. They used to babysit me when I was younger and help with our island when I was too young to help. When I was old enough to help on the island, they left and trained with these pumps. Don't worry. They aren't with the Rogues at all, so you can trust them."

They introduced themselves to me, hugging me. I was a little bit overwhelmed, but I rolled with it. Lily explained our situation, and Lucy, the blonde, piped up.

"So you're the Aozora boy. I know your parents. Your mum mostly. Well, I can tell you now your farms are still standing. The Rogues are dangerous but not stupid. They know how much the outer islands need those farms. However, Marhalm is fully under their control," Megan informed us, leaning against the counter. Lucy folded her arms and leant next to her, and carried on.

"Yeah. Pretty much every Cluster here is theirs now. They have started to pull people over and search for them. If you don't have the correct papers, then you may *accidentally* fall into the void." Lily and I exchanged a nervous look.

"Ya know, Amp, Lily really does like you if she is risking this much to help you." Lily went bright red, and I felt guilty. Lily was risking everything, and it was all because of me. I watched her face lower, embarrassed, but she looked up and shook her head. She mouthed, "Don't you even think about it." Yep...she knew what I was thinking.

"So, the situation is bad. If Marhalm is still a day's ride away, we still need somewhere to sleep the night. You know of anyone who would help and not turn us in," I asked, letting Lily recover from her embarrassment.

The girls smirked, and Lucy said, "Your name alone holds power around there. You're farmers. You're the heart of the nearby clusters. Without your family, these islands would all starve. It's like these water pumps. We hold power just because we know how to operate the machines. People will respect you."

Megan continued, "Exactly. The Rogues think they have control and think that people do as they ask, but they still rely on people with knowledge, like us. Without our water, your food, the builders...what are they really?"

"They're bandits who steal things and hurt people," I said.

"That's all they do. Hurt people. But if the right people knew where to squeeze, they get desperate and before you know it. You're in control of them," Megan explained. Lily raised her eyebrows as if she was signalling the girls to explain something else. Lucy sighed.

"Amp, your farm is the largest food supplier in this section. Lily's water and flowers, and White's water, are the largest water providers in the section...." I was slowly connecting the dots. It was a puzzle that suddenly revealed its answer. So this time, I finished what Lucy was saying.

"You want us to squeeze and take control because we control the essentials?" Nobody answered, which I took as a sign that what I was saying was right.

"Do you really think it will work? What is stopping them from training and finding new people to take over our farms and kill us? Then, they have loyal workers."

"Find the information they need you for," Lily perked up, taking my hand. I studied her face. In front of Megan and Lucy, Lily seemed so young and innocent. Lucy joined in, "Megan and I are going to arrange a meeting with the other White Water workers, and we are going to discuss our plans. We have other smaller farms who are planning to join us, and we would love it if you two both came." Lily answered, "of course, I will be there." But I was cautious.

I wasn't in charge of my family's farm; that was my dad's call. Skye was still missing, and my mum was the reason the Rogues were even searching here anyway. So I think I had a right to be careful.

"I... can't make promises," I said and then proceeded to explain my reasoning. Megan and Lucy shrugged.

"Well, if it isn't your call, then that's fine. Just...think about it. Anyway, back to helping you get back to Marhalm. I can call ahead to some contacts. You might be able to stay at theirs for the night. The people I am thinking of are only a half-a-day flight from Marhalm, so if you hustle, you'd get there tonight." Lily spoke next.

"I had made arrangements with Damian Hartford, but we are a day behind schedule. I was planning to head there with Amp." Megan quickly stopped her.

"No, no, no! Not him! He's a snake. Once upon a time, he would be your friend, but the moment Rogues came into these parts, he had been licking their boots. Trust me; he will turn you over without any other thought."

"Um, Damian...Hartford," I asked, feeling completely left out of the loop.

"He's a mechanic who knew my parents. I was meant to be a long-time friend, but if what Megan says is true, then I haven't got anyone else around here. We're out of the areas I have knowledge about. It's one of the reasons why I brought you here. I hoped Megs or Lucy could actually point me in his direction." Lucy scoffed.

"Yeah, good luck with him if you do try. Here, Megan, you think Ellie would take them in?" Megan thought for a second.

"That might actually be a good call. Her son is with the O.I.D., and she supports him. So we know she isn't with the Rogues. We can gift her a free canister of water, too, for her troubles. Speaking of which, how are you guys doing for supplies?"

"We have enough, thanks," replied Lily, "Um, whose Ellie?" Lily was just as unnerved as I was now. I don't even know these two girls, and now I am expecting a third girl to trust.

Megan answered, "She is a teacher. Lucy, go call her quickly." Lucy nodded and rushed behind the counter again and switched on a telepad. Whilst she did that, Megan carried on, "She lives in a tall building on the outskirts of Fronston. Carry on heading East from here, and it's an hour or two flight. Unfortunately, that does mean you need to fly high again." I was aware Lucy was now chatting with someone on her telepad. I gazed at Lily again for her opinion. She simply shrugged and said, "Do we really have any other choice? I trust Lucy and Megan's judgment." I trusted Lily's judgement in her choice of friends, and as a result, I agreed. Now we had to wait to see if *Ellie* would take us in for the night.

A couple of minutes later, Lucy came back smiling.

"She said, of course, you can stay there." I actually felt hopeful. I just wished I knew where Skye was. This whole time I have been assuming she is alive, but she may have been killed. She may have crashed into the void. I had to stop. I couldn't think like that, or it'll drive me insane. Instead, focus on the task ahead. Keeping myself out of trouble. Skye was capable of surviving on her own.

My arm ached slightly still from the other day. It's usually moving my arm forwards and back that triggered it. However, I had gotten used to the pain by this point, so it didn't bother me until I actually thought about it.

"Hey, before you guys get going, you may want to take these," Lucy mentioned, rummaging through drawers under the counter. She handed Lily and me small cards that read, '*Civilian License – Fronston*'. There was also a large number underneath.

"These are for Rogues, I'm guessing," I asked, studying them closely. The cards were light blue and didn't exactly have a lot going on.

"These are the *new* addition the Rogues are enforcing. Probably won't be long till these hit your area, Lily, so keep an eye out. If the Rogues stop you, then show these to them, and they *should* let you go. That is if you don't get recognised. Your face is plastered everywhere now, Amp. Now that I am looking at you closer, I realise you are on the posters the Rogues have put up. They seem pretty eager to find you. People will know who you are, so be…careful," warned Megan. To me, that sounded like she was getting ready to say bye.

"Thank you, Meg, and you, Lucy…for everything. Amp…" Lily stared at me, "We should get going. The sooner we are at Ellie's, the sooner I can relax a bit." She held my hand softly. "The sooner we find Skye too." Lily must have known that was playing on my mind. The girls hugged again, and we said our goodbyes, and before we knew it, we were flying…again.

PART 22

The good news was we were close to Ellie's. The bad news was Rogues had seen us and signalled for us to pull over. Two skiers, both discoloured and stained from various missions they had done in the past, hovered on either side of my skier as I flew. They man a weird hand gesture and point towards the closest island to us. Neither one of them seemed to appreciate me pretending not to see them and got even closer. Ahead, I saw two more on either side of Lily, and my heart sank when I saw they were armed with guns on their ones. I checked the two next to me, and they, too, had armed skiers.

At least Lily had the sense to do as they asked, and I didn't plan to leave her now. So, Lily and I placed ourselves down on an island that had nothing but a small patch of gravel surrounded by dirt. It looked like a bridge used to connect it to a slightly larger one that had ruins of an old building on it. Now they were two old supports that were slightly melted at the end that extended from our island.

I felt sick when I was asked to step away from my skier. We didn't have a choice but to listen and follow orders. After, Lily was taken to one side of the island, and I was taken to the other. A middled aged man with a very square jaw studied my face intensely and asked to see my papers. I said a silent thank you to Megan and Lucy, then took out the card. I showed it to them, trying to remember exactly what it said.

"From Fronston, are we," the squared-jawed man growled. I could feel his breath, and it smelt like gone garlic. He passed the card to his partner, who was one of the younger Rogues I have seen, maybe mid-twenties, the too-early thirties. The younger Rogue didn't seem to want to be there. He stood, half reluctant to hold the card, whilst the older man got back in my face again.

Every word sprayed more of his saliva over me, so I had to make a conscious effort not to throw up, which actually was a lot harder than I thought. I checked to see how Lily was doing, and she seemed to be talking a lot more than I was right now. I wondered what magic she was conjuring that would let her walk away from this. Me...I had no plan whatsoever.

"You look familiar," the man growled again. I was pretty sure he was trying to get my scent like a ravenous dog on the hunt. His nostrils flared non-stop.

"Sir, this checks out," the younger man said, showing my card. The older one sniffed and took another look at the card. He snatched it out of his hand and held it in front of me.

"What is your name, boy," I asked. I was hoping he wasn't going to ask that. I had to think on the fly. What if Lily says a different name to me? Then I would be screwed. Lily knew not to use my real name, and she would use a name that I knew and she knew. Mal-Chin? No, I don't look like him, and he is too well-known. Tyler? She met Tyler, and I knew him. I took the risk.

"Um...Tyler," I croaked. I sounded like a fourteen-year-old going through puberty, but I held my resolve. I had to act like nothing was wrong and that this was normal.

"Tyler, you say, hm?" the man circled me. He made me feel dwarfed, and I could see why people would cower to these men. But I wasn't about to be one of those people.

"Christina, I'd like to ask the girl a question!"

There was a murmur, and then Lily was dragged over, her arm pushed against her back. Rage was saturating my veins, but I kept my cool. The man eyed her up.

"Well, aren't you a pretty girl," he said to Lily, "I don't recognise you. Now...do you mind telling me the name of this young man here." He sounded like he was trying to be polite in a very condescending way. Lily looked at me and hesitated. I could sense her gears working away in her head, and she thought of an answer. After a short while, she smiled and said, "It's Tyler." There was a grumble, and then, "And what relation is... Tyler...to you." This time, she didn't hesitate to answer.

"My boyfriend. We were travelling back from the shop. Tyler was trying out his new skier." Did she say, boyfriend? Now I need to act like

I am Lily's boyfriend, which I guess shouldn't be too hard considering we had already kissed once. And I did really like her.

Christina kept muttering to the other woman who was with her. She had brown hair, and her face was manly looking. Compare her to the girl Christina was with. The other girl was actually fairly pretty, yet it looked like she was ready to push someone off the island at a moment's notice.

"Boyfriend's new skier. This looks rather modern for someone in this part. How did you afford it?" This time, he spoke to me. My mind went blank, and I could feel myself breaking out of character.

"Sir, you would probably like to see this," the younger girl said, interrupting. I was glad that I had a second to think about my answer; however, as soon as I saw why the girl interrupted, I was almost sick. In her hand was a piece of paper that was neatly rolled up. She stretched her arm out towards the older man and held the role for him to collect. He took it off her carefully. Then, he began to unroll it.

The silence was deadly, and he saw the paper. He took a look at it and then studied me. His face was concentrated at first, but it switched to a slight smirk. The smirk then developed into a booming laugh that echoed across the islands.

"Ah Tyler...or should I say...Amphorn Aozora...member of the O.I.D" That's it, the jig was up, and I was now about to die at the hands of a garlic-eating oaf. My first reaction was to run, but I had nowhere to run to. I couldn't fight them all off. For a start, garlic breath would out strengthen me. I sized up the other boy and figured I could take him. But then I had to worry about Christina and the other girl. Lily certainly couldn't take them both. I subtly felt my knife. I wanted to remain aware that it was there.

"Uh...damn... you got me. Hi," I said with a nervous laugh. I figured my best bet was to talk and distract whilst I thought of a better plan.

"You appear to be one of our most wanted. But this young lady here doesn't appear to be Skye. Who are you really," he asked Lily. Lily frowned at him.

"I am Lily Azalea. I am under Rogue protection due to my knowledge." She had so much confidence in her words that I was surprised when he questioned her. She said more information, and something seemed to sink into place for him.

"Fine, do not harm the girl. The boy, however, takes him." Christina tried to grab me, but my instincts said otherwise. I pushed my entire body weight into her. I rolled over the top and forced the younger girl back. She watched me, her gaze piercing me. However, she didn't appear to want to fight.

Garlic breath charged at me next, but Lily stuck her feet out, and he stumbled into Christina, who had just stumbled up. I had almost forgotten the younger man was there. He just stood still; he, too, looked conflicted.

Before I knew it, I was backed against the edge, Christina and the older man approaching me.

"Why aren't you attacking him," he bellowed to the younger ones. Both of them reluctantly stood forwards. I saw Lily try to pull the man, but he kept swatting her away. He warned that if she carried on, she would be having a visit into the void. She backed away.

Trying to dance around the skiers wasn't easy, but they were the only thing keeping them from just charging into me. But...that didn't stop the man from trying. I avoided two attempts before the third caught me. I flailed about as I was dragged towards a skier. Lily begged for him to let go and ran to me, but she was held back by the young girl. I'll give Lily credit, she was brave, but there really wasn't any point fighting. I let my body go limp, and I was dragged across the dirt.

"Get him strapped on, and we can get going. I need to deal with this annoying little...." He tried telling the young boy. Out of nowhere, there was a thump. For a moment, everyone was silent, abruptly after, a roar.

Blood poured down the side of garlic breath's head. I couldn't work out what had happened to him at first until I saw the boy with a long pole with a bloodied tip. The girl then let go of Lily and struck Christina, who fell onto the floor. She mustn't have anticipated the girl's betrayal because she was winded pretty hard. Almost right after, the girl kicked Christina, who rolled so close to the edge, she almost fell.

The man had come back to his sense and caught the boy's next swing. He gripped the pole and wrestled with him. Lily took her chance and helped me up, and told me we needed to leave now. But I felt bad leaving these two on their own. I told her to get ready and that I will be right behind her.

To the left, I was aware of Christina battling with the girl, but right in front of me, the boy had lost the fight. The older Rogue held the pole and pointed it at the young boy.

"I condemn you," he shouted at him before ramming the post through the chest of the boy. He screamed in pain and fell into a lump on the floor. I didn't wait anymore. As the pole went for another strike, I slammed into garlic breath. We smashed into a skier, which was the only thing that stopped us from rolling over. The skier, however, wasn't so lucky and toppled into the void. The man gripped my neck and squeezed, choking me so tightly that it felt like my eyes were popping. I tried to find a grip on him, but I was rapidly losing focus. I made a last-minute grab for my knife, but it was pinned under my body weight. Then, the grip loosened.

I was disorientated, so it took a second to process what had happened. All I heard was a shrieking rapidly, getting quiet. I looked over the edge and just about saw the man disappearing into the gas below. Lily was standing next to me, really pale behind her was a bloodied boy. I checked how the girl was getting on, but she was standing over the body that was no longer thrashing. She looked like she was crying.

"G... get out of here before more come," she muttered, but not looking at us. I had a feeling she was talking to us and not Christina. Lily helped me up, but she looked weak herself.

Before I left, I crouched next to the boy, but he was already gone. I couldn't bear to see the scene anymore, so I looked for my skier. Of course, my skier was the one that fell. So, I got into Lily's skipper, and with a gentle hum, we took off.

The hum of the engine felt like a cruel sense of calm. Lily persisted with her quietness, probably stewing on the events. I kept seeing the poor boy, the blood, the courage mixed with fear. I didn't want to say anything, but leaving the skipper in silence allowed time for the events to dampen our mood. I tried to think about what to say, but luckily, I didn't have to.

"Th...that was the first time that I...I have done that," Lily stammered, his eyes still forward, gazing into the distance. She seemed so far away that we narrowly missed bridges that would usually be easier to avoid.

"You saved me," I answered, trying to reassure her, "I think you saved that girl too." Now I was imagining the girl, alone on the island, with the dead young man, Christina, who was probably dead, and the older man, who had fallen into the void. She would also be hunted by the Rogues, forever named a betrayer. She'd probably be killed now if she didn't escape.

Either that or she would lie, blame it on us, and we would be wanted for murder. Neither situation is something I wanted.

"I killed him," Lily kept going, seemingly not hearing me or paying attention. I was going to say something, but it didn't feel right. Lily kept quiet, and so did I.

It felt like ages, but it wasn't. It was about fifteen minutes of pure silence when Lily sniffed and said that we were close and that we should keep an eye out for an island that matched Lucy's description. I was still paranoid we were being followed, but everything was eerily silent. Even the locals weren't buzzing about like usual. It was like they knew something we didn't. But that didn't matter because, in the distance, we found Ellie's Island.

It seemed like a quaint little place, and as we landed, Ellie had obviously spotted us. She had opened the door and was waiting for us. She had shoulder-length brown hair and a flower hair clip in her hair. She was older, my mum's age and had a silky flowery dress. Lily and I were welcomed inside like we were her kids. I was pretty sure she could sense something was up, as I had to do most of the talking whilst Lily was still remaining distant.

Once we had properly introduced ourselves and Ellie had given us drinks, I explained our situation.

"I'm so sorry you had to go through that," Ellie said, then swore about the blasted Rogues.

"Lily, your first time is always traumatising. When my son, Nathan, killed his first man, he couldn't stop crying for a week. I was on the telepad every day when he was in his room; he couldn't let it go." Ellie's words seemed to sink in because Lily finally stirred out of her trance.

"Did Nathan say anything about feeling sick?" Ellie let out a sympathetic chuckle which Lily also laughed at too. I hadn't noticed that she started crying until she wiped her eyes. They had been bloodshot all this time.

"Yep, all the time."

We sat chatting for about twenty minutes, and then Lily said she wanted to get some sleep. We were shown to our bed, which was on the third floor, and it didn't take long before both Lily and I had both eaten and fell asleep nice and early.

PART 23

I woke up cuddling Lily. She had cried some more and kept waking up in the night and then falling asleep again. I hated every moment of seeing her crying. She would bury her face in my shoulder and close her eyes, silently sobbing, and then eventually, her nervous breathing would slowly start to calm down. Next, exhaustion would take over, and she'd fall asleep.

My own mind was racing all night, so I struggled to sleep, despite the comfy bed. We had an actual mattress that was soft and comfortable and not a thin hard one. We both had sunk deep into it that it'll leave a mould on our bodies.

When I opened my eyes, the room was bright. My eyes felt heavy still, so I let them rest. Lily was still cuddled up. Her face looked peaceful, but I had a feeling inside her head right now wasn't so serene.

I didn't move until she woke up.

It took about half an hour, and I don't know if it was because I disturbed her or if it was natural, but Lily finally woke up properly. She had a soft smile when she saw me, but he eyes were still gloomy.

"Good morning, your majesty," I said to her, looking into her eyes. For a brief second, they flickered into a genuine smile but returned back to normal. Lily said good morning back, then readjusted herself against me. I found myself stroking her hair, which it turned out Lily really enjoyed. So when I stopped thinking I was annoying her, she frowned at me and told me to carry on.

I couldn't take my eyes off her. Even when she was sad, Lily was perfect in her own way. The fact her eyes were droopy and weren't filled with her usual joy and sparkle wrenched my insides that I had to do something to make her happy. I stopped stroking her hair so that she would look at me, and then I kissed her again. It was a few seconds of my heart rate rising, and I didn't want to stop.

I held her face and pulled away, but she didn't let me. She kept kissing me, but as much as I would love to keep going, I knew we would have to leave.

"Lily...we need to go," I managed to say, and she stopped. We both let out a nervous laugh, and I knew that she knew I was right. We needed to leave so we could reach Marhalm in time. The kiss had helped Lily focus more on the task ahead, and I could see the waves of sadness get buried below. Part of Lily came back.

"Amp...you need to remember something," she told me, sitting right up.

"Hm?"

"We don't know what to expect when we get to Marhalm. With the Rogues being there, actively searching for the sphere...things...may not be how you remembered them to be." I think she was expecting me to be the sad one, but I wasn't fazed. I had expected the place to be different and had already come up with a million different scenarios tha we could be talking into.

"I know. I'm just hoping we will find my parents and that they're okay. Also, I am praying Skye will be with them, asking what took us so long." Again, more amused smiles. Spirits were officially higher, regardless of our current state.

"Seriously though, Amp, expect the worse and hope for the best. We've both seen how ruthless these people can be. If they have your parents, then...."

"Lily...please...stop," I had to say, "I understand you want to help me, but I want to focus on the positives right now." Lily's eyes widened.

"Oh, I mean...yeah, of course," she said quietly. Her eyes then went back to normal, and she climbed out of bed.

"I'm um...going to get dressed. We need to leave soon. Ellie said she would have something for us to eat if we want." Lily remained quiet and didn't even bother to say much else. I asked her what was up, and she told me nothing. I could tell she was sad.

"Are you sad because of what I said?"

"No, why would I be sad?"

"I don't know. I don't want you to feel upset. I need you to feel good to keep me going. If you fall to the sad side, then what?"

"I upset you, and I figured I should stop talking," Lily said, sifting through a bag. She pulled on a large, dark red dress, and it took me a minute to realise that it was the same dress that she had worn when I first met her. I also questioned how she managed to fit the dress in such a small bag, but I let that thought leave my mind so I could focus on her.

"You not talking makes me upset! So…your majesty…please keep talking so that I don't get upset." I got myself out of bed and sat on the edge, bouncing a little.

Lily looked down at me timidly. Her hair was now brushed over one shoulder, making her look even cuter.

"That's really become our thing now, hasn't it," she asked. Lily then asked me to turn around so she could dress. I stared at the wooden bed frames and replied.

"Um, I guess so."

There was now only silence again, just shuffling of clothes.

"You could get ready too instead of just sitting there Lily explained.

She did have a point. I had just sat there awkwardly when I could have been getting myself ready to leave. So still avoiding looking at Lily, as hard as it was not to have just a tiny look, I took my own top off. It was a little sweaty and gross, so I felt so bad for Lily, who had to put up with that. I probably stunk, too, so I was now just paranoid constantly. Luckily, I had spray to help remove most smells in my bag.

Whilst spraying, I accidentally looked up at Lily. By chance, she had her dress on already, but I did catch her looking at me.

"Oi, hypocrite," I laughed, raising my eyebrows at her. She apologised but mentioned the scar on my arm. Although my wound from the whip was healed now, it had left a nice pink scar. My other arm still ached from being yanked a couple of days ago, but I chose not to bring that up.

"You also have a lot of bruises. Where did these all come from? They look new."

"They aren't new. I just bruise easily, so getting into fights probably doesn't help."

"You need to be careful, then. We can't have these muscles ruined by bruises, can we." Lily brushed her finger against my shoulder blades, which made my body shiver. My shoulders dropped and relaxed as I followed her, circling around to my left side.

"And this wound has barely left a scar. That is interesting." She pointed at the left side of my stomach, where a smaller wound used to be from the whip. Despite the fact it used to sting, the whip didn't do any real damage to my stomach. Lily touched where the wound used to be and brushed her finger up towards my chest.

"Guess we got lucky it didn't ruin these muscles either, ey?" It had only just clicked; she was flirting with me. At least, I thought she was. I panicked and ended up snorting by accident. There was a second of shocked silence before Lily burst out laughing. I'm pretty sure she was crying cos she was bent on the floor wiping her eyes.

"You…you just got demoted to a p... a pig," she laughed, barely being able to create a sentence without another round of giggling. My face was burning with embarrassment, so to hide it, I quickly dove through my bag and hid my face in my shirt.

"Oh, Amp, you are adorable," Lily managed to say, letting out another quick giggle.

"You really aren't going to let that go, are you?"

"Never! Do you always snort when a girl flirts with you, or is it just when you panic?"

I frowned at her, being made aware that my face was, in fact, bright red. After yesterday's events, I was just happy to see Lily smiling.

"I can't say it's ever happened before."

"What…a girl flirting with you or you snorting?"

"Both!"

I put on a plain grey cotton top with a black logo embroidered on the left side. I then had just a simple pair of jeans on because I didn't wear much else. Finally, another thin cotton jacket over the top of that. I looked similar to what people wore hundreds of years ago, but it was a look I liked. Plus, there wasn't exactly much option in the O.I.D store.

Before we knew it, we were ready for our last stretch of flight. Ellie let us eat egg sandwiches, which were the best thing we had eaten since I was last in Marhalm.

"You are both a pleasure. If you ever find yourselves around here again, you're more than welcome to stay the night again."

She hugged us both. It was a little weird as we barely knew her, but she did feel as close to my mum as I was going to get for a while.

"There aren't going to be too many clusters to get through, if any. So you should have a nice clear journey. You have my telepad number, so call if you need anything," Ellie explained before we all finally said goodbye.

Outside was really windy today. Lily had braided her hair before we left, which was a good job because otherwise, it would have been in her face constantly. Her braids fell in front of her, and I was obsessed. I'm pretty sure this is what love feels like, but I didn't say anything. Instead, I took Lily's hand and stood in the void again. Lily was quiet, also looking into the void, probably being reminded of the previous event. I squeezed Lily's hand and guided her to the skipper.

Soon after, we were flying again, the hum being the only sound about. We originally had the glass dome down, but the wind was too strong.

PART 24

Just as Ellie predicted, the flight was pretty easy. There were a few random islands that no one inhabited. At one point, we flew through an area with so many islands, above and below us, literally everywhere. Not a single one of them had buildings on them. It was all trees and grass, green trees and grass. Nothing was dead. Birds flew all around us.

"This place...this place is so pretty. I wish Skye were here to see this," I said out loud. I asked Lily to put the roof down; fortunately, the wind slowed. The first thing I noticed was how fresh the air smelt. I expected Lily to be happy, but she appeared puzzled, so I asked what was wrong.

"This isn't meant to be on our route. We must have been blown off course slightly, and we didn't realise. Blasted navigation." The news surprised me, but I didn't let it bother me.

"At least we are somewhere pretty. Perhaps we should look around. Someone might be about who can help us," I said, trying to keep the mood upbeat. Lily hit the dashboard behind her wheel and then agreed to my idea. She pulled the wheel back, and we ascended parallel to the cliff edges of the larger islands.

We gradually reached the top, and the view took my breath away. The island was solid green grass on top, with wildflowers scattered in an unearthly beauty. A bright blue river was flowing over the other side of the island, all starting from a bubbling source. Trees stretched over fifteen feet in the air, creating a tunnel of leaves above the river. Various species of birds hovered about, some perched on the trees, others pecking in the water. The sun was reflecting off the water, leaving sparkles everywhere. Towards the other side of the river, I could see rainbows from the spray of flowing water.

I suggested we check out the far end of the island we could see, so Lily took us over the top. The smell was so fresh, and the sound was gently trickling water that got louder and louder.

"Huh…a waterfall," Lily said in amazement when we passed the other side. This edge of the island had barely any rocks underneath. The river followed an outcrop where the water cascaded over the edge and righted the way down into a lower island. After a quick scan of the island, we saw a skier parked by the lake at the bottom. Right after, I noticed pipes stretching from the bottom of the lake and weaving their way up into the bottom of the big island. I assumed that was what was keeping the water flowing.

"We may as well go and see what that skier is," Lily suggested, taking us to the lower land. The sound of the waterfall was intense, although it was nothing compared to Lily's. We parked next to the skier, and a familiar voice spoke just as I was about to hop out.

"This is a cute place for your date," a girl said. Then, standing up behind the skier stood Skye with a beaming smile. I had a moment where I thought I was hallucinating before snapping out of it. I grabbed her and hugged her tightly.

"How many times am I going to lose you, Skye," I muttered, trying not to cry with relief.

"Hey, okay, Amp, not too tightly. You're acting like I was going to get hurt or something." I let go and held her shoulders. Her hair was tied back, and she wore a black cargo jacket and jeans. It was hard to see this was my younger sister.

"Um, where did you get the clothes from," Lily asked, joining us with a huge grin. Skye spread her arms and did a twirl, and checked herself out.

"These? Well, I lost the guy on the skier by flying under the islands, and my skier was beeping. Luckily, I had money on me, so I filled up my skier and got some food and a change of clothes. I figured a change of look would be a decent idea. I had really hoped you would have headed this way. I got lost and spent two nights here. I was trying to work out which direction it was to get to Marhalm but drifted northeast too much. I figured that we can't be too far off if we head southeast."

"You sound so much like mum right now, and it's scary. You even look like Mum with that on," I said. I was still trying to make sense of the fact that Skye was standing right in front of us.

She said, "Aw, I'll take that as a compliment. The question is, how did *you* end up here? You have a navigation device to help guide you." Lily lowered her head, and I let out a deep breath.

"That bad, huh?"

I recalled all of the events since we separated, including Lily kicking an older man over the edge. I could tell Lily was trying to hide as she decided to say she needed to sort out our bags. The only part I didn't mention was how close Lily and I had gotten. Skye was not bothered by the news of Lily killing someone and instead replied with, "That man killed at least one guy, and my guess many more. It's just karma if you ask me. Did you get the girl's name?"

I shook my head. Why Skye wanted to know the girl's name, I don't know, but I didn't press the matter.

"Did you have any issues with the Rogues?"

"Nope, pretty much a clean run apart from ending up on these beautiful islands. Speaking of which, where is this place? I've never heard of it before, and yet it's so close to Marhalm."

"I have no idea. I don't recognise anything. We are still a way off the middle islands. I'd assume we would be closer to the Dustram Cluster. That's northwest of Marhalm. So if we head east from here, we might end up in Dustram, and from there, I know the way back easily. But there is no guarantee that we are in line with Dustram."

"We could always look for the white swirl. Surely, if we are close enough, we will be able to see it," suggested Skye, picking at some flowers. She sniffed them, memorising their smells.

"White swirl? Also, that's a Dandelion," Lily interrupted. It took me a moment to realise she was watching us both talking. I bet she wanted to give us both time alone. Skye explained that the white swirl was the name we gave the strange white gases in the void below us, establishing a spiral-like shape. It was almost a daily occurrence at around four in the afternoon.

"Oh? And you think it will be obvious enough to see from here," Lily asked, crouching down next to some long purple flowers next to the lake. She inhaled through her nose.

"Lavender," she explained when she saw us looking at her.

"Oh, it smells really strong. And you probably wouldn't see it from here, but we can definitely see it if we get closer. I say, head east from here and slightly south, and we will be within the right distance. We may even end up in a nearby cluster we recognise."

Lily stood up and shrugged.

"Honestly, I am just going to follow your lead now. You know these areas more than I do, and it seems like between you, you can work out where we need to go." Skye banged on her skier.

"There is something I haven't told you both yet," she said, looking ashamed. Lily and I both raised our eyebrows.

"My skier is kind of busted."

"Huh? How," we both asked together. Lowering her head, Skye said, "The fuel tank had a leak, and when I tried to patch it up, I made it worse. That's the real reason why I haven't left this island. I'm so glad you actually came." I took a closer look at her skier when Skye stood, and sure enough, the metal was decorated with a large gash. Skye explained that she scraped it on the rocks of an island when trying to get away and also that she didn't realise how unstable it would be with a small hole.

I looked at Lily's Skipper.

"I'm guessing you're going to have to get in the back then," Lily answered, "but before we do anything, do you mind if we just explore these islands? There are a lot of flowers here."

"Oh, and lots of birds! One day I want my own bird," Skye butted in; clearly, her skier was old news now. Both of the girls looked at me as if I was meant to be in charge.

"Why are you looking at me for? I don't have a choice in these matters, do I?"

"Just being polite," Skye laughed, skipping over to the skipper, "there is a cute tree up the top, perfect for a picnic, that is, if you have food. I have kind of run out." Now I was really concerned.

"Skye, what would you have done? You couldn't leave the island. You had no food. You would have just died."

161

"Um, no," Skye butted in, quickly getting close to me, "we are farmers! We know how to farm things!" I scanned the island we were on, a gentle breeze rustling through the grass. The grass was at least half a foot tall.

"Uh-huh. Let's just get up to the top again."

Skye gathered whatever she could from her skier, including the key for whatever reason, and scrambled into the back of Lily's skipper. Lily and I joined her, and we began to rise.

"What would you both do without me, hm," Lily chuckled, slightly sarcastic. Her mood had changed again, and I couldn't work out what was going on. She was very eager to look at the islands, studying the waterfall and the trees. We even checked out the other areas, which weren't so green and were more rocky and gravelly on top. The formations were pretty interesting as some areas had such a large rocky underside that it created a shadow over small ones. We would stop, and Lily would study various flowers and rocks, then hop back in and move to another area.

"Okay, let's head up to the tree and grab some food before we leave," Lily suggested, now seeming content. I looked back at Skye, who shrugged.

"Why are you so interested in these islands," I asked as she touched down back at the top.

"Well, it's like my island, but different. I've never seen anything else like my island, so naturally, I am going to be curious." We all sat down and passed bottles of juices, various dried fruits, and tinned beans to each other. No one said anything and, instead, enjoyed the food. Only a few times, we had birds try to steal things or insects crawling on us. I discovered that Lily had a fear of bugs. She screamed when a small black bug crawled up her leg.

Skye laughed and said, "You're actually scared of bugs and yet love flowers? I wasn't expecting that!" Lily glared at me, brushing off the long grass that kept stroking her leg and then at Skye, who was happily chomping down on bread.

"They make you itch, they're gross, and the sounds are horrible," Lily explained. I could tell she was getting uncomfortable with discussing her fear because when she spoke, she came across as sharp and blunt. I quickly changed the discussion.

"So…um…we should probably consider leaving soon. We don't want to wait around here too long. If we can reach Dustram or even Marhalm tonight, then we will have a lot of time to talk about Skye's fears which I am sure Lily would just love to know." Skye went bright red,

"Don't...you even...think...about telling Lily!"

"Well then...I guess you had better behave yourself. Do you think you can manage that?" Skye sulked and packed up her things.

"Fine. But yeah, come on, let's get going," Skye said, being the first to stand up. I checked with Lily, who shrugged.

"Well, you won't get far without me, so I guess that's that, then." Skye had hopped in the front passenger seat of the skipper. I was about to protest but figured I was older, so I shouldn't. Instead, I helped Lily put a blanket back in the skipper, and then we both got in. It had gotten a little bit chilly, so Lily got the roof on, but the whirring hum could still be heard. Something about her skipper was so peaceful and calming. I could feel my eyes getting heavy despite it being early afternoon.

PART 25

"So we're looking for the swirl that is under Marhalm…ish," Lily questioned again. I could have been wrong, but it sounded like she slightly doubted us.

"Yep. Marhalm is further down into the void than Dustram is. So if we keep heading this way, we should end up seeing Marhalm in the distance anyway. But just in case, the swirl is almost guaranteed to be seen. Almost," Skye said, but I could tell she was barely clinging to our plan. I guess, the truth of the matter was, we were only assuming that we were close. But we actually had no real way of telling where we had actually ended up. We couldn't have been hugely off course, but the sheer emptiness of the islands gave me hope.

Marhalm had always seemed pretty isolated. Dustram was the only other cluster we really knew about. Everything else outside was only read about in books or spoken in stories by people who come externally. I know we have an aunt and cousin somewhere nearer to the middle islands.

My aunt used to travel with my mum when they were younger, but they both had kids and had to stop. We had visited them once when we were a lot younger; Skye would have been too young to remember anything. Even I had to scrape the bottom of my memory banks to find any memory of them. My cousin was older than me, easily in her twenties now, I would say; apparently, she looked just like her mum. Her name was Hailey, presumably named after the Haileyson Cluster that they lived in. Ha, even the name of the cluster sounded Middle Islandy.

The empty space between Dustram and Marhalm was pretty windy most of the time, as were all the empty spaces. I had worked that out whilst travelling a lot. Each time we were in the middle of a couple of clusters that were miles apart, we would experience pretty heavy winds. Back in the O.I.D library, Lily had explained that it was because of the way the islands were floating it created a wind barrier, and that led to a lot of winds being directed to larger areas. It is also why the gap between the inner islands and middle islands is almost impassable. The islands are so large and packed together that it all gets funnelled to the same area.

Talking about the wind reminded me of when Lily, Skye and I had a conversation about it back in the O.I.D. My mind drifted, and I found myself replaying the moment.

"But that would mean the islands will always be windy, and houses wouldn't be able to stand without being blown over," I said, my voice carrying around the library's café.

"But we're talking about the Inner Islands. If the stories and legends are correct, they know how the islands float, and they have full control over it."

"Surely, it's impossible to control nature! You may think you have it under your control, but it will always find a way to come out on top."

"Well, I guess that is going to be a problem for them to find out when the world decides that it has had enough." Skye came in, sweaty from her training session.

"I tell you what," she started, slumping into one of the wooden chairs between Lily and me, a piece of cake on a plate in hand, "Some of these *advanced* people are so dumb, they won't even fit in the foundation group." She looked at me and noticed I had my eyebrows raised.

"I mean, you're a leader of the foundation group. You're basically an advanced group," Skye corrected.

"Nice save," Lily chuckled. Skye thanked her and asked what we were speaking about. We explained our conversation, and Skye let out a loud laugh, which disrupted the silence of the library.

"The centre islanders are stuck-up rich people. If the wind wants to accidentally blow over all their houses, then I wouldn't complain. Do you remember how many times we had to repair our shed out the back or fix fences around our farms? That gets expensive so those rich people can get a taste of our lives," Skye said, slumping back into the creaking chair, "though, saying that, when we finally get home, and we can fly freely, I would love to see the Gully in person. Books just don't do the world justice when it comes to experience."

"Now that," Lily answered, "is something I agree with. Maybe we could all go together one day." Skye found something funny as she tittered and looked at the table.

"What," I questioned.

"Nothing," she answered back, her usual devilish grin across her face. Looking at me made her laugh again.

"Skye, come on...what is it," I begged, now getting frustrated at her annoying behaviour.

"Lily wants to spend more time with you," Skye said, before rushing back up to her feet, "I'm going to quickly head to the shop and get food before going back. I'm so tired. No doubt Tyler will still be about. That guy never leaves the room apart from food or training." Lily and I simultaneously rolled our eyes and said our goodbyes.

Suddenly, I was back in Lily's skipper. I must have fallen asleep because my eyes were heavy, and I felt like they were pasted together. My head was leaning against the side of the skipper, and the sound of Lily and Skye's were just echoes. I kept my eyes shut and listened to what they were saying.

"We used to stock up the machines that planted the seeds whilst my dad would drive the skipper that planted them. Amp only recently started to use the seeder, but obviously, stuff has happened since then," Skye said. Lily responded soon after.

"Oh, that's pretty cool. So your mum...she used to travel?"

"Yeah, she always told us stories before we went to bed. One time, she apparently saw a real-life horse and actually rode it! That just sounds so cool, doesn't it?" I couldn't see, but I could imagine Lily grinning. When she spoke, her tone confirmed what I was already assuming.

Lily said, "That is pretty cool. I've done my fair share of travelling about, though most of that was when I was too young to remember a whole bunch. With my parents not being around anymore and my shop and island, I can't really leave for too long. Even this...well, I am risking my entire island. I'm praying my friends I left instructions with will be able to maintain the flowers until I get back." Her tone died down a little bit, almost as if she had said something she was keeping to herself. Naturally, Skye answered back with a question.

"So you're telling me you came with us to help, knowing there was a chance that your flowers could die or your waterfall malfunctions or something?" The was only silence which I took as Lily's answer. Yes, she had risked the flowers to help us. I opened my eyes slightly, and the blue blinded me.

"Did you do it for Amp" Skye pestered Lily with a dumb question, so I was prepared for a negative reaction. But instead, Lily sighed and looked back at me. I quickly pretended I was still asleep for a couple of seconds before slowly opening my eyes. Lily's attention had returned to the front.

"The way you look at my brother, you really do like him, don't you," Skye asked, her voice now deadly serious. Another Shakey sigh breath from Lily, then, "Yes. I do." My chest felt like it was going to explode. It felt like my cheeks were burning, and I was pretty sure I was blushing. If the girls looked at me now, they would know I could hear everything. I knew she liked me already; we'd kissed. But it still felt like a freshly heated metal rod was pressing against my cheek.

"We…um…when you were away…Amp and I…kissed…a couple of times." I suddenly felt sick. I don't know why!

"What," Skye asked, flabbergasted, "Okay, I need *all* the details of what went on when I was gone." I couldn't see much of Skye's face, but I could see her right cheek was raised, which meant she was smiling pretty widely. Nervously, Lily explained our first kiss, which Skye kept insisting was extremely *cute* and *romantic*. After Lily explained when we were at Ellie's house and how things got a little bit more intense, Skye told her to stop, much to my relief. I didn't need my younger sister to know my making-out story.

"You do realise that was his first time ever kissing a girl."

"Wait…it was?" Lily was genuinely shocked, and I wasn't sure whether it was a good thing or a bad thing.

"Yep. He probably hasn't stopped thinking about the first kiss this entire time. Was he your first kiss?"

"No…he wasn't. My first kiss was when I was fourteen. A boy calls Calvin. I used to have a major crush on him. His family worked in the O.I.D., so I saw him a lot. He was fifteen at the time and worked out a lot. One day, he came home from his training and visited me. I was with my parents at the time, who were sorting out finances. Calvin told me he had a present and that he had saved up a lot of money for it. He gave me a rose."

"Aw, that's so sweet, though. I bet you already have loads at home."

"I do, but this one was special. Calvin had bought this one for me. Obviously, I was crushing hard, and my feelings took over. I, um…kissed him. We actually dated for a while." I didn't know anything about this Calvin guy, but I already didn't like him. I felt extremely protective of Lily.

"So, what happened to you guys?"

"Well…he moved away. We were together for about a year and a half until he moved further into the middle islands. He came back for a week or so when my parents died, but that was last year when I had just turned seventeen. I haven't seen him since."

"Do you message each other much?"

"Not really. He is always working, and I often have a lot to do."

"What are you going to do with Amp then when we get dropped off? I have a feeling Amp has been getting paranoid about that." Lily tapped her finger on the steering wheel. I waited, trying so hard not to make a sound.

"The islands we were on a few hours ago…I was thinking about… um…maybe…buying them." The news shocked me, and my head jolted, making a noise. The girls both turned to look at me. Lily was bright red., clearly embarrassed, and Skye didn't seem surprised and was still smiling.

"Uh…hi," I stuttered, sitting more upright. Lily quickly faced forwards as Skye asked how much of their conversation I had heard. I answered that I didn't hear much, but she didn't believe me.

"So you're telling me you are blushing for nothing, then?" Great, I was being interrogated by my younger sister. When did she learn this skill?

"I heard nothing," I repeated, but Skye wasn't buying it. I felt bad because Lily wasn't saying anything. Skye didn't break eye contact. I tried to stare her down, but I ended up breaking first.

"Fine, I heard the last five minutes or so." I don't know why the girls were acting like it was a big deal, but I found myself feeling guilty. After came the silence, which left the mood feeling awkward. Luckily, I spotted a familiar sight.

"It's the church on Dustram," I exclaimed, pointing to a silhouette in the distance. It was very hazy, but I recognised the bell tower's unique design. A cylindrical brick bottom with four rounded spires at the top and a bird in the middle.

Skye squinted and asked if I was definitely sure. I kept insisting. My memory of Dustram wasn't the best, but I knew that the church was easy to recognise.

Lily changed the course we were on and faced us towards Dustram. I felt hope. For the first time in a really long time, we weren't going somewhere new. We were headed somewhere actually close to home. The feeling that my parents weren't too far fuelled my eagerness to finally get home.

PART 26

Dustram felt completely different to what I remembered. That was mostly due to the fact that there wasn't much of the Dustram Cluster left. The once awkward silence was now just pure shock as we flew between the islands. Buildings were burnt to the ground; there was smoke still smouldering from the rubble.

There didn't seem to be anyone anywhere. There were no skiers or skippers. Some islands had clearly been destroyed because poles that had once attached islands to each other had one side buried in rock and the other jutting into the open air. Dust residue and rust were all that was left on the other sides.

It may have just been my imagination, but the void appeared to be a light shade of grey as if the brightness of the blue wasn't appropriate for the events that had taken place. The wind was calm, if not still. It felt like everything had frozen and darkened.

We approached the centre, closer to the church, and the situation really became clear. I figured the reason none of us spoke was that we had already guessed what had happened. However, when we saw the burnt skier with the Rogues symbol on the shattered fuel tank, we were still stunned. The more we looked, the more skiers we saw. Not all of them were Rogue skiers, either.

"O.I.D," Lily said, taking us to a complete stop near the church. The back end of the church was completely smashed to pieces. Something so innocent is now destroyed.

"Are...are there any...bodies," Skye asked like she was talking to herself. I didn't want to even think about the number of people who had lost their lives here, and for what? That still didn't stop me from scanning everything underneath piles of bricks or next to burnt skippers.

"Two…over there," Lily informed, pointing to some smoking ruins. Why I looked over, I will never know. I followed her finger, and my eyes rested on two bodies.

One was a woman draped over a fence, dried blood on her stomach and rubble nearby. The other one is an older man with a beard. He was buried under piles of wood. Half of his face and clothes had been charred. Suddenly, my picnic was now ready to come back up. They were just there, lifeless. Those two people probably had families who had no idea they were gone, and it's all thanks to some power-hungry psychopaths who value human lives the same as a building.

We kept moving, only to find more bodies.

The more I saw, the more I tuned out. Even smoke levels were getting pretty thick as we entered the residential area of the cluster. Well, what was left of it anyway. There wasn't a single building left standing. More islands looked like they had completely disintegrated and fallen into the void below.

"What do we do," Skye asked, again, only half focused on talking to us. Lily took the skipper to a halt, and we hovered above the void. All around us was pure carnage.

"There isn't anything we can do," Lily answered solemnly.

"What about survivors," she asked again, hopefully. She was desperately analysing every detail of every island, clearly hoping for some kind of movement.

"These have been gone for too long. We can check in the main cluster centre, but I don't think we are going to have any luck.

Skye sighed, sadness emitting from her face.

Lily took us over to the biggest island around, which had what looked like a larger building on it with a couple of shops indoors. We landed in a nearby parking area where a dozen other skiers and skippers were and hopped out.

I could taste smoke and feel the heat. The silence was deadly, apart from the occasional crackle from a wooden plank that recently caught alight.

Inside was a lot more normal. However, there were still signs of violence everywhere. This particular building appeared to be a small indoor market, with various stalls dotted all over the place. There was a main open area alongside shops that had been integrated into the walls. Most of them were selling clothes and various jewellery; however, there were some food stalls and also a mechanical stall too. I could imagine this bustling with life on a normal day.

There were bullet holes everywhere and unsold items scattering the floor. There were only a few bodies which gave me hope that most of these people escaped before whatever hit them came.

I held Lily's hand whilst we stepped further inside. Skye had already run in, searching every counter and everybody for signs of life. She looked over at us, angry and shaking her head.

"No one. Not a single person survived. How can someone do this?"

"It must be the Rogues who did this. There is O.I.D skier all over this place, which means they must have been fighting here," Lily explained, picking up a decorative bronze medallion that was once on sale. She played with it before returning it.

Suddenly there were voices outside. When I looked to see who it was, I saw a glimpse of a brown waistcoat.

"Shut up and hide. Rogues!" The girls quickly saw three people outside and darted to a nearby shop. I happened to go the other way to the girls, so I was now hiding on my own.

I didn't have much time to find a good spot. I dove over a countertop of a shop in the wall, and as soon as I crouched, there were footsteps.

"Take what you want, and if anyone is alive still, put them out of their misery," a person demanded. There were more sounds of rubble crunching under the feet of a couple more Rogues. One of them sounded like they were close to me. I held my breath, knowing full well that if someone looked over the counter, I would be spotted.

I brought my knees to my chest and held them, not making a sound. I pondered the idea of scooting over to find a better spot but figured I would be seen if not heard. The nearby person sounded like they were getting further into the clothes shop I was in.

I desperately searched around and saw a pillar I could reach quickly. It was wide enough for me to hide behind, and it seemed closed off from one side so that no one could see me. It would be a much better hiding place and is way less open. The only issue was the fact I didn't know where the person was, let alone where they were looking. If I risked a look, I could give myself away.

I heard the person rustling through a clothes rack. I took a quick chance to glance over the top of the counter. I saw a woman in a brown waistcoat with a red logo on display, taking random dresses on display and holding them against herself.

I took another look at the pillar I wanted to reach again and judged the run. I could be there quickly, but there was nothing stopping her from looking over my way. Once I was seen, I was pretty much dead. I crouched back down and searched the floor near me. I found a bit of brick that had fallen from a nearby wall and picked it up. It felt like it would crumble apart, but I still clutched it and peered back over the counter.

I saw a post that I knew would be a good distraction point, but then I saw that just outside the shop, more people scampered about. Any noise might cause too many of them to look over and ultimately spot me.

I didn't have a choice, and I took the risk. I waited for a loud noise, which came from someone tripping over outside the shop, and then I threw the debris at the post.

The was a cluck and smash. The woman, as I had hoped, switched to the post. Then, even better, she left the store to see what the commotion was about outside. I took my chance, and as silently as I could get, I bounced into my next hiding space.

I pushed must up against the white stone pillar and saw a tiny gap I could see through. I studied the place. At least twelve Rogues were here, and I had no idea where the girls were. Hopefully, they could get out safely. They had to have been able to get out a leave without me. I couldn't see my own exit plan yet as one person stood right by the market exit.

My hiding place was at least one shop away from being able to escape. I started to piece together areas I could duck behind, but everything was so risky. I'd have to be able to fly to avoid being seen. Then that gave me an idea.

I looked at the roof of the building. A metal beam stretched the whole way across in the middle. The drop wasn't too far, either. I judged that there was a few meters gap between the person guarding the exit and the edge of the beam. Even if I was to drop down, I would make way too much noise. Then I saw that at the end of the beam were frames. The frame outlined the triangular roof. That then hit a pillar that would be just next to the exit. I could do it.

It was a very dumb idea, but I went ahead with it anyway. I left my safe spot and quickly hid behind a rack of shirts. I then crept towards the edge of my current shop. This was ridiculous. It appeared that most of the Rogues were busy inside the other various shops that non looked over here. I guess they didn't fancy a change of clothes.

I was about to climb when I saw the guard facing my direction. He didn't see me, so I retreated back. Of course, he would see me. What sort of idiot would think he wouldn't notice? There goes my climbing plan. I looked for my next plan and saw Skye and Lily together in a shop selling ornaments.

The two of them were together behind a red curtain. They looked like they, too, were trying to escape unseen. I watched to see if I could work out what they were considering, but I couldn't. However, they noticed me. We had a silent conversation, trying to mouth words and pointing at various areas. We had a market stall between us, so the conversation was only half-seen.

Although I couldn't be sure exactly what was said, we came up with some kind of plan. From what I gathered, we would take turns throwing lures and get people where we wanted. We would rely on each other. Much better. Lily pointed at the shop next to me and put up four fingers, mouthing "four people." I'm guessing that meant four people next door. I checked the area around the girls and did the same action for the two on their right.

I had to hide a bit as a Rogue walked by. That pushed me to make the first move. I crept out and hovelled behind a market stall in the middle of the open part of the market. I felt really open, but I relied on the girls to tell me if anyone was getting close.

My first step was done. I held a mini figure of a kestrel that was supposed to be on sale and threw it as far away as I could. It landed just short of where I wanted, but it still did the trick. The two people near the girls had their attention caught, and both of them went to investigate. I did a quick search and beckoned Lily and Skye to move. They both rushed forwards and were forced to separate.

"We have new orders," a man shouted. He had a brown hat that had a dirty yellow strip around it. Just like the other Rogues, he had a brown waistcoat and a red pawprint logo on it. His voice seemed to make the place quiet. A few people stuck their heads out to listen.

"Turns out this skipper is Lily Azalea's, ya know, the flower girl. She was last seen with the Aozora siblings not long ago. So it's likely that she and they are on the way to Marhalm. Has anyone spotted them here? If not, we are to search this entire place for them. They can't be far if her skipper is here. Check everything!"

I swore, alongside a few other bad words. However, instead of the Rogues suddenly searching every nook and cranny, most of them left the market. Only a few stayed, which made no sense. Surely having Lily's skipper on this island meant we were still here. We couldn't exactly reach any other islands without it. Either way, this was better for us.

I took a chance to have a proper look around, poking up over the stall. It was a bit hard, however, as I had to tuck myself under a cupboard to avoid being seen by passers-by. I spotted two more people left. The best part was the guard was gone.

I was paying so much attention to the remaining people Skye scared the life out of me when she appeared next to me and popped over the top of the stall. It took every ounce of brainpower to stay quiet.

"You scared the life out of me," I whispered. Skye didn't care, as she had a plan.

"We can knock them out easily. Use their outfits and skiers to escape."

"Yeah, but what about Lily and her skipper? They would notice it was missing!"

"That's why we cause a distraction, and Lily will fly low. Below the islands, no one will look for her. She knows the direction we are headed."

"No! We can't risk that. We had already lost each other before. I am not going to r...."

"Amp, we have no choice. So you are going to take him, I will take the other. You ready," Skye said, picking up a metal pole. She began to creep towards the man on the right.

"I swear one of these days, you're gonna get yourself killed, Skye."

"That's what makes it fun," Skye laughed before swinging her pole. I wasn't even ready. I was too busy focusing on the fact Skye sounded like Mum did.

There was a ding and a clump. The man slumped to the floor in a bloody mess. The other had also heard the noise and was about to yell for help. So I rushed him, grabbing a piece of the torn purple curtain with golden-coloured stitching.

I wrapped it around his face and tugged. The shock meant that he fell into me, but I held tightly. His voice came out muffled and silent. There was a struggle when Skye bonked him on the head.

"You really need to stop hitting people," I told her, but I got an eye roll.

"They don't deserve any better," she grumbled, wiping blood off the pole on the curtain. Lily appeared out from her hiding place, looking at the scene with confusion.

"If you go around hitting everyone, you aren't any better than them," I answered back, trying to be aware of the fact we were now right in the open.

"So it's okay for them to hurt people, kill people and ruin lives," I replied.

"No, it isn't, but you're going to accidentally kill these people. If you start killing people, then who are you."

"Both of you just stop," Lily butted in, "you can have your sibling fights when you're home with mummy and daddy. Right now, you need to grow up and get out of here!" This side of Lily scared me. It was so stern and calm it made even Skye take a step back. We both looked at Lily.

"What," she questioned, shrugging, "you want to act like children, then I will treat you like kids. Amp, I've killed someone, so what does that make me?"

"So you're on her side," I said. I knew it was the wrong thing to say the moment it left my mouth. Lily shook her head.

"You really are unbelievable," Lily stated. She turned and walked towards the exit, and looked around. She told us there was only one person on this side and three skiers.

Skye looked at me and asked, "So, mister, no violence. How are we going to take this guy out?"

"What? You aren't going to whack him with a metal pole," I snapped back.

"Guys, please," Lily begged, "Put on their uniform. I'm sure you can keep him occupied enough whilst I get away...Now."

I did as Lily suggested in silence. I decided to just put on a waistcoat and hope it would be enough of a change that they wouldn't question me. Skye didn't put on anything as she *loved her clothes* too much. So it was down to my half-hearted attempt to look like a Rogue to convince this guy I was one of them.

Skye still wanted one of their skiers. They looked like an O.I.D skier that had been spray-painted brown with a logo on the back. Two large-barrelled guns were attached underneath the handle grips on all the skiers. It's pretty clear these things were not being used to shoot birds off the farmland.

I came up with a brief plan for what I was going to say, and I stepped out next to the man. He was younger, with a brown buzzcut and stubble. He seemed to be interested in an island below us with a crooked fence around the perimeter. He heard me approaching and looked over his shoulder. Then back on the island.

"Do you think that place was an animal pen?" The question completely threw me off, so instead of a response, a weird gargle came out. The man laughed and asked again. This time I put on a deeper voice. I still don't know why, then said that I didn't know.

"Do you reckon these people got the message? Personally, we should have just blown this whole damn cluster into the void. No one would miss it. It's so small." I felt anger bubbling up, but I was able to keep my cool.

"Yeah, um...what do you think they'll do to that other small one. Marhalm." He scoffed like I should know the answer.

"You really don't know? Jonas is going to blow that damn place out of existence once he gets the sphere. I heard they had just located the farm, but more O.I.D. reinforcements swarmed the place. I have a feeling they know about the sphere somehow."

My mind went to my mum and my dad. Were they still there? They located the farm. We are the only farm around, so I very much doubt they could miss it. Maybe he meant our house. O.I.D reinforcements. Does that mean there is a fight going on right now? Would Marhalm look like

Dustram when the fighting was finished? I found myself in a trance-like state next to this Rogue, who was now looking at me. It was like he was trying to work out who I was. I became aware of Lily's skipper humming to life, but I didn't look. I didn't want to bring any attention to the girls.

"Where are you based? You must be one of those newbies. I haven't met you before," the man inquired. His voice was now changing to slightly suspicious, yet he seemed so cheerful and casual.

"Um…yeah, I…um, can't remember his name, but I can describe the guy who is in charge of me," I stammered back. I quickly described the older man that Lily had kicked off the island. I would have described the man who had captured Skye and me all that time ago, but he could have been anyone. At least this older dude has someone working with him.

"That sounds like Ubel. You need to be careful with that guy. He has been through eight newbies in the last two months. I'm not sure why you'd be based way out here, but I guess all this new action is shifting everyone all over the place." The man seemed to be relaxed, if anything, he seemed to feel sorry for me. He put one of his paws on my shoulder.

"Hey, don't stick around here too long. If Ubel sees you with me, you may be the ninth guy he's had that ended up dead." He pointed to the skiers and told me to leave. In a daze, I did what I was told, glad to have an opportunity to leave. I wasn't sure what I thought of this man. He cared but was happy to see violence. Either way, I turned on a skier using a key from the waistcoat pocket. There were now only two skiers, which means Skye must have taken one. Lily's skipper was also gone. Now, it was time to find them before returning home.

PART 27

My skipper was rusted brown like a Rogues usually was. It had a red logo on the back. The two guns added extra weight, but the skier itself felt balanced enough. I had a helmet and goggles on, and I kept hearing radios from the Rogues talking about jokes. I switched the radio off and flew in silence.

Not too far in the distance, I could see a red and a smaller brown and black-looking spec flying just below the islands. I figured that was the girls, so I followed them. I couldn't see anyone looking down at us, which was good. I stuck close to the muddy, rocky bottom of the islands to make it even less likely to be spotted. It felt cold and was pretty dark, but I was happy to do this until we reached the middle stretch between Marhalm and here.

Speaking of getting dark, another day was coming to an end, and what a day it had been. It wasn't too long to Marhalm from here, which meant that by the time we got there, it would be night. I tried to imagine what kind of scene I was going to be greeted with. One thing was for sure; it wouldn't be how I remembered.

The girls didn't slow down, but I was able to catch up slowly. Lily's skipper was obviously slower than the skiers, so it was a gradual process. Lily had her roof down and was talking to Skye. It was very loud due to the skier's engines and the wind, so I wasn't sure how they communicated without the radios.

I kept checking the horizon, waiting for the dreaded shadows of Marhalm. I had waited so long for this moment, and yet I was now dreading it. I dreaded what I would be met with. I wanted to tell Skye, but it would be hard on a skier and yet too late to now stop. I hoped she didn't have high expectations of Marhalm. I hoped she figured out that it would not be the same.

The flight took forty-five minutes before the first islands came into view. I had finally caught up and was flying side by side with the girls in the dark. My favourite constellation, Scorpius, was really bright today too. I wasn't sure why it was my favourite, but it just looked pretty.

As we moved towards the islands that were rapidly getting closer, it became very obvious that something wasn't right. There were explosions and flashes of orange and yellow. We slowed right down, Skye looking at me in horror. I was so stupid. When I gazed back at Skye, I realised we were about to head into a potential warzone on enemy skiers. If we were seen by the O.I.D., they might shoot first and ask questions later.

Despite that, we had no other choice. We headed into Marhalm. I took the lead, Lily in the middle and Skye behind us. The main island we got to first was a few residential areas. They seemed okay. The usual scrap metal is laced together with rusted screws and nails. The explosions were on the other side of Marhalm, so perhaps the fight hadn't reached this far yet.

We began to encroach further in, the buildings so familiar and yet I struggled to recognise them. We came up behind the test centre. A couple of people were standing by the learning skiers, going through various checks. They must have been ignoring the fighting because day-to-day life was going on as normal. Even the cluster centre had a few people still about, despite the time of day.

We flew under the same bridge I almost failed my flying test under. I gazed into the void, thinking it could have been the end for me. If I had failed here, chances are, Skye and I wouldn't have been kidnapped. I wouldn't have a scar on my arm. I'd never have met Lily or the O.I.D. In some ways, it would have been boring, life carrying on like normal. But the Rogues would still have come. The O.I.D probably wouldn't have known about the sphere. Me passing the test could have potentially saved the islands.

I let that fuel me for a bit longer whilst being twisted between the tightly packed islands until we finally reached the other side of the centre. That's when we could get a clearer view of what was going on. There were around 20 skiers chasing each other around several islands outside of the centre. Our farm.

Our farm islands were swarmed with skiers shooting each other in orange flashes. The first thing I checked was to see our house, which was still standing. There were a few skiers parked outside the front, which certainly weren't ours. I beckoned to our house to the girls, and they understood. Together, we flew home.

Turns out, our shed was gone, which meant a perfect space for Lily to park her skipper. I didn't wait for anyone else. As soon as I landed, I tore my helmet and goggles off and rushed through the back door.

Men in O.I.D uniforms were all around the house, but I didn't care. I found the living room, and that's when I saw my mum. I was grabbed by a few people who thought I was a Rogue, but I shouted that this was my house.

My mum stopped her conversation. Her ears pricked up as she spun and faced me. Instantly, her face went into shock. Then, after a moment of silence, Skye came in behind Lily and me behind her.

"Hi, mum," I said, shaking off the O.I.D man. My mum held my face and then hugged me tightly. She opened her right arm and pulled Skye into us too. None of us cried, despite the fact we probably should have done. It was just a moment of pure relief. We had made it home.

"Where is Dad," Skye's muffled voice asked. Her face was buried in my mum's shoulder, but we all heard her. My mum pulled away.

"You're away for over a month, come home to war, and you ask where dad is? He has been taken to a safe place for now. I only came back to help with something. I assume you know what's going on here? Please, tell me exactly what has happened to you," my mum asked. Her dark hair sat over her left shoulder, and she was wearing a green cargo jacket similar to Skye's.

We took a seat, a few O.I.D. men still waiting around like bodyguards. We also introduced Lily.

"Please, call me Isra," my mum explained to Lily, giving her a mini hug. Slightly overwhelmed, Lily thanked her and sat next to me. She held my hand. No doubt she was extremely nervous. Between us, Skye and I explained everything, Lily providing a few details here and there if we needed them. My mum listened to everything and even asked to see the scar on my arm. When we were done, she nodded.

"Your father really wouldn't approve," she started, "but it seems like you had a lot of fun."

"I wouldn't describe it as fun," I mumbled, but Skye finished for me.

"It was pretty cool. There are huge islands, Mum! The O.I.D. is like a cluster on its own. Plus, the library there had so much information, not even I could remember it all!" I rolled my eyes. This is where Skye shows she's my mum's daughter. Once she knows we're safe, she just goes on about *adventure* and *taking risks for fun.*

"I can't believe this. Mal-Chin lets you get a flying license through them when you're underage for a normal one! I bet you could be out there right now, fighting and be absolutely fine!"

Skye kept going, bouncing on a dining chair like a hyperactive animal.

"I definitely could! Have you moved the sphere yet? Can I see it?"

"The only people who know where it is is me. You're lucky you got here now because these O.I.D people were preparing to take me to Dustram to get away from the fighting." The mood went dark.

"Yeah…no. We passed through Dustram. It was crawling with people, so that won't be a good idea. Why did they take Dad to a safe place and not you? Dad would never have left without you." I had to bring up Dad again because my mum was starting to make me suspicious. I wanted to work out what was actually going on here. I checked on Lily whilst Skye and Mum spoke.

"Something isn't right here," I whispered in Lily's ear. She shook her head subtly, agreeing with me. I carefully looked around, looking at the O.I.D. men. In the corner of my eye, I saw that Lily did the same. Then, her eyes lit up. At the same time, the man nearer my mum shifted uncomfortably.

"These aren't O.I.D. Two of them don't have badges, and one of them isn't wearing the correct uniform. He has a security uniform but not a soldier one," she whispered again, this time so quietly even I had to strain to hear.

"What are you two lovebirds gossiping about," my mum interrupted. My heart pounded. This was a trap, and it became very obvious.

"We were just saying how Skye kept getting the uniforms wrong at the O.I.D. She got everything mixed up," I fake laughed. Lily joined in too, and explained, "She thought security was soldier uniform at one point." Skye was very confused and tried denying it. But we repeated the statement again, looking at Skye directly and subtly gesturing towards the man behind me.

The soldiers were now looking at each other. We had blown it. They knew we were onto them. But luckily, the attention to the uniform made Skye naturally look at the men behind us. There was a moment when I saw that it clicked.

"Oh," Skye laughed, "of course! I remember now! You guys made me learn the difference between the correct uniforms so much that I could spot it anywhere. Even Tyler was better than me a first, and that's saying something." I wasn't sure how much my mum knew of the O.I.D., but she also clocked on to the fact that something was wrong. She was smart like that, able to read the room.

"Amp, why don't you show Lily your room? Maybe you could show her your night light that you could never sleep without," my mum suggested. I knew exactly what she was doing. I took Lily's hand.

"To be fair, it's a very pretty lamp," I laughed, standing up and taking Lily with me. I guided her to my room; that was exactly how I had left it. The soldiers remained where they were. Once inside, I shut my door, locking it.

"My blue lamp, where is it," I mumbled to myself, quickly searching around my room. It took a second, but Lily started half-searching around. She was more focused on the room itself.

"I've just met your mum; now I am in your room," she said out loud like she was in a daze, "We've done it!" Her tone worried me.

"What," I asked, still half listening but looking for my lamp. That's one thing I could not remember where I had left it.

"You're home. Now what do I do," Lily asked again. I stopped. My heart sank. For the next few minutes, the only thing I could focus on was Lily.

"Oh...um...I don't know."

"Amp, I can't just leave my island alone for too long. It'll take me a while to get back home." A second of silence later, I found my words.

"Then you need to go! We'll find real O.I.D. people to go back with you."

"But you? Us?" I kissed her.

"Be my girlfriend…officially," I asked her. I held her face with both of my hands. Her face and lips were just as soft as ever. My heart wasn't racing. It was just normal.

"Wha…wait…what," she stuttered, frozen on the spot. Lily looked into my eyes, hopeful but sad.

"Be. My. Girlfriend," I repeated again sharply, "then you will *have* to see me again."

"But…the distance," she asked. I switched and held both of her hands, still gazing into her bright green eyes.

"Go and get things in order. I'll do the same. It may be a couple of weeks, maybe a little longer, but we will see each other again. I will move to your island if I need to! I want to be with you!" Lily clung to every word I said. She broke the gaze and watched her feet shuffle. Our breathing had become synced, both very long and deep.

"You promise me you will see me again," Lily asked.

"Of course, I promise. It'll be sooner than you think," I answered softly. I lifted her head back up gently, making her look at me. Her eyes watered, but she still held the gaze. We had a few moments of nothing, but I felt the urge again. The urge to kiss her. I did. I pulled her chin towards me, and our lips met again.

"Then yes," Lily started, breaking away, "I will be your girlfriend!" I was so lost in the moment I forgot why we were in my room.

"Um, sphere! Lamp," I managed to say, letting go of Lily.

"Yes, duh! We gotta deal with this first, then me home after." Together, we tore my room apart, searching under everything until I was able to find a small, navy-blue lamp covered in dust.

"I have it," I exclaimed, showing Lily. As I brought it up, a glimpse of gold caught my eye. Gold that wasn't there before. On closer inspection, I realised that where the lightbulb should usually be, was the golden sphere. It was stuck under the lampshade so that it was barely visible. Lily smiled and said, "That's a pretty good hiding place." I was pretty impressed, but I didn't have time to think.

"My mum must have come back to find the sphere and move it when she heard about the Rogues. These guys must have somehow convinced her they were here to help but actually wanna take it from her. We must have got here just in time!" I kept my voice quiet so no one could hear.

"Well, what now? We need to get this away before they can take it...." Lily started, but at the same time, there was a scream. Then a crash and another scream.

Still holding the lamp, I smashed the door open and was greeted by Skye and my mum with a gun to their heads and an arm around their throats. Lily trailed close behind.

"We know you have it, mister Aozora. Give me the sphere, and they'll go free," A man demanded. He had a plain black uniform with a navy blue 'O.I.D SECURITY' etched into it. My mum shouted for them to let Skye and us go and take her, but she was ignored. I was asked again at the same time as the guns were being pushed further into their head. My hand wrapped around Lily's, the other holding the lamp.

"Now, mister Aozora, or they die, and we will take it from you ourselves after you and your girlfriend die. Miss Azalea, your right to our protection has been revoked, and orders for your arrest have been issued. However, if you turn over the sphere, you will be let go."

"No," Lily said, "you don't have it." My body automatically took over. I took a couple of steps closer and extended my arm holding the lamp.

"Amp, what are you doing," Skye said through gritted teeth. Then she winced as the arm around her throat pushed in harder. The man took the lamp, and I let go.

"There we go," he said softly with an eerie calmness, "nice and easy." Skye tried to struggle, but she was now choking. The guy with the lamp slowly left the room, backing out and nodding to everyone.

"Keep her and kill the rest!" His last words restarted my entire body again. I launched myself at the man holding Skye and tugged his arm. I managed to loosen it enough for Skye to slide underneath, hitting him in the crotch on the way down. He clamped forwards, holding where he was, and I slammed his face down into the floor. He didn't move. Then, Bang.

A gun fired. I checked, and Skye. We were fine. Lily was fine. The other person let go of my mum, whose breathing was shaky. Then I noticed the blood pouring out her neck. She slumped to the ground, and I rushed to catch her. A second later, the man with the gun left with nobody following him.

"M...mum," I said, panicking and demanding Lily to grab a towel. She disappeared for a second and came back with two. I grabbed them and held them against her neck, pushing them down.

"It's okay. Just stay awake for me, yeah," I tried to say, but I could feel my tears catching my voice. But it was too late. My mum had lost too much blood already, and the twinkle in her eye had gone. Skye and I begged my mum to wake up for a few more minutes, but Lily had to pull us away.

"She's gone," she told us, placing a hand on my shoulder. Crying, I looked at the scene. I knew she was right. Then I let go. Blood now covered the floor, and the towels were saturated.

Skye leant over to mum, not holding the towels but crying instead. She kept repeatedly saying mum, please which just made my heart ache more. The sound of two skiers leaving the island rattled the house, and Skye lifted her head. Her watery eyes narrowed.

"I'm going to kill them," she stammered through gritted teeth, sitting upright, poised.

"Skye...no. Don't" I knew exactly what she was thinking. I sniffed away my running nose and prepared myself to grab Skye.

"I...am going...to kill them," she repeated. This time she shouted and leapt to her feet. She then ran out the backdoor where she parked her skier. I ran after her, leaving Lily alone.

PART 28

I wasn't able to stop Skye from taking off in time. She had already taken off by the time I had got to her. Lily followed me to the back. I looked longingly at her, my hands still covered in blood.

"I have to stop her. Do you think you can find help? Bring them back here? I'll meet you back here as soon as I can." I was half asking and half begging. Lily told me to go, which I did. I strapped myself into my skier, goggles, and helmet. I even switched on the radio. So far, nothing has been said. I took off as quickly as I could and left home once again.

I was able to see Skye rapidly catching up with the man who killed our mum. The frustrating thing was that I couldn't catch up even at top speed. I could only keep up. I attempted to yell her name but to no avail. My voice was lost in the wind. I could feel my chest burning and my brain whizzing all over the place. I was dizzy and couldn't focus. My breathing was speeding up. I could feel myself losing grip on the handles. My skier was starting to dip. I yelled for Skye again, this time for help. She kept flying, and I could see her getting further away.

Out of nowhere, there were several loud noises. Gun sounds. It took me a moment to realise several O.I.D skiers were chasing a nearby Rogue.

Despite it being night, I could still see they had spotted me, Skye, and the man ahead of her. They would undoubtedly be after us next, not realising we are one of them and not a Rogue. In a way, that had regained my determination to catch my sister before she did something she regrets.

Luckily, the nearby gunshots and flashes of orange also distracted Skye enough that she slowed down. It was like it had taken her mind away for just enough that I could make ground. Enough that she could hear me yelling her name again. She looked behind her and saw me, which did the trick. She slowed right down.

On the radio, I heard, "Package is secure; moving to safe space Delta." I didn't have time to determine what that meant, though I guessed it was to do with the sphere. I was pulling up next to Skye, who had no helmet or goggles. She had torn it off. I thought about doing the same, though I couldn't when hovering.

"You need to stop, Skye! Land down there, and we can talk," I shouted, pointing to an island below us, but Skye shook her head.

"Please, Skye," I begged, "I want to punish them too, but I won't. Could you imagine Mum's reaction if she saw what you're going to do?"

"Mum is dead because of them," she screamed back. Her hair flapped in front of her face making it hard to look her in the eye. But I did. I could see that she had been crying. Her eyes were puffy and red. Nothing was breaking my focus now.

"I know, and I am just as angry and upset as you! Skye and O.I.D are headed towards us, and they don't realise we are with them. Land…talk to them. We can punish the people responsible with the O.I.D's support, but we cannot manage this on our own!" I was telling the truth, and my words affected Skye. She looked desperately at the man flying away, blending in with the night sky.

"Argh, dammit!" Skye whacked her handlebars and headed down to the nearby island. It was one of our islands. It had a crate on it with a tree to the side. There was a decent size flat area, easily big enough for five skiers and five people to fit on comfortably. Usually, a large skipper would land here, but that didn't matter.

Skye touched down next to me and unbuckled herself. I did the same and hugged her. She broke down crying.

"You're exhausted, you're tired, and you're strong, Skye," I said, rubbing her arm. I had watery eyes myself. My chest had a lump, and my only comfort was holding my sister. I had to stay strong for her. The truth was, I wasn't strong at all. I was a wreck. The fact that it was a matter of time before Lily went home only made things worse.

We hugged for a short while until we were disrupted by four skiers landing on the same island as us. It was a very tight fit now. However, they made it work. Real O.I.D. soldiers powered down their skiers and got off.

"Hold it," one man said, taking a better look at us. Skye and I were defenceless, huddled together.

"Please, we're with the O.LD. We took Rogue skiers," I explained, ripping off the waistcoat I took of the body in Dustram.

"Miss Aozora. Mister Aozora," a familiar voice said. Skye's sobbing stopped. She, too, recognised the voice.

"Mal," she asked uncertainly. She looked up, and her face lit up. Quickly she wiped away her tears and stood upright. A quick sniff and a hair fix later, she looked almost normal. Usually, seeing Mal-Chin would frustrate me, but honestly, I was glad to see a friendly face. A face of a man who was here to help. He took off his helmet and revealed his stern face. To make it even better, when the other soldiers took their helmets off, we were greeted by Darcy, Tyler, and one of Mal-Chin's right-hand men... women...Do you say right-hand woman? Either way, it was a woman.

"What are you guys doing here," I asked, still holding Skye's hand. I switched between them all.

"Looking for you two," Tyler answered, smirking. Mal-Chin and the woman glared at him, and Tyler quickly retreated back in line next to Darcy. He apologised, then apologised again for speaking.

The air grew chilly, and the moonlight was the only thing illuminating us. Their dark uniforms made it near impossible to see them correctly.

Mal started to speak.

"What he says is true. Right after you left, I received new orders. We were to head to the Aozora home, retrieve the sphere, and get it back to the O.I.D before the Rogue did. However, we found Miss Azalea there alongside your mother. I'm sorry for your loss." There was a moment of silence. I hung my head, looking at my feet whilst Mal-chin carried on.

"From what I am aware, you gave the sphere away, which means the Rogues have now got control over it."

"I didn't just give it away," I snapped, now facing down the man in front of me. I was aware of Skye behind me, ready to stop me from lashing out. Despite my tone, Mal didn't flinch. He looked me dead in the eye.

"I have Mister Flynn and Miss Wilkins with me due to personal request. They know you, and both volunteered for this mission, knowing that you were both directly involved. The mission is not over, and now, our mission is also yours. Both of you are going to join us in retrieving that sphere, no matter where it will take us."

I had to take a moment to process that. Darcy and Tyler actually volunteered? And they did that because they know us? I figured I should feel honoured, but reality says that they're too inexperienced, as are Skye and me! For us, this was a suicide mission. I looked at my friends and then at my sister.

"But, what about our dad? What about our mum? What about Marhalm? We can't just let the Rogues take over this whole place!" It took a second to realise Skye was talking.

"I will do this mission. I really will. But I want to make sure my mum has a funeral. I want to see my dad, and I want to know my home is safe." Skye had calmed down a lot.

Her crying had paused. With her new clothes and her hair up, my sister looked like she was ready to take on the world. A new fuel to keep her going. But no matter what her face said, I could tell her heart ached. She was still a little girl who was grieving and scared.

I spoke next, saying, "If Skye is going with you, then so am I. I'm not about to let her out of my sight. But she is right; we have to deal with our personal problems first." There was a cold wind picking up now. I felt a chill go down my neck. The wind was picking up, too, like it often did at night around our islands.

"I should probably introduce you to Kella. She also volunteered for this mission. Kella, would you like to say anything?" The woman stepped forwards. It was hard to see her in the dark, but I could see her hair was tied back. She stood upright instead of slouching. When she spoke, she had a sharp, concise, and clear tone.

"You four have next to no experience between you. However, between Mal and I, we have plenty. Of course, take time to grieve. I have seen plenty of losses in the past. In the meantime, we need to work out our next point of call. With regards to your home, the Rogues have no reason to be here. We believe that now they have the sphere, all resources will be dedicated to completing that part of their mission. As you may have noticed, the Rogues are pretty quickly moving away from these islands. Now they have the sphere."

Tyler hopped on the spot, and even Darcy kept moving. It was now getting frigid. Tyler surprised me, as he used to not stop talking, but now,

I wasn't sure if he had grown up, liked Mal-Chin or was simply scared, but he remained silent. Silent until he was spoken to.

"Tyler, stop jumping. Skye, Amp…the rest of the O.I.D are pulling out of Marhalm. They do not have the manpower to remain where they do not believe the threat is high. Would it be possible if we could take shelter in your home for now? We can have some people take your mother to your father, where you can go and see them as soon as possible," Kella said. She was way more relaxed than Mal-Chin.

I had an inkling that only she had the right to be so casual and informal around him. If anyone else did, he'd go mental at you. It did make me curious how she would be if I was as casual with her.

I didn't want to drag us all back home, but equally, I didn't want to stay away anymore. I was torn. My chest burned, and my emotions ran rampant. I was still holding Skye's hand, which I felt squeezed mine. I pulled her into me and hugged her with my one arm. I felt her head moving. She was looking at me. We took deep breaths together, filling ourselves with oxygen and letting out fear and grief. We agreed.

The next few minutes were a blur. The six of us got back onto our skiers, and I took the lead. I landed in the same spot where I did before. Lily's skipper hadn't moved, which meant she was still here. I wasn't eager to rush in. I was expecting to see my mum's bloody body slumped on the floor, but there was nothing. Nothing apart from Lily wiping the floor. Her solemn eyes watched us arrive, so she stood up. She stood up and hugged me so tightly that I let out a grunt. I wrapped my arms back around her. Mal-Chin and Kella came through, then a nervous Tyler. Darcy seemed to want to stay outside.

"I moved her body and cleaned up the blood. There are people who'll be here shortly to move her," Lily said gently. She looked like she had been crying herself.

I answered back, now just talking to Lily.

"Thank you. Do you mind if I go and talk to Darcy? I'll catch up with you in a bit." She kissed me, not caring that everyone could see and told me that she was going to help Skye sort people into rooms. She said that she would sleep with me again to make room for everyone else. I wasn't about to complain.

Our lips touched again before I then headed back out. I found Darcy propped against the dirty wall, her knees bent against her chest.

She was fiddling with her telepad, the same thing she used to do back in our room. That seemed like ages ago now.

I sat myself down next to her, but she didn't move. She kept her focus on the small, blue holographic images floating about the telepad. I joined in, working out what she was doing.

"Where is this place," I asked her, pointing to the few islands that were projected in front of us. Just like before, in our room, small skiers and skippers flickered about the islands and moved whenever Darcy moved her hands.

After my question, Darcy typed that it was just a random place on a strategy game she plays. It apparently helps keeps her mind sharp and ready to come up with plans. I was so fascinated that I just kept on watching her sweep her hands in various movements. Every now and then, a blue, flickering image of a skier would start to shoot at another skier. The one being shot would then fall and spiral down until it would phase out and disappear. I guessed that meant they were out of the game.

Eventually, I said she never got to finish her story. Darcy froze, pondering her response. Without any head movement, she eyed me up, probably working out whether she should tell me or not. I figured that Darcy thought I was worth it because she swiped away her game in one motion and pulled out her mini keyboard again. The telepad switched to just a plain blue light projecting in front of us. The girl began to type, her choppy dark hair illuminated by the glowing light.

Inside, I could see the yellow light flickering and some chattering. I think Lily was talking to Mal, though I couldn't be too sure. Despite the scrappy walls being very thin, the wind whistling through various scrap metal pieces made it hard to hear.

I looked about our island. The various skiers parked precariously near the edge of our tiny island. Where the tatty shed had previously been, Lily's skipper stood, the shining red breaking up the monotonous night sky. I felt dreary, my mind centring on the action that happened with my mum. I became vaguely aware of Darcy checking on me. My eyes were puffy, and tears fell. I found my head resting on a flat part of an old, run-down piece of farming equipment used to help spread the seeds evenly across the fields.

I wanted to doze off right there, but I refused. I forced my eyes awake until I was prodded by Darcy. I sat back up and readjusted my seating position. Where the glow was once blank, a wall of text now appeared.

"My mum sold my brother and me to the Rogues when we were babies so that she could be free from them. My dad was killed just before we were born. I was raised in a family with extreme views about the islands, views that meant people being hurt. As I got older, I formed my own opinion. My brother followed their views whereas me, I hated everything they stood for. Control people with fear is the best way to keep people in check. Taking more money from everyone and reinvesting to make a bigger, more condensed area that only a select few can use. If someone steps out of line, punish them in cruel ways to teach them a lesson. That's where I went wrong."

I read her text aloud; it was slowly scrolling down as I went on. The new information was enough to awaken me more, the burning feeling under my eyes phasing out slightly. I rubbed my eyes to keep myself going. Darcy had pulled her legs even further into her chest, trying to make herself as small as possible. Clearly, she didn't usually tell her story that often.

This quiet, introverted girl was raised by Rogues. Her whole childhood was her being morphed into these people. Darcy had a better understanding of the Rogues than any of us.

Darcy hesitated to continue but worked up the courage to write more. She swept away the text before and kept writing more. My heart was racing for her. I was never one for comforting someone, so I did whatever felt natural. I placed my hand on her knee. She flinched the moment I made contact, and I thought that perhaps I had gone too far. But she calmed quickly and finished typing.

"As I got older, I started to voice my opinions which resulted in being punished a lot. I was locked on an isolated island, and I was whipped. I started telling people at school, and other kids would go against the rogues. Eventually, I had gone too far. They took my tongue, so I couldn't talk anymore."

As soon as I read the last part, she swiped it away and held her knees. She placed the telepad in her pocket alongside her keyboard. I took this as a sign of no more questions. Just quiet.

I was not expecting that to be the reason for her to have no tongue. I wasn't sure what I was meant to say, so I just slouched back again next to Darcy. Her dark, hollow eyes were fixed on the distant islands. She appeared so frail and pale the more I looked. Her eyes were sunken. How had I never realised how sad she seemed? She always appeared so quiet and mysterious, slightly weird but relatively cool. It felt like a mental veil had been unravelled, and her true colours had been shown.

Together, we sat in silence.

PART 29

When I woke up, I was met with the familiar sight of my room. There was my tatty cupboard where my helmet and goggles used to sit once upon a time. Next to it were my books, only three of them stacked on their sides. Dust sat on them now, so clearly, they hadn't been moved since I left.

I rolled over in my bed and right away felt the pins and needles in my legs. I swung one leg over the edge of the bed, the quilt still covering the other one, and hoped the tingling would go away. My other leg budged and kicked Lily accidentally. She was next to me, and both of us were barely able to stay on the bed because it was so small.

Lily groaned, and the bed rocked as she, too, rolled and faced me. Her smile was soft, and her eyes sparkled, despite not being open very wide. Her hair was messy, but that didn't matter.

"I can't believe you tried to sleep outside," she murmured, closing her eyes again.

"I wasn't supposed to," I argued, and Lily sniggered.

"You and Darcy both fell asleep outside! I don't blame you. It had been a very long day. A lot had...happened." Lily's voice trailed off, leaving a tense feeling lingering.

The more awake I became, the more I realised my mum's death wasn't just a nightmare. She really was gone, and her body had been taken to a safe area. Mal-Chin had said we would be allowed to see them soon and that we needed to rest, mentally and physically.

Apparently, Darcy is going to help with our next plan to locate and retrieve the sphere. All personnel is to be kept in the dark as much as possible, and only a select few can know any more details about the mission. My guess is that too many people in the O.I.D knew anyway, so the effort was pointless.

Lily wasn't going to be around for too much longer, so she didn't really have a role in the plan. Tyler was just extra muscle. Skye and I...well, our job was to find out as much information about the device as possible. Skye had told Mal that we loved reading and learning about things, so I figured that was his reasoning behind it.

Right now, though, my role was to be an older brother. I wanted to spend the day with Skye, making sure she was okay. Knowing her, she would spiral into a frenzy of work. Skye wouldn't allow herself to grieve and, instead, would force herself to work as a distraction. I could hardly blame her. I'd do the same thing, except I am trying to be more responsible for Skye. I need to look after her. We've both been through way too much, and things would only get more challenging.

I finally hauled myself out of bed and sat on the step by my window. I pushed against it, and as always, it was stiff. I bashed it harder, and it eventually gave way. Blasts of cool, gentle wind floated around the room. I watched the islands, getting a glimpse of the aftermath of the fighting. There weren't too many skiers out.

Many islands were still somewhat normal; their rocky bottoms still cast shadows on the islands slightly below. However, many buildings appeared to be knocked over or destroyed. I couldn't see how extensive the damages were, but hopefully not too bad. The only way I'd find out was when we went and saw it for ourselves.

Lily didn't say anything else. She had most likely fallen asleep again. I didn't want to wake her, so I chose to head into the living room and see what was going on. I heard a few voices chattering away, but they were reticent, even though the paper-thin walls.

My door creaked open, and inside were Mal-Chin, Skye, and Kella. Skye was handing them a cup, probably tea. As soon as she spotted me, Skye asked if I wanted something. I declined and stood to the side. Skye seemed scarily in a good mood. I didn't want to say anything in case I triggered her, so instead just hovered casually against a wall. I said good morning to the guests who were sitting on the couch.

"How is everyone," I asked, trying to be as normal as possible. In truth, I had no clue what I was doing or saying.

"I'm pretty worn out, but other than that, I'm great. And you, Amp," Kella said, accepting Skye's tea. She smiled with appreciation, thanked her, and took a sip. The boiling water caused her to pull a quick face and chuckle right before it went back to a usual, polite smile. Right after, Kella placed the tea on a table to the left that had been moved there from my parent's room.

I replied back to her that I was feeling better than I did last night but that I was still processing what had happened. I automatically checked on Skye again, who was still rushing around the kitchen, seemingly ignoring the conversation behind her. Looking at her now, Skye was just like my mum after my dad, and she had an argument.

My mum would obsessively clean or try to help people as a coping mechanism. She would handle it well for a few days, but suddenly she'll drop and burn out. If there is one thing I learnt from that, there was no point trying to stop the first part, so being there when she crashes would be way more beneficial. So, if this is what Skye was doing, I had a few days to prepare before things settled in.

Mal-Chin took a quick sip of his drink and then said, "As you are both here, I'd like to discuss a report about Marhalm with both of you. That is…if it's okay." He waited patiently until Skye, without turning around, said, "Yeah, of course!"

Nervously, he proceeded.

"So, this morning, Kella and I had reports that the Rogues haven't fully left Marhalm. Despite having the sphere device, they appear to still have interest in the cluster. We aren't sure what possible reason they could have other than a power move." His voice trailed, but I asked him to keep going.

"We believe they mean to destroy Marhalm as a way to create fear and power."

There was silence, but Skye broke it quickly.

"So, let's stop them? Why are we just waiting here."

"Miss Aozora, unfortunately, this isn't our mission. We are telling you out of courtesy. This is your home, and we trust that…."

"No! Our mission can wait! My home, Amp and I are home, can't! If the Rogues want to destroy it, then they have to go through me!" There's the impulsive Skye I was expecting, but I agreed with her.

"Skye's right. We've just lost our mum; we don't want to lose our home. I'm not about to sit here and do nothing!" My words were left to hang in the air. The only sound was the clunking of plates and cups. Skye had now started wiping down the surfaces, Kella watching her with a deadpan expression. Mal-Chin's was set, too, watching Skye's excessive scrubbing.

It took Skye a moment to work out that everyone was watching her. She paused halfway through removing a light brown stain on a cupboard, her hand hanging mid-air, and looked at us three.

"What," she asked grudgingly, now glaring at our guests.

"What do you suppose then? If you were to stop these people from erasing your home, you need a plan. You against an army that is growing by the hundreds, if not thousands, by the day," Kella questioned, leaning forwards. She now appeared more amused than anything. She had her elbows on her knees and held her own hands, flicking between Skye and me. I was now leaning against a doorway leading outside, so I was in view of Mal-Chin and Kella but also in view of Skye too.

At Kella's response, Skye looked to me for help, uneasy.

"Well, um, do we know where their nearest base of operations is? Maybe we could start there," Skye suggested, putting down a dirty, wet rag on the side and putting all her focus on the conversation.

Mal-Chin laughed and gestured for her to carry on.

"So we storm over there, then what? We blow them all up," Kella asked, a smile creeping on her face. I could see that Skye was just going to keep burying herself in a hole.

"Look, we get it! We don't know what we're doing, so stop being sarcastic, especially to my sister. Instead, offer to help us because if you don't, we're just going to go anyway. If you have a plan or any ideas that can help, then please, we're all ears." I stood up closer to Skye with my arms crossed. Their smiles drifted back into a more serious look.

The silence lasted much longer than it should have. No one wanted to speak first. Skye and I kept our eyes on the other two whilst they kept checking each other.

"For people who are supposed to be good at plans and leading…ha, well, a fat lot of help you are," I snapped, not knowing where I was going with it. Luckily, the perfect opportunity arose to switch the attention from me because Darcy was hovering in the door frame of my parent's old room, a telepad in her hand. I wasn't sure how long she had been there, but her face told me that she had heard enough of the conversation to know what was up.

Skye had also noticed her and exhaled, grabbing the cloth again and trying to scrub the stain, this time with more force. Upon being noticed, Darcy stepped closer to us, cautiously looking at Kella and Mal-Chin, then back to me. She lifted her cube up and beckoned me over. I rolled my eyes at the two on the sofa and headed over to Darcy.

She slouched down against my bedroom door, and I sat down opposite, my back not too far off the sofa's back. Darcy turned on the telepad and placed it between us.

As usual, blue holographic islands flickered in the air. She quickly made a few actions with her hands, moving the islands. It looked like she was zooming out because more islands appeared and shrunk smaller and smaller, making room for yet more islands to flicker into view. Soon, they stopped, and Darcy pointed towards an island with a house on it. I studied it, and then something clicked. I looked at the other islands around them and realised they were all very familiar.

"This is Marhalm," I said, half in awe and half intrigued. I searched and saw all the markets and the island I once thought was significant. Some of the islands began to change red, some darker than others. Once almost half of them had changed colour.

Darcy took out a second cube and her mini keypad. A plain blue light emitted from the second telepad, and then Darcy started to write. I read what she wrote out loud but quietly.

"The red islands are controlled by Rogues. The darker it is, the more Rogues there are." I took another look at the map. Most of the islands near me were light red or blue, including many of our farm islands. However, the centre was dark red, the darkest being the far end of the market near the middle of the cluster.

"So, most Rogues in Marhalm are still in the centre? So much for leaving," I said to Darcy, who was too busy making more hand actions and moving things around. Skiers whizzed around, and she moved a few herself, then typed more.

"It's a bad move on their part. The outer islands of Marhalm are all clear of Rogue presence, mostly as they're your farms. That means it gives us space to squeeze them out. You want them out; you'll force them out. There isn't enough of us to do it, but with Mal-Chin and Kella's help, we may be able to pull it off."

Darcy's fingers were a blur when she typed. However, it did mean she could say what she needed to quickly and show off what she was talking about. Sure enough, the red parts of the map were all central, exactly where most of the people were. All the outer islands of Marhalm were blue.

"What would stop them from just coming back with force," I inquired. I crossed my legs. I liked where this was going. Excitedly, Darcy typed again. Clearly, she had expected this.

"As soon as we drive them all out, we launch our mission into the middle islands to find the device and make a racket along the way to get their attention. Any smart person on their side will want to stop us before we have a chance. If we move enough and have the right distraction, the middle islanders will naturally want to fight them off themselves. We will simply blend in and make out mission a lot simpler and give the Rogues a tougher time. More and more resources will be needed to fight off the middle islanders, so they won't bother Marhalm anymore."

"Darcy, you are a genius! We need to tell Mal and Kella!" Darcy being happy felt unnerving, and yet her excitement was infectious. The empty void inside was slightly filled with the idea that a plan was in the making.

Darcy agreed to tell the others, which made Skye stop cleaning again. She was itching to go now, but Kella and Mal didn't share the same enthusiasm.

They spoke between themselves for a bit and then addressed us.

Mal-Chin spoke first, saying, "The plan is a good plan, but it does require us to potentially use up resources the O.I.D. doesn't have around these parts. It'll be too much of a strain, and we could lose other areas if we sent some resources this way. That also doesn't consider the fact that they may attack from the outside too. We surround them then they surround us. Suddenly we're the ones stuck in the middle with most of our resources. It won't work."

"Oh, come on, Mal! Help us think of something then because it's a better plan than what you have come up with."

"Amp, please, be quiet for a second. We have an alternative plan that you two are the key part of. If you want to save your home, well, you two will. However, it is risky and could put you both in danger," Kella said, standing up. Her mind was now ticking, as was Mal-Chin's."

"As if we haven't been already. What are you thinking," Skye asked, her body bursting with newfound energy?

"You both have a very big reputation, right? Your family feeds the cluster, and these Rogues killed your mother. Use that to get them to fight for us."

All noise stopped again as the words lingered between us. Slowly and clearly, Skye clarified what Kella said.

"So...you want us...to rally up the innocent people...to fight the militarised Rogues...to save Marhalm?" Kella nodded and slouched back.

"Yep. Pretty much."

"Innocent, nonmilitary people," Skye asked again, her eyes widening, fixed on Kella. Once again, Kella nodded.

"Well, it's your home. We have no people to spare. So tell me, miss Aozora, what would you suggest we do then?" This time it was Mal who sat forwards, elbows on his knees.

"I agree that using innocents isn't ideal, especially people you know. But we do not have enough men to spare. Sure, we have a handful of men, a few spare modified skiers, but it won't be enough."

"Actually...it is," I said. I wasn't too sure it'll be a good one, but I had a plan forming. Everyone faced me.

"We make it voluntary for one. Explain the situation to as many people as we can before we are hunted down by the Rogues. If we have them causing a mess from the middle, they'll need more people getting closer to the middle to help restrain everyone. That's when our limited people will attack them. They'll be too focused on them and trying to destroy Marhalm. They won't expect us to take them out." Once they're out, we go to the centre." I waited for the counter, but nothing came.

"Volunteering only, and everyone involved needs to have everything to them told. No Lies," Skye demanded, which I took as an agreement to the plan. Darcy also nodded, showing her approval. Now it was a case of waiting for Kella and Mal-Chin.

I could tell we won Kella over because she, too, faced Mal-Chin.

He said, "Fine. We will start as soon as possible! I know you both wanted time to grieve, so as soon as we are out, we can backtrack towards where your father is. But it will take a lot of effort from all of us." As soon as he mentioned starting as quickly as possible, I thought about Lily. My goodbye would be imminent. Suddenly, the plan didn't feel like such a good idea. A knot formed in my chest, my mind now full. I felt a hand hold my arm. Soft and light, but very supportive.

Coming out of my daze, I was aware of the group being disbanded for now and that it was Skye touching me. I pulled her into me and hugged my sister tightly.

"I know you're thinking about Lily," she quietly said so no one could hear. I stayed quiet.

"If you want to sta…." she tried to stay, but I stopped her.

"No, I'm coming with you, Skye." I felt her gently smiling cheek on my chest.

"Well, then you have the motivation to get yourself home and get this mission over with then, ey."

PART 30

The rest of that morning felt tense. Tyler had been made aware of the plans once he had awoken from his slumber. He was nested in a few blankets inside a smaller room we used to use for storage. He insisted on letting Darcy have her privacy, which I am sure Darcy appreciated.

The group all got into their uniforms whilst I went to see Lily again. Everyone shuffling around had woken her up too. She has half dressed already, fixing her red dress in place with a red ribbon around her slim waist. At first, she looked a little shocked to see someone walk in, but when she saw it was me, she relaxed. After helping her zip her back up, which she clearly didn't need my help with, I explained the situation. The same thoughts I had obviously troubled her, too, because her bottom lip stuck out and her eyebrows dropped

I was pretty much stuck with Lily, collecting all my things and packing them in a small satchel bag that hung around my shoulder. We didn't say too much, just enjoying each other's presence. Lily didn't have a good deal of stuff with her as most of it was still in her skipper.

I had arranged to go gather some food from our farm that we kept in storage a few islands away. Lily tagged along with me, knowing that we wouldn't have much time together. I wasn't sure how much we had, let alone how much produce was good to consume still, but anything would be good. Skye had taken Tyler to go and get spare juices, leaving Darcy, Mal-Chin, and Kella to arrange and finalise the plan.

It was only when Lily and I were closer to some of our farming islands we could truly see the damage the Rogues had caused. A lot of my family's islands, once grassy around the edges and muddy in the middle, were now dry and crumbly, definitely not crop-ready.

Lily was sympathetic, knowing how much time it would take to get the islands anywhere near ready to plant things again. My guess was that my parents didn't have a lot of time to keep everything all maintained with us being gone, let alone with Rogues coming around. I had no idea how much they interacted with them, but being the main reason the Rogues were here, I imagine it was a lot.

A bit further along, past a few more islands of ours, I caught glimpses of the cluster centre. Although we were far out, we could still see Rogues pacing about the central islands, probably controlling stuff. I consulted with Lily about ideas of getting in there and speaking to people. Her best idea was to just do it. Go about your typical day, don't stick out, but when no one is nearby, start spreading the plan. It wasn't the best idea, but it doesn't make a difference.

We landed on a muddy farming island that had multiple sheds built up in an open area. One had a few metallic pipes headed towards the farm, which was also dried and brittle, and the other shed was simply a wooded shack that had rotting wooden braces holding the roof up. There was also a wind turbine between them, rapidly spinning about in the air.

Lily parked her skipper next to the second shed, near a large fence panel with twelve slats. A weird memory flashed up as we did, so I remembered when my dad and I put that there. A few years ago, we had fences around the farms, but we removed them due to high winds blowing them over. Most of the wood from the fences was recycled into more homes for other people or more shed to store things in. However, this one particular panel was left behind accidentally for ages. My dad and I finally got around to getting out of the ground and left it by this shed, planning to use it for something. But we never did so; instead, it lives here now, many years later.

The familiar feeling of stepping onto my farmland again felt like a weird dream that I was living with Lily. She appeared to be interested in the layout of the farm and asked questions about the pipes that spread between the various islands. I told her that our main water tank was in there, which provided water for the farms. Usually, they'd be making a lot of noise if they were working, but clearly, it was as the only thing to be heard were a few birds and distance skiers.

I took Lily inside the bigger shed that had no pipes. It was dark, the only light coming from a small cut-out in the wall between two shelves that expanded along the back wall. The floor was dry, dusty, and dirty, with ripped bags that had been stepped on so many times it was half covered by the floor itself. Small pebbles and stones dotted the ground, making it fairly uneven.

I had hoped we had enough stuff stocked up, but produce wouldn't usually last too long as it would rot and get mouldy.

We did have a small fridge to the right, but we hardly used it as it was expensive to run. Most of the time, my dad would sell the stock at the market straight away or do island deliveries using our skier trailer. It's rare to see them, as most people use skippers. Skier trailers were large buckets that hover behind the skier, attached with metal rods, so you're towing it behind. It costs a lot of fuel to keep running, so they quickly became out of fashion.

It turned out that we didn't have anywhere near as much food as I had originally hoped. There would be enough to last our group of five, excluding Lily, as she wouldn't be there for at least three nights. I did also want to leave Lily with stuff for her journey home, though. Oh, and also as a way for her to remember me. We're dating now, so she won't forget me, but the thought was there either way.

We spent the next ten minutes clearing the shack out. Lily's skipper was loaded with a few loaves of bread and various vegetables. A smaller bag had been filled for Lily too, which she was very appreciative of.

Once we finished at the shed, we headed back home. Within those few minutes, the number of Rogues seemed to have increased by a lot. It looked like some form of rebellion had started, and we weren't even there yet. Typical Marhalm, being the one group to rebel.

We stuck with our job and landed back home. We very quickly caught everyone up with the situation that we saw whilst packing bags and skier containers with food and juices. It looked like Skye had had better luck with the juice as she and Tyler came back with plenty of juice to last a long while. Mal had been able to organise a few troops who happened to be close by, so Kella had been sent over to organise them around various areas. The sight of a few O.I.D. people had the Rogues riled up, hence the small riot-looking scenes.

Darcy had her cube map open, adjusting it every now and then. She kept taking notes down on her other telepad, checking more holographic islands. Mal explained that she was working out the best site for Skye and me to get out once we were inside. At the rate people were kicking off in Marhalm already, we really wouldn't need much influence to get people really moving. The main purpose of us going would be to get the Rogues to follow us now. Maybe catch them off guard too, but I have a feeling they're preparing for everything.

The next hour was chaos. I stood in the corner, watching my house go from the farmer's family house to the H.Q. for a rebellion.

Lily finished moving the last bag before telling me it was time. Time for the part I was dreading the most. Our goodbye.

She hugged me tightly. I squeezed her to the point she laughed and had to tell me to let go.

"You'll see me soon enough. Remember, I own half the O.I.D., so I'll be watching your progress from this end, even if you can't see me," Lily stated. This gave me unwavering reassurance that I would hold on to every single moment from this point onwards. She then kissed me before we headed outside. Her skipper was all ready to leave. She had said her byes to everyone already except Skye and me. Skye hugged her and stood by my side as Lily got into her skipper. The hum of her engine whirled on. The landing gears were brought up as she rose off the island, waving at us. Then, just like that, she was gone.

Skye had her head on my shoulder, gazing into the distance at the many islands. Most of them were ours, though there were a few residential islands too. They all floated so peacefully, blissfully unaware of the events occurring just around the corner of the house.

"It's weird to think how different things are going to be, how different things already are," Skye spoke, now looking at the skiers they were going ride shortly.

"Why did I have to have lessons to get my skier license, and yet you got a military skier license when you're younger than me." Skye lifted her head and shrugged.

"I'm just better than you," she laughed," Come on, we have to go over our plan one last time."

The plan was simple enough. Skye and I will get as many Rogues into the centre by getting the locals to rebel (they seem to already be kicking up a fuss), then the limited O.I.D. will fly in, take out what they can, with as minimal damage possible. Then our group will head into the middle with them chasing us. This wasn't going to be easy.

Mal-Chin gave us all a quick talking too. Then finally, one by one, they all started to leave. We had our plans to reconvene later, but, in the meantime, it was down to Skye and me. We had painted over our skiers now so that they were as similar to the O.I.D ones, but naturally, we personalised them slightly to make them seem more us.

Skye's had a Lotus flower painted over the old Rogue logo. The skier itself was now plain black, too, just like mine. She wore her new clothes, her hair up. She was ready for anything.

Me, I had an old Rogue skipper that had been salvaged and sent over to us. I had painted it black too, and to cover the logo, I had put a red lily, which did look girly, I admit, but that didn't bother me much. It had meaning, which is what mattered.

Skye and I were the only ones left on our island. It was down to me to lock up. We had spent so long to get here, over a month now and yet now, we were ready to leave again. This time though, we planned to leave, and we were going to be gone for a long time. We took one last look at home before Skye, and I finally took off ourselves. The history and events that had happened there, we now left behind.

Within minutes, we were in the cluster centre. We didn't exactly follow any laws; we ignored all the flying lanes, which made the trip a lot quicker than I remembered. We flew pretty close and caught the attention of a lot of people as we landed. Also, right away, we had waistcoated Rogues approaching us. Straight away, we could tell they wanted to apprehend us. But just as they got ten metres in front of us, someone with a squeaky voice shouted, "Amphorn? Skye?" I knew that voice straight away.

"Ray," Skye said excitedly, not paying any attention to the Rogues.

"Where have you been? Your parents have been worried sick!" We didn't have a chance to explain as a waistcoated man grabbed me.

"You're coming with me," the man boomed, trying to pull me away. However, Ray, the short, white-bearded goblin man, shoved him off me.

"Who do you think you are," he squeaked, standing between the Rogue and us. A few more people heard the commotion and crowded around us.

"We are taking charge here, laying down the law. These two are wanted and are going to be taken in," the Rogue informed again. More men joined him. A circle had now formed around us. I could hear whispers in the crowd. More and more people noticed it was us. Skye must have had the same idea. If we were going to say something, this was the chance. She stepped forwards, staring the man down.

"You kidnapped us when we were at the market. Not only that, but you also then tried to torture us, arrest us, and kill us several times and for what reason?"

I joined in, addressing the crowd, saying, "These Rogues have been killing and enforcing their *law* all across the outer islands on the southwestern side of Skilands. But their version of justice is blowing up and wiping out entire clusters. Just yesterday, we flew through Dustram, which has been completely destroyed. When we finally got home, they killed our mother!" I felt a lump in my throat, but I remained strong. Skye held my hand, her eyes looking like they would be slaughtering the Rogues in front of us. I had a feeling that she held my hand so that I would stop her from doing something stupid.

More muttering from the group.

"Lies," a female Rogue shouted, marching towards us, but more people stepped in and stopped her.

"Skye and I are on a mission, a mission that will bring these bandits down and stop them from destroying more land."

A random man shouted for the Rogues to leave, and out of nowhere, a mental bar was thrown at them. Right away, the crowd rushed them. Skye and I took that as our chance to back away into skiers.

We took off and got a look from above at the situation. The skier parking area was overrun. Around ten Rogues had batons out, hitting against groups of people. A couple noticed us and pointed. Straight away, Rogues were on the radio. It didn't take long before we were on the run from heavily armed skiers.

Skye and I had expected this, and we had made our plan. We had a private chat about this part. We had guns on our skiers, and we had both said we were prepared to use them.

We made sure we had flown away from islands that had people to avoid any casualties. Skye couldn't resist. She shot into the void, attracting attention. We got more than we asked for.

Gun sounds that weren't ours echoed through the islands, and suddenly, we had armed skiers shooting at us. We didn't count how many, but we weaved our way around the various islands. The Red Rogues didn't care about damaged buildings being torn to pieces by their guns. Too much damage, so we took the fight down lower. But again, this was planned because as we whizzed under the rocky underside of an island, an O.I.D skier raced out and shot towards the Rogues. Two of them started smoking and began to decline into the void. Skye and I stuck together as we pulled up and around the next island's bottom. We made a loop and took a chance to shoot at an unexpected Rogue. He instantly went up in flames. There was a scream. I wasn't sure which one of us it was hit them, but that was sure death. I didn't stick with that for too long.

A handful more O.I.D soldiers appeared, tearing through the pursuers. The one leading the front peeled off from the group and approached us. They lifted their goggles, revealing Kella. We nodded and gestured the way to go for our next plan.

The three of us kept going, leaving fighting behind. We approached more shooting where four O.I.D skiers were fighting off five Rogues. Skye, Kella, and I joined the fight, easily wiping out the opposition. When it was over, the group met in the middle. Mal-Chin, Darcy, Tyler, and another person were around. Mal-Chin did some actions, and the stranger headed to join the fight. The rest of us headed towards the open spaces, ready to begin our next mission into the centre.

PART 31

I will tell you now it is a lot easier to travel around the Islands when you have military support and protection. Our group had chosen to stop on an isolated island quite a few miles away from the Dustram Cluster. We were supposedly meant to reconvene and go over our next part of the plan before the pursuing Rogues caught up.

Darcy and Tyler didn't make too much noise, keeping quiet and keeping to themselves. Every now and then, Skye would talk to Tyler, but for the most part, Skye would be talking to me.

"We can still see some of the smoke from here," Skye said solemnly, pointing in the distance and planting herself next to me. I followed her finger, resting my eyes upon the blooming fires in Dustram that still hadn't settled. If anything, they looked like they had gotten worse since Lily, Skye and I were there yesterday. Maybe the rush of Rogue's presence had led to the spread of the fires somehow.

"I wonder if they are looking for us over there," I wondered out loud, gazing into the horizon where we had just flown from. We were initially followed by quite a few people, but they gradually peeled off and left us to fly freely. Although no one said it, that was a concern for all of us. These bandits would never let anyone go that easily, especially if we were outgunned and outmanned.

Mal-Chin and Kella both agreed that if we were to reach our first destination, the place where my mum's body was headed too and where my dad was hiding, then we would need to confirm we had lost the Rogues for good. We could always get their attention again later.

The six of us spent approximately five minutes on the island. Darcy had been called over for her opinion on the next phase.

Apparently, Tyler, Skye and I had no part of this and were just here for muscle. Skye started to become agitated, crossing her arms and tapping her foot whilst, behind us, Mal, Kella, and Darcy were fiddling around with telepads.

"I just had a thought," Skye said, pausing her tapping.

"And what will that be," I said, half trying to eavesdrop on the other conversation taking place.

"Marhalm are going to be without much food if we don't work on our farm."

Although I knew her concern, I had already arranged a plan for that. I had just forgotten to bring it up with Skye.

"Kella has got some people to work on our farm for us; keep it going whilst we aren't here. It was something we were going to talk to Dad about when we saw him. Marhalm will be fine, Skye."

Pure relief flooded her face.

"Oh…good. You could have mentioned that before I got worried."

"Well, we have been kinda busy," I pointed out, now able to pick up more words from the others.

"If we head inwards, then we can cut them off and take it before they cause too much issue," Mal-Chin argued.

"We'll have time to get it later. It won't be fair for them," Kella said back.

"It's their duty. I'm sorry for them, I really am, but this is just more important."

There was a furious clicking sound which I guessed was Darcy, then silence from the other two.

"Fine," began Mal, "we will carry on with getting these two dropped off. Then we will…."

"No dropping them off. We all stay and pay our respects. You can't just leave them out. We can make ground on them easily, interrupted Kella.

I had become aware of Skye and Tyler also listening to the voices that were pretty much at normal volume now.

"Just tell us what is going on," my sister shouted, her agitation finally letting loose, "Our plan was simple enough, so if you have an issue, then it involves all of us!" She gestured to Tyler and me as she stepped towards the three. Kella frowned at Mal-Chin, nodded at Skye, and asked Mal to tell us.

Reluctantly Mal informed us that the sphere was not as far as we thought. It was a few miles away, and we could cut them off.

"And I told him that we need to get you two back with your father first. The sphere can wait. Darcy agrees."

Skye recoiled from Mal, looking shocked and let down. I met her arm and held her hand, telling Kella and Darcy that we appreciated their support.

"This is ridiculous," Skye moaned, headed to her skier.

"Um, I, for one, think we should leave the sphere for now," Tyler perked up. No one answered. There was an eye roll from Mal but nothing else. And just like that, we were back on our skiers, ready to go and see my dad and mum.

Ingram Content Group UK Ltd.
Milton Keynes UK
UKHW010000250423
420706UK00001B/18